# AN ABRUPT DEPARTURE

# AN ABRUPT DEPARTURE

## A BLEEDING HEARTS VALLEY THRILLER

### P.D. WORKMAN

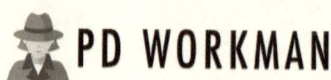

PD WORKMAN

ISBN: 9781774688663 (KDP Paperback)
ISBN: 9781774688670 (KDP Hardcover)
ISBN: 9781774688694 (Lulu Paperback)
ISBN: 9781774688687 (Large Print)
ISBN: 9781774688700 (Digital)
ISBN: 9781774688717 (Auto-narrated audiobook)

## A BLEEDING HEARTS VALLEY THRILLER

Welcome to Bleeding Hearts Valley, a standalone series of interconnected thrillers in one twisted midwestern suburb.

*Keep coming back to Bleeding Hearts Valley to uncover more dark secrets. But before moving in remember, you can never trust your neighbors.*

Unhinged, *by Danielle Fear*

I Saw You Sweetheart, *by Erica Damon*

An Abrupt Departure, *by P.D. Workman*

*To the Survivors*
*who struggle*

# CHAPTER
# ONE

She hoped she would never see him again. And she was terrified he would never return.

Each time she drifted back into consciousness, her body ached all over, and she wanted to move. She had never realized before how lucky she was to be able to walk around and do whatever she liked. Even in circumstances where she was expected to behave a certain way and had felt herself trapped, it was nothing like what she was faced with now, lying in that dim, dank room.

Even when she had felt like she didn't have any choice in her old life, when she was supposed to sit still and be quiet and listen to someone drone on in a meeting or lecture, she'd still had choice. She could change her position whenever she felt like it. Move her arms and legs. She could even get up and walk out, murmuring an excuse if she wanted to be polite, and go to the restroom. Or even go home. What did it matter if someone got upset or angry? That wasn't the end of the world.

Now, she would have given anything to be able just to change her position, stretch her shoulders, or sit up. But she could barely move a muscle. The manacles dug into her flesh, rubbing her wrists raw.

She wanted him to come and release her from her bonds.

Give her something to eat. Walk her to the bathroom. She didn't care if he stared at her. She would put up with that. She wouldn't even complain. She would be perfectly easy to get along with, do anything he said.

But at the same time, she never wanted him to come back again. If he didn't return, and she died there, lying bound on the bed, at least it would be over. She wouldn't have to cower in terror before him, worried that anything she did, anything she said, looking at him too long, or having the wrong expression on her face could set him off. He would scream and rant, get in her face, hit her or twist her arm or something else that would have her screaming in agony.

He had taken her sweetheart from her, and she knew in her heart of hearts that she would never see him again. Never see her boyfriend with that loving, devoted puppy dog expression on his face. Never catch him in a poignant moment as he stared off into space, not realizing that she was watching him.

She felt like her heart had been torn right out of her chest. He was gone.

She feared that in another day or two, she would be too.

And she feared that she wouldn't be, and it would go on forever.

# CHAPTER
# TWO

The landlord, a man of average size and build, much like Graham himself, might have been handsome if he had bothered to clean himself up. But Marcel was a greasy, sloppy pig of a man. His hair was greasy and stringy, longish but not down to his shoulders. His skin glistened with oils as if he had greased himself up before Graham had arrived. He wore a shapeless, decades-old band t-shirt, the worn name and picture no longer discernible, with stained gray sweatpants. He had probably been sitting in front of the TV in them for a month or two.

He gave Graham a pleasant smile and unlocked the apartment door. "Marissa recommended you," he said. "I don't usually like hiring outsiders, but she said that 'Hall it Away' had done a good job for her. She said you're a hard worker and she was impressed with your work on her barn."

Graham nodded. "I like to be productive. Work with my hands. My parents brought me up to know the value of hard work."

Marcel nodded in agreement. "Young people these days just don't get it. They are afraid of hard work. You have to commit to a job. Be willing to put the time and effort into it. Sitting around in the basement playing games isn't going to get you there. I don't know how they think they are going to get anywhere in life."

He swung the door open and they entered the apartment. Graham could tell from the warm, stale air that it had been shut up for a few days. But luckily for both of them, it didn't stink. Sometimes, when people abandoned a place, they left food in the fridge or even on the counters. Vermin got into them. You walked into a place like that, buzzing with flies, crawling with ants, the stink of rotting meat and sour milk combining with other unknown substances to ferment into something truly vomit-worthy.

Or sometimes it was vomit.

Or dirty diapers.

Graham was still new to the business, so he hadn't experienced some of the things he had heard about on message boards from more experienced junk removal experts. Dog or cat carcasses. Toilets that had continued to be used long after they were clogged up and overflowing. Or not used.

Human beings really could be disgusting.

But the little apartment Marcel walked him into was not like that. Abandoned, but not disgusting.

"I need all of the personal items removed," Marcel told him, turning in a slow circle to survey the apartment contents. "The large furniture can stay. I can rent it furnished. But only the large pieces, and only if they are in good repair. I'm not a slumlord."

"Okay," Graham agreed. "Just give me a minute to look around, and then I can give you a quote and get your signature on my standard contract."

Marcel nodded. He went into the kitchen area and opened the fridge to double-check that there was no food about to go bad in it, while Graham took a quick turn through the other rooms—two bedrooms and a bathroom—to get an idea of how much he would need to haul and how much he would be able to sell or recycle. The job would take a few days; that much was clear. Marcel's tenants had not taken much with them when they had abandoned the apartment. There were still clothes hanging in the closet, blankets and pillows on the bed, and some toiletries abandoned in the bathroom. From the looks of the empty spaces in the drawers, closets, and bathroom, they had packed two to four suitcases and left everything else behind.

More work to clean up, but also a good opportunity for a profit.

Graham returned to the kitchen and set his computer tablet on the counter. The clean counter. Even though they had been leaving, the tenants had wiped down the kitchen after their last meal.

"Okay, just give me a minute..." Graham plugged numbers into the quote sheet and turned it around for Marcel to see. "How does that look?"

Marcel glanced at the total and nodded. "Very reasonable," he approved. "Are you sure you can do it for that much? You aren't going to add on extra surcharges for dump and recycling fees?"

"The price is guaranteed," Graham assured him, indicating the red lettering next to the signature line. "You will not be charged any extra fees."

"Okay, then," Marcel agreed. He used his fingertip to sign the quote. Graham pulled up the second document. "These are my usual terms. Do you want to read through that?"

Marcel scrolled through the agreement, doing no more than skimming the headings. Not surprising. Most people didn't even bother to do that; they just gave the screen a few flicks to scroll to the bottom and signed it.

Marcel finished skimming the document and signed it. "Great, so you will have it cleared out before the beginning of the month so I can show it and get someone in here on the first?"

"It will be ready to show," Graham agreed.

"Excellent," Marcel approved. He gave Graham a nod and a ready smile. "Hall it Away."

# CHAPTER
# THREE

Maybe "Hall it Away," playing off of Graham Hall's last name, was too cute for a junk removal business, but Graham liked it, and his clients seemed to find it memorable, at least.

Of course, it was only spelled the right way on half of the correspondence he received. People were too quick to correct H-A-L-L to H-A-U-L without realizing why it was named that way.

Before starting on Marcel's job, Graham needed to pick up some additional supplies. When he had started the business, he had not anticipated how quickly he would go through things like heavy-duty rubber gloves. He also wanted to take his truck through the auto wash after the previous day's load. He liked his vehicle to be an advertisement for the business and wanted people to associate Hall it Away with a sense of renewal and cleanliness rather than something dirty and smelling of the dump.

It was very different from how he had envisioned his life path ten years earlier. Back then, he figured he would be living "the good life" by now. Sipping expensive whiskey seated in a club chair with buttery soft leather cushioning his backside at the end of a long day speculating on the markets. Wearing only the most expensive bespoke suits, surrounded by people who knew how successful he was.

But he hadn't anticipated the kind of stress that went along with handling the kind of transactions he had. He had seen the glitz and glamour of the high-finance lifestyle and had not antici-pated the gut-wrenching feeling of a huge loss. Or the relentless backstabbing that went on, camouflaged by smiles and compli-ments. He hadn't anticipated all of the people who looked like friends, but were actually bloodthirsty sharks.

He was glad to be out of that business and far away from his origins. He was better off where he was, tucked away in Bleeding Hearts Valley, running a junk removal business that, in a month, made only a fraction of what he had previously made in a day or in a single transaction out east. It was better to have left the stress and anguish of that life behind him and be doing hard physical work with his own two hands.

Graham pulled his truck over in front of Scarlett's Secrets, a thrift store he had passed a dozen times but had never ventured into. He had told himself more than once that he needed to make Scarlett Stone's acquaintance. Their businesses could be synergis-tic, but he didn't know whether she would see things the same way. He ducked under the lower branches of a tree that needed to be trimmed back. The newly leafed buds smelled green and fresh, and clusters of red, tubular flowers had just emerged a couple of days before.

A bell tinkled over the door as he stepped in. The interior of the store was pleasant and well-organized. Good lighting, even without the sunshine streaming in the front window. Everything seemed clean and tidy, with the racks not pushed too closely together as they were in so many of these stores. He could see vintage and antique finds lined up on the shelves on one wall. Beneath the glass in the display cases by the cash register was jewelry too valuable to display where people could easily walk off with it.

The woman behind the cash register, checking a price tag,

was in her early thirties. She had dark hair twisted up in a knot or loose bun. She adjusted her square-framed glasses to look at him, and he saw her glittering green eyes for the first time. He drew in his breath sharply.

"Good morning," he greeted briskly, keeping his voice warm and cheerful. "You must be Scarlett Stone."

She straightened her red flannel shirt, raising her brows. "Must I?"

"Well... I guess you could be an employee rather than the owner," he admitted, his cheeks warming slightly. "But you look like you own the place."

"Yes, I do," she agreed. "And you are the garbage man."

He winced at the label.

"I'm not a garbage man; I'm a—"

"Sanitation specialist? Isn't that what they call it these days?"

"I don't collect the garbage," Graham told her firmly. "I am a junk removal specialist. I help people organize their homes or other buildings and clear out their unwanted possessions to make room for the stuff they love."

"I don't need your sales copy. You are a garbage man," she told him flatly.

Graham shook his head, smiling. She was being irritating and disparaging, but he kind of liked her blunt attitude. He shrugged off any sting left behind by her words and walked up to the register. He put out his hand.

"Graham Hall," he introduced himself, "Hall it Away junk removal specialist. Garbage man."

She gave him her cool, dry hand. "Nice to meet you, garbage man."

Up close, he could see that she had a small diamond stud nose ring.

"Nice to meet you, Miss Stone."

She waved this away. "Everyone calls me Scarlett." She folded her arms and looked him over critically. "So what are you doing here? I assume you're not looking for a wardrobe upgrade."

Most of her clothing stock appeared to be women's clothing, not unusual for a thrift store.

"Another time, maybe," he said with a smile. "I just wanted to introduce myself and see... whether there is any possibility of us doing business together in the future."

"Oh, I see. You've decided you don't want to be competitors?"

Graham scratched the back of his head as he tried to figure out the best way to handle the conversation. He had gone into it without a script, unsure how she would respond to his approach. He hadn't anticipated that she would recognize him and know that he was already selling reusable goods that he removed from his clients' homes that were not destined for the dump or recycling. He had a small junk shop in the front of his warehouse. Not on Main Street like Scarlett's Secrets, but off the beaten path.

"I am about to do an apartment reclamation," he told her. "I just did a walk-through on it. A couple took off without notice to their landlord. They left behind a lot of good-quality name-brand clothing, bedding, and room decor. The stuff I sell from my shop runs more the way of small appliances, building materials, and tools."

"Uh-huh." Her arresting green eyes glittered. "And what do you want from me?"

"I am wondering whether you would be interested in buying the clothing and soft furnishings as a lot. Say, ten cents on the dollar for what you could sell them for."

Her chin came up as she considered the offer. She had clearly been expecting him to hold back more for himself. Maybe expecting forty cents on the dollar.

"I only take donations."

"I see. And you wouldn't consider paying a small stipend as... a finder's fee? I don't expect this to be the only time I will come into good-quality stock like this. I'm not talking about stuff stored in an attic for a hundred years or that is moldy, holey, or smoke-damaged. It's well-cared-for, high-quality merchandise."

Scarlett tapped her pen on the top of the display case, thinking about it some more.

"I don't want to agree to anything sight-unseen," she said finally. "I'll make a decision when I see it. And not just a sampling. The whole lot."

Graham nodded, letting out a small sigh of relief. "Of course. I'm not expecting you to agree without seeing anything. I just wanted to float the idea and see whether you would be interested. I can try to sell it out of my store or travel to the city to find a buyer, but I think since it falls well within the type of stock you are selling, we may as well keep it 'in the family' if we can." He gave her a warm, friendly smile.

"I'll take a look at it," Scarlett agreed coolly. "But we are *not* family."

# CHAPTER
# FOUR

Graham couldn't blame people for seeing him as an outsider. It was true. He was. He had lived in Bleeding Hearts Valley for less than a year. He was as green and "other" as could be. But he had hoped that moving to a small town would be good for him. He'd heard all the stories about how close small towns were, how close the friendships were, how people really cared about each other and knew who their neighbors were, unlike in the big city.

So far, that closeness formed a barrier that kept him on the outside. He didn't have any good friends. A few people who would talk to him at the bar without turning up their noses at him, but those friendships did not extend beyond the walls of the bar. He didn't know his neighbors. And did anyone care about him?

No.

But it was only his first year. Graham had to have the patience to wait it out. Some people in Bleeding Hearts Valley had lived there for generations. He couldn't expect them to see him as part of that community after only a few weeks or months.

Graham pushed the encounter with Scarlett out of his mind. He had succeeded in his approach. Scarlett had not turned him down flat, but had said she would look at what he had to offer. If he could sell clothing and soft furnishings in town rather than having to go to the city or just donate them to a recycler without getting anything for them, it would improve his bottom line. Anything was better than nothing.

He still had a few things he wanted to finish up before starting on Marcel's abandoned apartment. The next job would not be nearly as pleasant as the meeting with Scarlett.

Marty Ballantyne lived in a brand-spanking-new mansion in Gold Heart. He had been eager to have his father Mark's modest bungalow cleaned out so that it could be sold, and he could sever ties with his past and reinvent himself as a lifelong member of the Bleeding Hearts Valley elite. He had looked down his nose at Graham, treating him, as Scarlett had, as the garbage man, dirty and beneath his notice. Graham was happy to take his money and had been sure to charge him premium prices.

Now Graham was back for the surcharge he had assured Marcel he would not have to pay.

Sometimes things showed up in cleanouts that families wished had not surfaced. But they didn't know or had forgotten them after they were buried so deeply.

Such was the case for the Ballantyne family. And wasn't that too bad for snooty old Marty, who thought it was funny to wipe his feet on everyone else, despite the fact he had not come from money? He probably had more debt than assets, only pretending to be rich while he ruined his credit rating. Eventually, he would declare bankruptcy, only to rise like a phoenix from the ashes a year or two later, a totally new man, again spending money like it was going out of style.

Graham rang the doorbell on the stately mansion with columns—freaking Roman columns—in front. The gardens were planted with fragrant hyacinths, and the mature trees in the yard must have cost a fortune. The door was answered by a maid, who looked Graham over and shook her head.

"I'm sorry, no solicitors." She started to close the door again.

"I'm here to see Marty. He'll see me."

"Mr. Ballantyne is tied up."

"I wish he *was*," Graham said, his lip curling in a scowl. "Tell him that Graham Hall is here to see him. It is urgent that I speak to him right away."

She opened her mouth to argue.

"He will regret it if he doesn't take this appointment."

She hesitated, searching his face for clues, then finally conceded.

"I'll let him know. If you'll just wait for a moment while I check to see if he can see you." She motioned for Graham to come inside and sit on one of the comfy couches in the lobby/reception area. There were a lot of white furnishings and a big two-story window that looked out into the stunning gardens. Graham did not sit down. Even if he hadn't wanted to stay sharp and alert rather than sinking into one of the pillowy-soft couches where he would undoubtedly get drowsy and stupid. His guts were tied in knots that would not release until he had dealt with this issue.

It was a few minutes before the maid returned and nodded to him. "Come this way, please."

He followed her back to the same office he had met Marty in the last time. A large, dignified room paneled with dark wood, bookcases covering most of the walls, a big desk that probably weighed a ton, and an executive chair that could have been a throne, it was so large and imposing. The last time, Graham had sat down on one of the guest chairs Marty pointed to and found himself seated significantly lower than the kingly Marty, having to stare up at him as they dealt with their business. A cheap trick to emphasize his dominance.

This time, Graham refused the chair and stood in front of the desk, considerably taller than the seated man. This time he had the advantage. He looked down at the corpulent man and could see Marty's hair was thinning, despite his valiant attempts to hold back the tide of time.

"What is this all about?" Marty demanded. "I don't understand this nonsense. You convinced my maid that you had some-thing very urgent and important to discuss, but I know I don't have any pressing business with you, so what is this all about?"

Graham brought out the leather-bound portfolio he held under his arm and placed it on the desk before him.

"Sometimes when I do a cleanout, I come across things that were forgotten about, or buried so deeply that family members didn't know about them when I was hired."

Marty's bushy brows knitted, and he shook his head. "What?"

"Sometimes, I come across things that are very valuable."

Marty's eyes lit up at the thought of receiving something valuable from Graham. But he was cautious, not immediately accepting Graham's words at face value. Which was smart, because that wasn't the way they were meant. Marty probably realized that his dad had never owned anything of any real value in his life.

"What do you mean? What could you find that was valuable?"

"This isn't something with a high intrinsic value, like jewelry or cash. In fact, the market for this sort of thing is fairly limited."

"Stop talking in riddles."

Graham pulled a photograph out of the portfolio and snapped it down on the dark wood of the desk in front of Marty.

It took only a fraction of a second for Marty to recognize what it was. He recoiled, and his eyes flashed up to Graham, horrified.

"Where did *that* come from?"

Graham just looked at him.

Marty shook his head in denial. "That wasn't my father's."

"I found it in his house," Graham said flatly. "Who else would it belong to?"

Marty licked his lips. He swiveled his chair around to face the long credenza behind him. He opened the doors to reveal several cut glass bottles and tumblers. He poured himself a drink and did not offer one to Graham. He wet his lips. He looked at the picture and took a couple of long swallows, closing his eyes against the burn of the liquor.

"Maybe a previous resident," he said offhandedly, with a shrug that tried to persuade Graham that it was true, and he was unconcerned about the picture or any of the others in the collection that Graham had stumbled upon.

"I checked the land titles records for the house," Graham said with a smile. "It belonged to your father for sixty years. Which definitely covers the time when these pictures were taken. They couldn't be more than thirty years old." He met Marty's eyes. That was, of course, the period during which Marty himself had still been living in the house.

Marty wiped his sweating brow and cleared his throat.

"I'm sure we could come to some kind of arrangement," he said with difficulty.

"Good," Graham smiled his approval. "I was sure that you were a generous man."

"But this is a one-time offer. One payment only. You provide me with all of the... items. We never speak of this discovery again. Protect the reputation of my dearly departed father. One time only."

Graham didn't say anything for a long time, watching droplets of sweat beading on Marty's temples. Making him suffer in anticipation. How would Marty's life change if he had this threat hanging over his head for years to come?

"Fine," Graham finally conceded. "Because I am such a nice guy and respect your family's sterling reputation, I will limit it to a one-time payment. I think that... ten thousand would be an appropriate amount."

Marty choked. His face turned bright red. "Ten thousand? Are you kidding? I'm going to call the police and report you for attempted blackmail. This is ridiculous. I thought I would be nice and give you a little bit of 'go away' money for your trouble. Because you came to me rather than going to the police or the media. But ten thousand?" He blew out his breath in a whistle. "No way."

"You would call the police and let them see this? And... the other pictures?"

"I wanted to protect my father's reputation. But it's not worth that much."

"Fine, then. Fifteen thousand."

Marty's eyes bugged out. He poured himself another glass, this one larger, and gulped it down. "You get out of my house," he ordered. "I will not be blackmailed. I don't ever want to see your face again."

"Twenty thousand."

Marty went still. He swallowed. He wasn't showing any sign of impairment from the amount of liquor he had slammed down. Graham could almost see the gears turning. Calculating how much Graham knew and the damage he could do if he started circulating those pictures. To the police, the media, Marty's cronies. They would do incredible damage to his reputation. He would probably have to leave town. And as Graham had learned, it was a very tight-knit community. Marty did not want to leave the town and everything he had built there. He would not be nearly as wealthy in the big city. He wouldn't have a big house with Roman columns. And no one would do business with him.

Marty opened a desk drawer and withdrew a small, long binder. He opened it to reveal a stack of checks. His hand did not shake as he carefully filled out the next check in the series. He filled in the stub to indicate that it was a cash withdrawal. No name. No indication who he had paid. Not unless the police dug into his records one day to trace the financial transaction. And there would be no need for the police to do that if Graham and Marty were both satisfied with their transaction and Marty didn't find himself under investigation for some other crime.

Marty tore the check off and handed it to Graham. His hand was still as steady as a rock. He had better nerves than Graham had given him credit for. Graham took the check and opened his leather-bound portfolio. He inserted the check into one of the pockets on the left side and removed a stack of pictures. He put them on the desk in front of Marty.

"Photography is a dangerous hobby," he advised. "I would suggest you don't follow in your father's footsteps."

A snarl formed on Marty's lips, but he did not say whatever he was thinking or acknowledge Graham's advice.

It was an expensive lesson. Graham hoped it was worth it. For now, he would let Marty keep his secret, but he would be watching for any signs that Marty was still pursuing his nasty hobby.

Because they both knew which room those pictures had been hidden in, and it had not been Mark Ballantyne's room. He had probably never known anything about his son's proclivities, or he would have disposed of the evidence long ago.

Marty had never gone back to retrieve the pictures for his own use or disposal, so maybe it had been an experimental phase for him, and he had outgrown his taste for prepubescent bodies.

But Graham still had copies, and he would wait and see.

G raham took his truck through the car wash and wished he could stop and shower himself, washing off the feeling of filth coating his skin and leaving a bad taste in his mouth. But he had a lot to do, and going home to shower would just break up the day too much, and he wouldn't have time to do the tasks he had planned. After polishing his windows and mirrors with a chamois, he looked at his watch and decided he had time to hit Bitter Bites to buy a Big Stinky sandwich. He could eat while he worked.

Then, with the key Marcel had given him in hand, Graham returned to the abandoned apartment. It would take a few days to complete the job, and he wanted to turn it back over to Marcel as soon as possible to make good on his promise to have it done in time for Marcel to rent it back out for the following month. He didn't want to cost the man a month's rent. If he did, Marcel would remember that the next time he had another cleanout job and would go to someone else.

It was a pleasant environment, which Graham could not have said about all the job sites he worked on. In fact, most of them were worse. Some of them much worse. With a bit of airing out, the abandoned apartment felt as if the tenants had merely gone on a trip and would be back any minute. But Graham knew that was not the case. Marcel had tried repeatedly to get in touch with the tenants to find out what had happened and where they had gone.

But the message they had left for Marcel was pretty straight-forward. "I'm sorry," scrawled on a piece of paper and left on the kitchen counter, weighted down with two sets of keys. Sorry that they hadn't given him notice? Sorry that they had left all of their crap behind in the apartment for Marcel to take care of? Or for something else?

Graham had brought a stack of moving boxes up to the apart-ment, and assembled several of them now, enjoying the produc-tive feeling of getting the job organized, the sound and smell of the packing tape as he pulled it across the seams of the boxes to ensure that they wouldn't come apart or open in transit. He labeled each box neatly.

- Dump
- Scarlett
- Warehouse
- Donations
- Recycling
- Hazardous

And then he got started. The fridge first, the contents of which would go straight into the garbage. Although he fished out a few pickles to go with his Stinky and munched on the sand-wich and pickles as he worked. The kitchen cabinets provided a few unopened cans and packages of food that could be donated to St Francis, the local homeless shelter. They appreciated any food items they could get. If any of the bedding was not up to Scarlett's thrift store standards, it could also be donated to St Francis.

Graham was diligent about keeping everything he could out of the landfill. Cans of food and blankets did a lot more good at

St Francis than buried with the rest of the refuse of Bleeding Hearts Valley.

He found several prescription bottles with pills still left in them in the cupboard. Graham tossed them in the Hazardous box, which he would take to the fire station for disposal. Some people simply flushed old medications, unaware they would end up in the town's water supply. People thought water treatment destroyed all the chemicals they flushed, but of course, it didn't. They filtered the water, treated it with chlorine and ultraviolet light to kill any pathogens, and then it was considered drinkable once more. Most cities' water supplies had detectable amounts of SSRIs and other medications. Graham didn't want to contribute to the problem.

The Big Stinky was delicious, as usual, and was gone by the time Graham finished emptying the cupboards.

He moved into the living room. The soft furnishings would go to Scarlett, the lamps joined the small kitchen appliances in boxes destined for Graham's warehouse and storefront. Magazines and newspapers went into the one labeled recycling.

Books were always a question mark, as they could range from worthless to priceless. He would have to take them back to his warehouse to sort and evaluate. Mass-produced paperbacks could be donated or pulped. Anything that looked old, unusual, or expensive went into a box he took into the city every few months to be evaluated by a buyer. Sometimes they were valuable. Sometimes they were not. It was always a crapshoot.

Graham always had plenty of reading materials on his bedside table.

There was an e-reader on one of the bookshelves. Graham turned it on, expecting it to be old or inoperable. But the splash screen showed that it was fully charged and had last been read just a few days before. Had the tenants overlooked it because it was on the bookshelf instead of left out on the coffee table or a side table? He contemplated it for a few moments before putting it to the side.

How big a hurry had they been in when they had left? Had they been running from something or someone? Were they in trouble with the law? A bookie or loan shark? A stalker?

He found a neat stack of mail on the coffee table. All recent. A few bills or offers. He studied the names on the envelopes.

Ashley Carter
Ethan Quick

Graham didn't recognize either name. Not people who ran in his circles.

Not that he had any circles yet. He recognized a few people when he stopped for a drink at Poison, the local bar. He knew some of the local business owners or municipal leaders. The names of his neighbors. Names that he had seen in the Bleeding Hearts Chronicle.

Not people he actually knew. He sighed. One day, he would know people again. He would have friends, people he could go to when he felt like a chat, had news to share, or questions to ask. But that day was in the future. If he had been more proactive, he could have had friends by now. But he had felt too raw and vulnerable to reach out to people when he had moved to Bleeding Hearts Valley.

Maybe he was healing, now that he was thinking about reaching out to people again. His dissatisfaction with the current state of affairs was a good thing.

# CHAPTER SIX

She had thought that maybe he wouldn't return this time. Maybe he had vented his rage enough to satisfy whatever need he had within himself to commit violence and would forget that she was even there. He was like an animal, and maybe that inhuman part of him wouldn't even keep track from one day to the next that he held her captive. He would just walk out the door and never come back again.

Her lips were parched, her body had stopped screaming in pain, and she felt numb and removed from herself. She was ready to go. Just to drift on, out of that life, and become a part of the universe. Drifting, her eyes half closed, she fantasized about seeing her grandmother again, but she didn't really believe in heaven or an afterlife and discarded the idea after a while. Just to be removed from her prison would be enough.

And then she had heard his key in the front door. He had moved something in front of the broken back door to keep it shut when the wind had started to blow, though she could still hear it banging over and over as it swung against the obstacle and the air moving through the house made it cold, especially at night.

Fully awake now, she stiffened in anticipation of his arrival.

She thrashed around, despite the fact that she had accepted the inevitability of her own death. She didn't have control of her body. Not like a seizure, when she was unaware of what was happening until it was all over, but like someone else was in control of her motor functions, and she had no control over whether she fought him off.

He entered the room with a whoosh of cold wind and moisture, the fresh smell of rain filling the room. He shut and locked the door, bolting and chaining it. He carried a couple of heavy grocery bags and set them down on the kitchen counter. The open space concept of the sixties-era house allowed her to see everything that went on in the food prep and dining spaces from where she lay in the living room. It reminded her of a cabin, but it wasn't. It was just an old house that had never been modernized. The old avocado green appliances had apparently been replaced with a white fridge and stove, and a microwave had been added, but other than that, it probably looked very much the same as it had sixty years ago.

Her captor unpacked a few items from the grocery bags, but he appeared to be breaking down. The effort of appearing normal and thinking logically while he had shopped for the groceries had probably taken too much effort, and now the monster wanted out. He growled and muttered to himself, repeating phrases to himself under his breath as he tried to pull out and arrange all of the goodies he had bought. Before long, he abandoned the project and crossed the room to look at her.

If she had been able to talk, she would have told him not to look at her. Just to leave her alone and go away, and let her die in peace.

But he wouldn't have done it, even if she had been able to tell him that.

"What have you been doing?" he demanded.

As if she might have been up and around and getting into mischief. She just stared at him.

He pulled the tight gag out of her mouth. She opened and

closed her mouth gently, her jaw clicking and cracking from being displaced for so long. He yanked down on her chin and reached into her mouth to remove the balled-up rag. She gagged and thought for a minute that she was going to throw up.

But she hadn't had anything to eat or drink, so there was no chance of losing her lunch. Some burning yellow acid, maybe, but she had a feeling that even the juices in her stomach had dried up in the time she had been lying there.

"How could you do this to me?" the monster screamed in her face. "How?"

It had scared her the first day. And maybe the second. By the third day, she had learned not to be afraid of the screaming. It was just noise. She paid no attention to it now, instead analyzing his behavior like he was a new, unfamiliar species. What made him behave the way that he did?

What drove him? What would change him? Calm him?

She didn't know if there was an answer. He was so far gone that there was no pattern, just random impulses in his brain that drove him from one thing to another, without ever getting the satisfaction he needed.

He screamed at her some more, then walked away. He paced around the room, looking out the windows, opening and banging shut the cupboards without taking anything out. Then he returned to rummaging through the shopping bags again, calmer. He found a bottle of water and twisted the cap.

Despite her acceptance of her fate, being assured of and at peace with her own death, her body reacted at the sight of the water. She could smell it all the way across the room. Her mouth started to water even though she was sure there was no more moisture left in her body.

He walked across the room and offered it to her. She opened her mouth like a baby bird peeping to be fed. He trickled water in. A lot of it just spilled down her chin and soaked into her shirt. She closed her mouth and swallowed painfully, trying to get some of it down. Her mouth and throat were so parched and sore, it felt like they would crack open.

She opened her mouth again and he trickled more water in. This process was completed several more times until her stomach hurt. She was still thirsty, if that was what the excruciating feeling could be called, but if she drank any more, she would throw up, and what good would it be to her then?

She closed her eyes and sank back into the couch.

She didn't try to talk to him, to ask him, "Why?"

She had done that the first day. She had tried to make sense of it. To come up with a logical reason for everything that had happened. But how did one make sense of something that was so erratic and illogical? She was sure he couldn't explain it to her if he had wanted to. He was driven by something within himself.

"This is madness," he muttered, as if he could read her thoughts. He paced back and forth across the room, putting the water bottle back down in the kitchen and searching for something that was not there.

"You can't trust 'em," he said to himself. "You can't trust anyone. They all turn against you."

She licked her lips and wished that he would forget to put the gag back on again when he left. Not so that she could scream for help. Just so she could close her mouth properly and not have to deal with that disgusting rag being stuffed back into her mouth again.

After more pacing, he approached her again. He shoved her onto her side and grabbed her arms to unlock the handcuffs that held them bound. She fought back against him. Bad things happened when he unlocked the handcuffs. She didn't want to go through it again.

But he didn't give her the choice. He ignored her weak struggles and unlocked one bracelet, freeing her arms. She brought her hands to the front. They didn't hurt yet. Not until the circulation started to return. They were just numb and felt as though they belonged to someone else. The other woman was controlling her body, fighting to stay alive when she just wanted to die.

He reached down to cut the plastic zip tie that bound her ankles together. She didn't kick him or try to stand up to escape.

The initial part of the release was routine. He would pull her to her feet. Once she could take her own weight, he would lead her to the bathroom. There, she could relieve herself, even splash a little water on her face.

But after that...

That was when the brutality would start.

# CHAPTER
## SEVEN

It was day two of the apartment cleanout. Graham had finished with most of the kitchen and living room. There wasn't much to do in the bathroom, so he started in on that. Most of the time, he considered everything in a bathroom to be garbage or hazardous chemicals. It was pretty quick just to throw everything out. A pair of gloves to protect himself from anything disgusting, and he just went to town.

But the apartment was pretty clean and inoffensive, so he took more time in the bathroom than he normally did, considering the towels for the thrift store, putting a curling iron and blow dryer in the warehouse box for his storefront, and seeing whether there was anything he wanted to keep for himself in the toiletries and cleaning chemicals. Reducing the bottom line was what it was all about. The fewer expenses he had, the more profitable the business was, even if he didn't have a lot of jobs lined up.

Then it was time to begin on the bedroom.

He already knew that the clothing and bedding would go to Scarlett's Secrets. Or at least, he would show them to her. He was pretty sure she would snatch it all up in a heartbeat. There was a lot of brand-name stuff, and it was all in very good shape. Ashley had known how to pick and take care of her clothes.

He brushed aside his concerns about why Ashley would leave so much behind. They had obviously been in a hurry and had not been able to pack very much. He had used the same logic to explain the presence of pictures of the newlyweds and Ashley's family in the living room.

There were no family pictures of Ethan, other than the wedding pictures. Maybe the apartment had originally belonged to Ashley and Ethan hadn't yet populated it with all his memories. They might be in a storage locker somewhere.

It *was* odd that Ashley would leave family pictures behind. But maybe she had taken a few select ones with her. If they had to fit everything in a small car, she had to be selective about what she could take with her. And if she had the photos on her phone or in a cloud account somewhere, she could get them reprinted wherever she settled next.

When Graham dug into the boxes on the shelf of the bedroom closet, he came across their wedding book. He looked through it, studying each page with a growing sense of unease. It was so carefully put together, with mementos as well as photos. Mementos that could not be stored in a cloud account.

Was there a reason Ashley would not want her wedding album? Maybe they had not left together. Maybe one-half of the couple had decided to leave. Maybe Ashley had been the one to write "I'm sorry" and left her keys behind. And then Ethan had decided to follow suit, perhaps pursuing her, begging her to come back. But he had known that they would never be coming back to this apartment again.

Graham shook his head. "I don't care why she left the wedding album behind," he said aloud.

He had a job to do, and it was not psychoanalyzing Ashley and figuring out why she had taken some items with her and not others. His job was to clean the apartment for the next tenant.

They didn't care why she had left. Marcel didn't care why she had left.

Graham couldn't care about it either. He would do the job he had been hired for.

The marriage had dissolved. Or it hadn't, and they had been on the run and couldn't afford to take the bulky book with them. Or Ashley had forgotten that it was in the closet, thinking it was in a storage locker somewhere, or that her sister had it for safekeeping, or she had been so focused on getting out quickly that she hadn't even thought of it. Or maybe she thought she could come back and get her personal items from Marcel in a month or two.

Graham put the book to the side. He would figure that one out later.

He didn't want to work on the bedroom. He needed a break from its intimacy. He decided to work on the multipurpose office and guest room. They had not stored too much junk there. Many people's spare rooms were filled to the gills with junk. They didn't have the time or energy to sort it, so they kept adding to it, shoving one thing after another into the space.

Graham left the couple's bedroom and walked into the smaller bedroom. Pull-out bed for guests. Desk, chair, shelves. There was no computer tower under the desk; they probably both used laptops or tablets, taken with them. A two-drawer filing cabinet. That would probably be quick enough to empty. Old bills could go straight into the recycling bin. He opened the first drawer and grabbed a handful of folders. They were primarily bills and other financial papers, as he had expected. Most people didn't even store those anymore. They could look them up online or download them to their hard drive. No need to store a paper copy, too.

A couple of books fell out of one of the file folders Graham had grabbed. He bent down to pick them up and slowly straightened. They were passports. Handling them gingerly by the edges, he turned to the identification page and looked at the expiry dates. They were still valid.

Who would abandon their apartment and leave their passports behind? Those were not easy to replace. Of course, they could have forgotten all about them, just as Ashley might have forgotten about her wedding book, but would they really? The questions were piling up. Leaving behind family pictures, wedding album, passports, e-reader, and all of that brand-name clothing? Had Ashley and Ethan really been in that much of a hurry to get out of the apartment? And if so, why? What had driven them out?

He looked around uneasily, as if whatever evil had chased them out was lurking behind him, watching his progress.

The apartment was quiet and still. He could hear distant noises in other apartments, but the soundproofing was not too bad.

Graham forced himself to turn back to his work. He looked through the drawers. It didn't appear that the couple had taken anything with them. The insurance papers, school records, and tax filings were there. There were no obvious gaps or empty folders to indicate they had removed anything.

He looked at the desk, where he had already noted that there was no desktop computer. But there were chargers. Why would they take their devices but leave the chargers behind? How would they charge those things when they ran out of juice? It didn't even look like they had taken one or two chargers that worked for multiple devices. There were no empty spaces on the power strip.

Graham walked back into the bedroom. He was no longer bothered by the fact that he was invading their bedroom. Now, he rifled through everything at high speed. He pushed the unmentionables around in drawers without any regard for how he was messing them up, checking underneath for anything that might have been hidden. He ferreted out jewelry boxes and bags and anything else that had intrinsic value.

Yes, he found valuable items in cleanouts all the time, but

those were jobs where detritus had built up over the years, and they had been forgotten about. Estates where the heir had no idea what had been left in the house.

Not a couple of newlyweds who couldn't have been living together for more than a year and hadn't had the time to forget what they owned. When Graham had decided to ditch his own apartment and his old life, he had prioritized his passport, jewelry, and electronics. If Ashley and Ethan were on the run from something, they would need anything easily converted into cash. If they were in trouble, they might need to leave the country.

It didn't make any sense.

# CHAPTER
# EIGHT

Graham sat down on the couch in the living room and took a break to call Marcel.

It took a few rings for the man to answer, but then he did so with a chirpy greeting.

"Ah, Mr. Hall It Away. Don't tell me you are done already. I expected you to take at least another day."

"No, I'm not done, but I'm making good progress. I just had a few questions for you."

"About what to take and what to leave?" Marcel guessed.

"No. I think we're on the same page there. But there are a few odd things about how the apartment was left."

Marcel made a dismissive noise. "You wouldn't believe the things people leave behind sometimes. It's nothing to worry about. Just keep going."

"Are you sure they abandoned the apartment?"

"Am I sure? Of course I'm sure. They left their keys. How did they expect to get back in?"

"I know. But... they left their passports."

"They forgot about them. Just make sure they are shredded so no one can use them."

"They didn't leave you with a forwarding address? Did you try their phone numbers?"

"Of course I did! And no, they did not leave a forwarding address. They're gone, Mr. Hall; they didn't want to be contacted. They just wanted to disappear. It happens. Probably in trouble with the law or some leg-breaker. They just picked up and left."

"Without their passports?"

"Sure. People don't think of that in the moment. They're panicking. Maybe they remember later, but then it is too late. They're not coming back here to ask for them. They'll just have to get new ones. Say that the old ones were stolen."

"All of Ashley's family photos and her wedding album."

"Not what you think about when you are in a panic."

"Jewelry, some of it high-end. And all of those clothes."

"Mr. Hall. Graham." Marcel sighed. "I understand why you are worried, but you don't need to be. They are gone. They are not coming back for any of this stuff. If there are valuables... I suggest you and I divide them up between us."

Graham would not be splitting his profits with the landlord. Not when he was the one doing all the work. He did not respond to this suggestion.

"You're absolutely sure that they left of their own choice?"

There was a beat of silence. "What do you mean, 'of their own choice'?"

"What if they were forced to leave? What if... they didn't take off? What if they were..."

"What? Kidnapped?" Marcel demanded in a tone of disbelief.

"Well, yes."

"Then why would they leave a note and their keys?"

"Well... if the kidnapper wanted you to think that they had left of their own volition."

"I think... you have quite an imagination, my friend. There is no sign of violence. I walked through that apartment myself. There's no blood, no chairs knocked over, no drag marks or scuffs on the wall. Nothing at all to make me think that maybe someone kidnapped Ashley and Ethan. They just took off, Mr. Hall. I am sure of that."

"You're *sure*," Graham repeated.

"I'm sure. If you'd been a landlord as long as I have, you'd understand. There's no whiff of anything illegal or violent going on in that apartment. They just abandoned it. Took off to pursue a new venture. Wanted to disappear. Who knows. But it isn't anything for us to worry about."

"Okay," Graham finally conceded. Marcel was far more experienced than he was. He had been clearing out people's junk for less than a year. Marcel had been at his business for years. Listen to the expert. He hadn't gotten ahead in life by ignoring the experts.

"Great," Marcel approved. "Back to work for you."

Graham chuckled. "Not in a hurry, are you?"

"The sooner the job is done, the better. You get it done today, and maybe I'll even give you a bonus."

# CHAPTER
# NINE

Graham wasn't going to have the job finished that day. He could push and have everything out of there by midnight if he didn't mind being too exhausted to do anything else the next day.

But it wasn't worth it for him to push through the job that quickly. Even if Marcel paid him a bonus.

But exhaustion was not what was stopping him from finishing. He just couldn't continue without being sure that Marcel was right.

He left the apartment and knocked on the door across the hallway.

At first, it appeared that no one was home, but eventually, there was a noise within, and the door latch clicked. The door opened just a crack, and a sliver of a person was visible, one eye applied to the crack to see who was there.

"Who are you?" a cracking voice demanded.

"My name is Graham, ma'am," he introduced himself, hoping that the person was a woman as he guessed. It wouldn't do to "ma'am" a mister. "I'm working with Marcel, your landlord, to clear out the apartment across the hall."

She looked him up and down and considered this for a long

moment before opening the door a few more inches so he could see her better.

An old woman with scraggly gray hair. She had a worn and stained housecoat wrapped around her. Maybe he had woken her up, and she was normally more presentable. She looked like the old witch out of a Hansel and Gretel book.

"What happened to them?" She nodded to the door. "They moved out?"

"Yes. Did you know them well?"

"No. Just saw them coming and going sometimes."

"You didn't ever hear them? They didn't argue?"

She stared at Graham. "Why would they?"

"Well... I don't know. Most couples do at some point. Get angry or drunk, a little out of control, don't realize other people can hear them."

"No. Nothing like that."

"Did you ever talk to them? Discuss the weather when you were both picking up your mail...?"

"They seemed like a nice couple," she said. "What are you accusing them of?"

"Nothing at all. I'm actually a little worried about them. Marcel said they moved out, but they left a few things behind that made me wonder if something had happened to them."

The neighbor rubbed her nose, then opened the door a little farther, inviting Graham to enter.

She motioned for him to sit at the kitchen counter, where a couple of tall bar stools were parked. Her kitchen table was piled high with paper and detritus, as was every other surface Graham could see in the living room. The apartment smelled of dust and stale coffee.

Someone would be calling Graham when the old woman died. And it would be a much bigger project than cleaning out Ashley's and Ethan's apartment.

"I am Myrtle," the woman introduced herself, again wiping her nose and then holding out her hand to shake. Graham ignored the extended hand. She eventually lowered it and boosted herself up onto the other stool. Graham was afraid she was going to topple right off the other side, but she knew what she was doing and sat perched there, peering at him nearsightedly. Several pairs of glasses were probably sprinkled about the cluttered apartment.

"What do you think happened to them?" Myrtle asked Graham. "They seemed like a nice couple. They brought me a Danish, sometimes, when they had been down to Holes. I never asked them to; they just started doing it, bringing an old lady something to brighten her Saturday mornings."

"That *is* nice," Graham agreed. He had no idea people did things like that. One of those friendly, small-town gestures he had heard about. "To be honest, I don't know what happened... did they tell you they were going away? Or that they were having any trouble?"

"No. They didn't say anything to me. They just... one day, they were there, and then I realized it had been a few days since I had heard anything from them. I mentioned it to Marcel and asked him if they had gone away. He said not that he knew of..."

And then he had checked, Graham guessed. First, he made a few phone calls, knocked on their door, and finally let himself in and found the apartment abandoned. So Myrtle was the first one who had noticed their absence.

"When was the last time you saw them?"

"Oh, I don't know. Last week sometime. Maybe... Saturday, when they brought me my Danish. I can't remember if I saw them after that or not."

"Were they packing? Did you see them with any suitcases?"

"No, I didn't see. But I'm not a nosy neighbor. I don't spend all of my time watching my neighbors. I have plenty else to do." She made a short motion to indicate her apartment. Clearly, she had a lot of projects on the go. Plenty to keep her attention on other things.

"Yes, of course. I didn't mean to make you think I was being critical. I was just hoping to get some idea of when they left, and if... well, if it was voluntary."

Her forehead wrinkled in a frown of concern. "What do you think happened to them? You don't think that... someone did something to them, do you?"

"I don't have any evidence that anyone did anything to them. You didn't see anyone going into their apartment? Any visitors they might have had in the past week or so?"

"No. Nothing. I don't know what happened. But... if you think something happened to them, you should report it to the police."

Graham was not eager to have to talk to the police about anything. Hopefully, he could find something out just by talking to the neighbors, and if one of them thought that something might have happened to Ashley and Ethan, they could report it themselves. Or maybe Marcel would report their absence.

But Marcel wouldn't. He had already made it clear that he wanted Graham to just clear out the apartment and not worry about the possibility that the couple had not left voluntarily. He had his own reasons for not reporting the disappearance. He just wanted to keep everything simple and keep his business running smoothly.

"Were Ashley and Ethan friends with anyone else in the building?"

"Oh, I don't know. Ashley was friendly to everyone, but I don't know if I ever saw her with anyone other than Ethan. And Ethan... well, he was very shy."

"Oh, was he?"

"You didn't know them?"

Graham shook his head. "I'm pretty new to Bleeding Hearts Valley. I've only been here for a few months. I never met either of them. I was just hired by Marcel to clean out the apartment."

"Well, it's very nice of you to be so concerned when you never even met them." Myrtle rolled her head back and forth, considering. "They were not very much alike, but you know the saying—

opposites attract. Ashley was friendly and outgoing and showed a lot of concern for other people. She is a social worker, you know, in the city. I could never do something like that. She must see the most heartbreaking cases."

Graham grimaced. "Yes, you're right. I don't know how people can keep at it for years. I would be done after three weeks."

Myrtle laughed and nodded. "I might last a little longer than that, but probably not a lot. But you can see how her caring nature affected her career choice and her choice to do little things like bringing an old lady a Danish for no reason."

Graham nodded. "And what did Ethan do?" He had seen pictures of the two of them. Ashley, with sleek blond hair. An understated beauty with her Midwest charm. Little to no makeup, just a smile and stylish clothes.

Ethan had looked broody even in the pictures. Dark hair and eyes that were deep-set and vulnerable looking as he held Ashley close to his side. Graham allowed a flight of fancy that Ethan saw himself as Ashley's protector, and she saw herself as his.

"He was an artist." Myrtle chewed on her lower lip. "That was what they said, anyway. I never actually saw him paint anything. I never even saw any art supplies in their apartment. I think maybe he was *unemployed* and they just didn't want to tell anyone that."

She rolled her eyes and looked back toward the door and the apartment beyond it.

So much of society's value of a person hinged on their monetary contribution to their household, how high in their company they managed to rise, and other such capitalist measurements. Once upon a time, Graham had thought he had it all made. He was raking in the money, was climbing the ranks in the company, and was considered a rising star by many.

But that was then. Now, he was the *garbage man*.

# CHAPTER
# TEN

Ashley and Ethan had occupied the apartment at the end of the hall, so they only had neighbors to one side, and Myrtle across the hall. Myrtle looked around vaguely when various clocks began chiming around her apartment. "What time is that? Five o'clock? Ian and Robin should be home soon if they aren't already. They share a wall with Ashley and Ethan, so they might be able to tell you more than I can."

"Ian and Robin," Graham repeated, nodding.

"They are both young men," Myrtle told him. "You *know*..." She made an "airy fairy" motion to ensure her meaning could not be mistaken. "Both very nice, but not very... ahem." She cleared her throat.

Graham did his best to avoid smiling or laughing at her. "I understand," he assured her. "I have a cousin like that. I'll be careful."

"Oh, yes," she agreed, nodding her head wisely. "That's good, then."

Graham said goodbye to Myrtle and let himself out. He heard the locks and bolts engaging as he walked down the hall. He approached Ian's and Robin's apartment and knocked politely. Hopefully, he was not interrupting their mealtime. He could always go back to cleaning up the apartment if they were occupied and get back to them once they finished eating.

There were voices within the apartment, and Graham heard one calling out, "Coming, coming, one minute..."

The door opened with a whoosh. The young man who appeared in the doorway had short brown hair and glasses, and a loud, blue patterned jacket paired with a striped t-shirt. Graham had caught sight of him in the elevator the day before. They looked at each other for a moment, the young man trying to place Graham.

"Hi. Graham Hall. I'm working next door, getting it cleaned out for Marcel."

"Oh, you are Hall," he said in a high, dramatic voice. "It's the neighbor," he called out to his companion. "I am Ian." he looked Graham over. "Well, you have undoubtedly had a busy day over there and are tired and sweaty." He gave a private smile and winked at Graham. "What can Ian and Robbie do for you?"

He opened the door wider and motioned Graham in.

The other man was busy in the kitchen. He had shoulder-length blond hair and was dressed all in black. He had no visible tattoos, but Graham had no doubt he had some which were currently covered by his leather jacket. Not what Graham would have considered kitchen attire, but to each his own.

Robin raised his brows, looked at Graham for a second, then returned to his meal prep.

"I guess you heard that Ashley and Ethan were leaving?" Graham suggested.

"Hear about it? No. They never said a thing. I would think they would at least tell us and say goodbye, but they just disappeared. One day, they were here, and the next, they were gone."

"Do you know which day they moved? When was the last time you saw them?"

Ian looked at Robin, who did not provide any suggestions. "Well, let's see... I know they were here Sunday morning. They were having a rather... outspoken conversation while we were still trying to sleep." He sighed deeply and rolled his eyes. "But that's the last time I remember seeing or hearing them. Monday night... Robbie mentioned that they didn't have the TV on. They usually had it on after supper. Sports shows, mainly. Ashley liked her sports."

"Ashley did?" Graham was surprised. Usually it was the husband who commandeered the TV for sports after dinner.

"Yes, Big football and baseball fan. And anything else if football or baseball weren't on. Big Wild fan."

"Wild?"

"Hockey," Ian laughed. "Minnesota Wild."

"Oh." Graham shrugged. "I don't follow it. So... no TV Monday night?"

"No. Nothing since then. Right, Robbie?"

Robbie nodded as he read the back of a jar of Alfredo sauce. "Nothing," he agreed. A soft, low voice.

If they had disappeared later Sunday or during the day Monday, it had now been five or six days. Graham's stomach felt as heavy as a brick. A lot could happen in that length of time. A lot. He read the news. He watched TV. The first forty-eight hours had already passed. The second forty-eight too. If they had been abducted, the chances they were both still alive were very low.

"And they never told you they were leaving or that they had an opportunity out of town or anything like that?"

Ian and Robin exchanged looks. Robin paused in his meal preparations, thinking.

"Nothing, I'm telling you," Ian insisted. "You would think that they would at least have said something. You don't just walk off and not say anything to anyone."

"And leave everything in your apartment behind."

Ian's eyes flashed with interest. "Everything?"

"Looks like they packed a few bags, but they still left a lot behind. Clothes, jewelry, passports."

Ian and Robin both looked at Graham, their eyes wide.

"What?" Ian demanded. "Jewelry? Passports? That doesn't make any sense."

"That's what I thought. But Marcel said it's nothing. People leave things behind all the time that you wouldn't expect them to."

"Well, that's not right," Ian disagreed. "Are you telling me that... they just walked away with a couple of suitcases, and left everything else behind, including passports?"

"And their wedding album."

Both men shifted uncomfortably and looked at each other.

"A girl doesn't just leave her wedding album behind," Ian said. "Not unless she's leaving *him* too."

"How had things been between them? Was there... trouble in paradise?" Graham suggested.

"Well, I don't like to say," Ian said in a gossipy tone. He motioned for Graham to take a seat at the table. Bright red chairs and a yellow table. Graham wouldn't have put them together, but the combination worked.

Ian leaned in closer to Graham. "I mean, they were a couple. They had discussions. Some of them louder than others. Everybody loses their patience sometimes. People can't be one hundred percent compatible. I would have said that they were still trying to make it work. But Ashley walking away..." He shook his head. "No, I wouldn't have expected that."

# CHAPTER
# ELEVEN

"What did you think?" Graham pressed. "You thought that they were pretty stable as a couple?"

"Yeah. I didn't think they were to the point where either of them was willing to break it off. They both seemed really devoted to each other. Willing to put in the hard work on the relationship. You need that, you know? You can be compatible and not put the work into it, and you'll end up breaking up. Or you can be incompatible, and if you put the work into it, you still might be able to make it." Ian looked over at Robin and smiled.

"We are not incompatible," Robin said.

"No." Ian smiled again, a little bit of color flushing his cheeks. He shrugged. "We're not. And I don't think Ashley and Ethan were either. I think they just... they were a new couple. They needed work. Needed to find out how to make it work with each other."

"Do you know how long they had been married?"

"Not exactly. A few months. Maybe a year. Not two." Ian raised a brow at his partner.

Robin shook his head. "No, not two," he agreed. He reviewed his mental records and shook his head. "I can't think of anything that would pinpoint it... maybe when they leased the apartment."

"Was it their first place together? Was that when they first moved in with each other?" Graham asked.

"They were together before that, but not long. It was their first *real* place. Since they officially tied the knot and started living together as man and wife."

"I can ask Marcel."

"Yeah, he might be able to tell you," Ian agreed. "Marcel doesn't think anything happened? He thinks that they just decided to move out without telling him? Marcel never told me that. He just said that they had moved out and that some stuff needed to be cleaned up before the apartment could be rented out again. I just thought... maybe some holes in the wall and repainting. Maybe an old TV to be hauled off to the dump. I didn't think that... it was everything. That they just took off and left everything behind."

"Marcel said people do that. He's not concerned."

"But he should be," Robin said forcefully, surprising Graham. "Anything could have happened to them. How can he not see that?"

Graham nodded vigorously, glad someone else could see it from his perspective. "Exactly. That's what I don't understand. I mean, I get that he doesn't want to get the police involved. No one *likes* to have to go to the police with something like this." Certainly, Graham didn't want to go to the police. He wanted someone else to step in and take over on this. "But they could have been abducted. Murdered. We don't know."

"There isn't anything..." Ian gave an exaggerated shudder, "Anything *creepy* over there, is there? I mean, like, blood? Or something that was bleached? Or a knife missing from the butcher's block?"

"Don't be dramatic," Robin snapped. "This isn't a game. They *could* have been killed. They could have been robbed or kidnapped. At least their bodies weren't left in the apartment." He paused and swallowed, and Graham had a feeling he was trying to force down his own shudder and keep everything on an even keel. "So they could still be fine. But why would they go away and leave everything behind?"

"Not everything," Ian reminded him. "They did take suitcases with them. They could have taken the most important stuff... and what was left was just stuff that was less important or that they had forgotten about."

Robin shook his head. "Passport and wedding album," he reminded Ian. "There's no way they forgot both."

"But it wasn't a robbery," Graham said. "There was a lot of valuable stuff left behind. It took me two minutes to find Ashley's jewelry. If someone had broken into their apartment or forced his way in, they would have looked for anything they could liquidate quickly. Cash, computers, jewelry. But the jewelry was still there. If it had been a burglar, he would have at least gone through the bedroom drawers to find her jewelry."

"Then it wasn't burglary. Or robbery, or whatever. But that doesn't mean it wasn't murder. Or abduction." Robin insisted.

He was putting Graham's own fears into words, so it was hard to argue, even playing devil's advocate. Robin was right. The young couple being murdered or abducted fit with the facts in a way that a voluntary departure or robbery did not.

"Someone else could have packed the missing suitcases. Just thrown a few things in to make it look like they went on a vacation or took off voluntarily. And then it would take the police a long time to start looking for them, if at all. Maybe until their bodies were discovered in some lake or a shallow grave."

Graham swallowed. "We can't assume they are dead," he said firmly. "For the purposes of our discussion, they are still alive. Maybe not doing very well, but still alive."

They were all silent for a few minutes. Robin went back to his silent meal preparations. The smell of garlic frying filled the air.

"You never heard anything?" Graham asked. "A big fight, an altercation, furniture being thrown around, anything like that? Strange voices?"

"No," Ian shook his head slowly. "Sometimes they had arguments, but nothing like that. Nothing that I would have guessed was violent. Not on either side," he added abruptly. "I know that women can be abusive too. You can't assume that the man is always the aggressor."

"What did they argue about?" Graham glanced in the direction of the apartment he had been cleaning out. "Could you hear that through the walls?"

"No," Ian shook his head with regret. "I have no idea what they were arguing about. The usual, I would assume. Money. She wants to go out, and he wants to stay home. Pressure from their parents. Her time of the month. Couples argue."

Graham shrugged. He had been in few romantic relationships, but that about covered it. Disparate backgrounds, family members and traditions, finances. It could all add up, increasing the pressure, until things reached a boiling point.

"Myrtle across the hall, she said that Ethan didn't have a job. He was an unemployed artist. So that must have led to financial pressure."

Ian looked amused. He pushed his glasses up. "That old biddy has no idea what's going on," he told Graham. "She never leaves her own apartment. She rarely talks to anyone. You're lucky she even knew who they were."

"She said that Ashley and Ethan brought her Danishes. So they must have stayed to talk now and then. She doesn't seem unfriendly."

Ian's expression softened. "That's just like Ashley. She's such a sweetheart. Always thinking of other people. She *would* befriend the old hermit."

"So they must have talked. She knew that Ethan was an artist. Unless that was made up too."

"She said he was an artist," Ian agreed. "Ashley did, I mean. But I never saw anything that he had done. You're going through the apartment. Have you found any painting supplies? Sculptures? Anything at all? Even a few old sketchbooks?"

"Not yet," Graham admitted. He hadn't been through everything yet, but there was no obvious studio space, easel, art supplies, or finished works. There was no original art showcased in the apartment, just some mass-produced posters to brighten the area up.

"So... starving artist? I wouldn't think so. Ashley might want people to think so, but I don't think that was the case."

"What did Ethan do, then?"

"He had a job," Robin contributed. He removed pasta and sauce from the stovetop and chopped chicken pieces from the oven where they were warming, and started assembling their meal, setting out three plates without a word of invitation. "Ashley helped him to find something through her connections."

"What kind of job?" Graham didn't protest the assumption that he would eat with them. His mouth was watering and his stomach growling. If he didn't eat with them, he would have to go out to get something. And the food smelled really good.

Robin took a big bowl of dressed salad out of the fridge and set out salad bowls for each of them so that the chilled salad didn't have to touch the hot pasta, possibly causing the leaves to wilt.

"What kind of job?" Robin repeated, casting his mind back. "I think... it was something at an office. I would have thought that it would be something in light industrial. Working outside. Or maybe a retail shop that needed some additional hands. As far as I know, he didn't have any education. But it was better than that. Initially, he was excited about it and thought it was a great opportunity."

"So maybe it was something that used his artistic skills?" Graham suggested. "If Ashley said he was an artist and she was the one who connected him up with this job, maybe it was some kind of commercial art job. And he was excited that it was something that he could bring his talent to bear upon."

The other two men nodded. Robin sat down with them and motioned for them to eat, digging in himself.

The salad was crisp and not soaked in dressing. The chicken Alfredo was prepared to perfection. Graham would never have expected the black-jacket-wearing man to be a culinary genius, but he definitely knew how to pull a meal together. It was delicious.

"So, was he happy with his job?" Graham asked. "And was Ashley happy with hers? Myrtle said that she was a social worker. Or did she get that wrong too?"

"No, that's right. She must have been very good at it," Ian said. "I told you, Ashley was lovely. Cared about everyone, always checking in to make sure that they were okay and doing little things like buying Myrtle Danishes without ever being asked. I think that is how she met Ethan, too. Through her work."

"He was... one of her cases?" Graham frowned and tried to make that fit with the narrative. What kind of social work did she do? What if she worked at a halfway house or some other job with criminals, and that was how she and Ethan had met?

"No, no, not like that," Ian laughed. "He did volunteer work at a shelter where she worked. Something like that. He wasn't homeless, at least I don't think so. He helped out. Soup kitchen or something, maybe. I'm not sure what it was. But you know, she liked him, decided he was so sweet and shy, and before you know it..." Ian sucked a bit of sauce off his finger with a popping sound. "Bob's your uncle."

"And was that here? At St Francis? Or was it in the city?"

"I don't think Ashley ever worked at St Francis," Ian said. "So it must have been in the city."

"Is she a Bleeding Hearts Valley native?" Graham asked. "Is her family here?"

"She's a Bleeder, all right," Ian agreed. "Her family moved away, though. I think her parents went to Florida. Ashley went away to school, and I don't think they figured she would ever come back here after she was done. It's not exactly... the up-and-coming place it was eighty years ago." Ian laughed.

"But she did come back here after school to live and work."

Ian nodded. "Obviously."

"But not because her parents or boyfriend were here."

"She must like it or something," Robin said. "I can't imagine why." He looked at Graham. "You're a newcomer. Why did you come here? What exactly was it that attracted you to Bleeding Hearts Valley, and why did you stay here? Why didn't you run away screaming after a couple of weeks?"

Graham chuckled. "I was looking for somewhere quieter. A slower speed."

"Well, Bleeding Hearts is that," Ian acknowledged.

"Other than—apparently—people can just disappear for no reason," Graham observed.

"Well, I wouldn't say that is normal. I don't think we've ever had a neighbor disappear before, have we, Robbie?"

Robin shook his head. "I don't think so. Not that we noticed."

The conversation drifted as they ate the salad and pasta, savoring every bite. Robin uncorked a bottle of wine to go with it, and though Graham wasn't a big wine guy, he thought it paired nicely, and nodded his appreciation.

They all leaned back in their chairs after eating, satiated and a bit sleepy. Graham thought about the job that still awaited him next door. He should get back to it. He knew he wouldn't finish it today, but he should put in a few more hours if he wanted to get it done on schedule.

But besides the bone weariness he felt at the thought of tackling the job once more, something else prevented him from returning to the task. The discussion with Ian and Robin confirmed his feelings were not wrong or exaggerated. They felt the same way he did. The things the newlyweds had left behind signaled that something sinister might have happened. Maybe Marcel was right, and Ashley and Ethan had just walked away from their lease, but Graham couldn't help feeling that even if they hadn't been killed or kidnapped, they had been chased off in a hurry, forcing them to leave everything else behind.

"What are you going to do about it?" Ian asked, leaning forward in his seat and picking up his cup of coffee for a sip. "Are you going to go to the police?"

There wasn't much that Graham wanted to do less.

He rubbed his forehead, hoping that somehow, Robin would jump in and say that they should do it. Or that they would call Marcel and talk him into doing it. Anything that would take it off Graham's plate.

"Do I have to?" he asked plaintively, like a child being told it was bedtime.

"Yes, Graham, you have to," Ian told him with a chuckle. "You know you do."

Graham swore. He really did not want to. "You're the ones who knew them. Shouldn't you do it? I never even met the people. I can't very well say what their state of mind was and if this was something they would be likely to do. How can I second-guess what Marcel has to say? He knew them. I don't."

"You're the one who can tell the police what Ashley and Ethan left behind. If we were to try to make a report, all of that would just be hearsay. We don't know anything directly except that they aren't there anymore, and Marcel said he has to get someone else to rent the unit."

"He should have reported it when he first found out that the apartment had been abandoned," Graham groused.

"Maybe," Ian agreed with a shrug. "But he didn't, and he won't. So it's up to you."

# CHAPTER
## TWELVE

Graham wished he could just wait until the next day to make the report. Maybe once he slept on it, he would come up with another solution. And even if he didn't, at least he would have felt a little less emotionally wrung out and it would be easier to just treat it as a routine chore that needed to be done.

But if he waited until the next day, it would cut into tomorrow's work. He would have less time for the cleanout. And he wanted to start fresh in the morning, without the specter hanging over him.

After thanking Robin and Ian for the unexpected repast, Graham forced himself to drive to the police station to report the disappearance of Ashley Carter and Ethan Quick.

The police station was small but well-lit and modern. A window had been cracked open adjacent to the waiting area, making it smell fresh. There were still cops on duty writing reports, answering phones, and shooting the breeze in the open-concept room beyond the reception desk where Graham was required to check in and make his request.

"I've never done this before," he told the short female cop who stood there looking mulish. "I'm a little nervous and I don't know who I'm supposed to talk to."

"What's the problem? You need to file a complaint? Had a car accident and need a sticker?"

"Uh, no. Nothing like that. I wanted to... file a missing person report, I guess. They make it look so easy on TV. You just walk in and tell them that someone has disappeared, and they take care of it..."

"Who is missing?" she asked tiredly. "Your wife?"

Graham had a feeling that if it were his wife, she would just tell him to go home and wait. And to behave better so that she wouldn't take off again.

"No, no. I'm not married. It's... a young couple. I'm doing some work on their apartment. Or their former apartment. And... I think that something might have happened to them."

"What makes you think that?"

"They disappeared, and there are a lot of valuables and personal items that they didn't take with them."

"Who says they disappeared?"

"The landlord called me in to do the work because he said they had abandoned the apartment. But when I started to do the work... it seems like they didn't leave it voluntarily. Their passports are still there, for one thing. Their jewelry."

She looked at him, pursing her lips. It seemed like she, too, thought it odd that they would abandon the apartment but leave their passports and valuables behind.

"What do you think happened to them?"

"I wish I knew. I'm afraid that someone might have taken them, or harmed them, and then tried to cover it up by making it look like they had just abandoned the apartment voluntarily."

She tapped her pen on the desk a few times, thoughtful, then finally nodded. "If you'll have a seat and wait, I will get one of the detectives to talk to you."

"Thanks."

The last thing he wanted to do was to sit down again and waste his time staring at the wall or scrolling his social media accounts.

But he did as instructed and sat in one of the uncomfortable chairs in the waiting area. He waited, watching the woman to see what she would do. She didn't seem to immediately spring into action, raising the alarm and immediately recruiting a detective to take Graham's statement. She typed on her computer, maybe sending a message to the designated detective. Or maybe typing up her lunch order for the next day. She answered the phone a few times. She didn't speak loudly enough for Graham to hear what she might be discussing.

After watching her for a while, he finally dug out his phone, checked his email, looked for any stray text messages he might have missed, and settled on his social media accounts, wondering how long he was going to sit there waiting.

At long last, he was approached by a pair of shiny black shoes.

"Mr. Hall?"

He looked up at the owner of the shiny shoes. The police detective was dressed tidily in a light blue shirt, dark navy pants, and tie, loosened at the neck, and looked as world-weary as any cop Graham had ever seen on TV. His name bar said Det. Joiner, and he looked ready for retirement if not already past his qualification date. He had a wrinkled face that had seen a lot of sun and lots of gray in his temples and sideburns.

"Yes, that's me," Graham agreed, standing up and offering his hand.

Detective Joiner gave him an uninterested handshake. He sighed. "Follow me."

He led Graham to an interview room that looked nothing like the interrogation rooms he had seen on TV. It was carpeted with a dark blue, low pile. The chairs looked freshly upholstered instead of just the plastic and metal tubes of the chairs out in the waiting room. Maybe they used different rooms to interview witnesses and suspects who might throw up during an interrogation.

Graham sat down across from Joiner. Joiner didn't say

anything at first, then wiggled his fingers in an invitation for Graham to explain why he was there. "Go ahead."

He again went through a similar spiel to what he had given the woman at the reception desk. Joiner sat there without any change in his expression, no sign of what he thought of Graham's story. He didn't write anything down or pull out a voice recorder. He wasn't playing with his phone, but Graham felt his mind was far away.

Graham finished with the bare bones of the couple's disappearance and looked at Joiner, waiting for his response.

Joiner coughed into his fist. He shrugged his broad shoulders. "Sounds to me like they are voluntarily missing," he said. "There's nothing we can do about that. No laws have been broken."

"But they could be in danger. They could already have come to harm."

"It doesn't sound like there is any evidence to suggest that."

"Well... no. I don't have any evidence they have been harmed, but do you need that? Aren't the circumstances of their disappearance enough for you to look into it? See what you can find?"

"What are we supposed to do? You haven't discovered anything that suggests they were abducted or harmed."

"You could try to find out where they went. Maybe talk to their employers and find out if they have a mail forwarding order. I don't know. Talk to their extended families, and find out if they have been in touch. Or if they know how to reach them. It shouldn't be too hard to figure out if they were just going on a holiday or moving to the city. They will not have just dropped off the face of the earth."

"You have tried to reach them?"

"Well, no. I don't know them. But Marcel, he said that he tried calling them, and couldn't get either of them on the phone. He didn't have an address to forward their mail to."

"And he isn't concerned about it? Why isn't *he* in here making a report?"

"He thinks that they just abandoned the apartment. But they didn't. They left their passports there. Their valuables. Does that sound like someone who just decided not to let their landlord know they were leaving? Why abandon it? They weren't behind on the rent. They didn't owe him anything. They could have just told him that they were moving. They could have packed up their apartment and given him a forwarding address for anything that arrived for them after they left. Why disappear?"

"We don't need a reason. There is nothing against the law in them disappearing. They can do that any time they like."

"I'm not saying they broke the law. I'm saying it wasn't voluntary. Something happened to them."

"You have no evidence."

"That doesn't mean I'm wrong."

"Maybe not," Joiner said with a shrug. "But there is nothing I can do about it. I'll keep my ears open for any rumor of something that might have happened to them. But don't hold your breath. Chances are, they just decided to start fresh somewhere else. People do it more often than you would think."

*Did they indeed?*

# CHAPTER
# THIRTEEN

It was late by the time Graham got back to the apartment. He really didn't want to get back to working on the cleanout, but he didn't have much choice. He needed time the next day to put on the finishing touches that would set him apart from other junk removal specialists and make his business shine so that Marcel and the others Marcel talked to would hire him for future jobs. If there was one way to spread goodwill and get good reviews and referrals from a client, it was by going that extra mile and putting on those last finishing touches.

If he wanted the time to do that and still give Marcel enough time to get people in to look at the apartment and sign a rental agreement before the first of the month, he needed to finish the bulk of the work tonight and just have the removal and final touches to do the next day.

It was a self-imposed deadline. Nothing catastrophic would happen if Graham took an extra day to finish. Marcel would still be grateful.

He tiptoed down the hall past Ian and Robin's apartment and opened the door very quietly as he stood in front of Myrtle's door to get back into Ashley and Ethan's apartment. He flicked on the light switch and closed the door gently behind him. It looked like it needed a lot more work than it did. He knew that if he put a few hours in, he would be ready to haul the sorted boxes away tomorrow.

He returned to the bedroom, where he had the most work to do. He started with the bedding and the clothing hanging in the closet, folding everything neatly and piling it into the boxes. Having stripped the bed, Graham decided to flip and rotate the mattress so it would be ready for the next tenants.

And that was when he found the journal. While he had done a quick check of the bed before to make sure there was nothing hidden under the mattress, the book was pushed much farther over than he would have expected. Maybe Ashley had dealt with nosy parents or an intrusive partner in the past and had learned to push it well past where most searchers would check. That was smart. Still an obvious hiding place, but too far out of reach to find in a casual search. Anyone looking for it would go on to search the rest of the room and apartment without ever finding it.

Graham sat down on the bed for a moment to flip through the journal. The same uneasy feeling came back tenfold. Maybe she would forget about her passport, something that she only used once every year or two on vacation. But her journal? Something she wrote in regularly? Would she really forget that when she was packing? Even if she were upset about something else?

He couldn't see it. If she were under duress, maybe. If someone were forcing her to leave with him, she might have left it behind. But not if she were leaving voluntarily.

He stopped at a random page and looked at the next entry.

When I got up this morning, the apartment door was open. Not just unlocked, as it has been a couple of times lately, but actually standing open a couple of inches.

I asked Ethan about it. He was the one who is supposed to be checking to make sure that it is locked each night so that we can both go to sleep knowing that we are safe and secure. He got angry and said that of course he had locked it. He wouldn't leave it unlocked so that anyone could just walk in. He said it was his job to protect me and make sure nothing bad happened to me.

I feel comforted and uneasy at the same time. Did he just forget? Or does someone else have a key to our apartment? That weaselly landlord, Marcel? Maybe a building maintenance man? Or was it someone who doesn't have a key? Someone who can pick locks? A cat burglar?

Nothing has been taken. Each time I have found it unlocked, I have checked on the stereo and computer equipment, my jewelry, and anything else that might look like a good target for a thief. And none of that stuff has ever been touched.

I guess from now on, I need to be the one to check the doors. Then, at least, I'll know whether it was locked or not. Ethan can be so absent-minded sometimes. It's not his fault, I know, just ADHD or thinking important thoughts about other things. But I need to know that we are safe. And if we are not, I need to know that too.

Graham looked up from the journal and looked around the apartment as if he might be able to see something that reflected what he had just read in the journal. He looked at the door, with its series of locks. He had always thought that people didn't lock their doors in small towns. They thought it was safe just to leave them unlocked. Everyone trusted their neighbors.

But that hadn't been his experience in Bleeding Hearts Valley. Instead, there almost seemed to be an atmosphere of distrust. It expanded far past just trusting your neighbors to stay out of your business and keep an eye out for any trouble.

Here was evidence that something *had* been going on with Ashley and Ethan. It wasn't proof of whether they had been kidnapped or had left of their own volition. But it confirmed to him that something had been wrong. Something had gone wrong weeks before Ashley and Ethan had disappeared.

# CHAPTER
# FOURTEEN

Graham never did make it home that night. There was a lot of work to do, and he kept stopping what he was doing to read journal entries and try to figure out what had happened to the young couple. Some of Ashley's entries were light and cheerful, reporting on routine happenings, how things were going with her work, and touching moments with Ethan that were so saccharine sweet that Graham doubted whether they had really happened the way Ashley reported them.

He fell asleep on the stripped bed, which wasn't something that he would tell Marcel.

Graham wouldn't have thought he would be able to sleep so easily, considering the horror movie script that Ashley seemed to be recounting. It wasn't just the unlocked apartment door. That was just the beginning.

When I got home from work today, everything had been moved. I tried to show Ethan, but he just couldn't see it. It wasn't obvious. Not like last week when the chairs had been turned around backward. This time, it was more subtle. All of the pictures and knickknacks moved over a quarter of an inch.

The dimmer switches on the lights set to the wrong level. The organizer trays in the drawers put back in the wrong positions.

Ethan just shook his head and said, "Are you sure?" like he didn't believe anything had been moved and couldn't see it himself. I know that guys don't see things the same way as women, but are they really that clueless? Could he not see everything had been moved?

I suggested that we might need to move away from here, and Ethan just snapped about how hard it had been to find a suitable place to live, and he wasn't going to go through all of that again. Like it just wasn't worth the extra work it would take to live somewhere safe.

Graham put the journal to the side, even though his brain insisted he needed to sit down and read the rest of it. But he still had work to do. Marcel didn't believe anything had happened to Ashley and Ethan, so Graham needed to complete the project. If he held it up, not only would Marcel file a complaint against him with the Better Business Bureau, but he would talk negatively about Graham to prospective customers.

Hall it Away needed to get more good reviews and referrals for Graham to keep building his fledgling business and make it sustainable. If he got a negative reputation now, he might as well just pack up his truck and move to another state, because he wouldn't be able to get any more business in Bleeding Hearts Valley.

After all of the work he had done to get everything set up, he wouldn't let that happen.

He finished packing the boxes and started carrying them down to the truck. He could manage quite a few on his hand truck at once, but Ian and Robin saw him in the hallway and insisted on grabbing a couple of boxes each and hauling them downstairs by hand.

"It will be easier to just take them down on my cart," Graham pointed out. Rather than saving him any work, they were just making extra work for themselves, doing something they didn't need to. But the two men just beamed at him, happy to be putting some sweat equity into helping him.

"I thought I heard you back last night," Ian said. "But it was late. Were you there again?"

Graham nodded. "Yeah. I was working pretty late. Sorry about that."

"No, it's okay, man. It didn't keep me up. I just thought I heard noises. But they were too quiet to identify. I just had a feeling that someone was over there, moving around."

"Did you ever notice that with Ashley and Ethan? Someone up moving around at night?"

"Uh... no, not usually. They went to bed in good time and didn't get up too early. They were good neighbors that way."

"Did Ethan sleepwalk?"

"Sleepwalk?" Ian shook his head. "No, not that I knew about. But I really wouldn't, would I? How would I know if he was wandering around at night? As long as he wasn't making noise, I wouldn't have any idea."

"What if he left the apartment? Would you hear him if he was in the hallway?"

"Well..." Ian looked at Robin, who shrugged. "I guess I might have heard him then. But I don't remember hearing anything like that or Ashley mentioning it. I think she would mention it if he was out wandering at night. Mention that if we ever heard anything, we should wake her up or something."

It had been a long shot. Graham hadn't expected a positive answer or anything that might contribute to his understanding of what had happened with the newlyweds.

He forced a smile in response to Ian's questioning look.

"Just wondering. It would have explained some things. That's all."

But not everything Ashley had written about in her journal

had happened at night. Some of it had happened when she had been at work during the day. Some of it had even happened when she and Ethan had been home, alone in the apartment.

Was someone really that bold? Brazen enough to come in while Ashley and Ethan were in another room to scare Ashley?

Had he been trying to scare her out of the apartment? To get her to move? Or had there been an even more sinister motive? Maybe he was trying to break Ashley and Ethan up. Perhaps he was an ex-lover or someone she had turned down. Even someone who had made a pass at her in a restaurant or gas station. It wasn't necessarily anyone she had even noticed.

"So you filed a police report?" Ian asked. "What did they say?"

"Oh." Graham stopped loading boxes into the truck and wiped sweat from his face, realizing that he had not told the men the results of his visit to the police station, and they had been patiently waiting for him to fill them in. "Sorry, yeah. Not much happened, unfortunately. I did go to the police station and tried to file a missing person report, but they didn't think that there was enough evidence that anything had happened to them and wouldn't open a file. The detective said they had just walked away, and we had nothing to prove otherwise."

"Oh." Ian frowned, brows lowering and mouth turning down. "I thought they would at least take a report. I mean... all of the stuff that they left behind at the apartment."

"It's the note and the keys. If it wasn't for those, I think they would look into it. But leaving a note saying that you are sorry, along with both sets of keys to the apartment, that makes it look like they just walked away from the lease. If there was a broken door and no sign of them, no note, no keys... maybe they would do something about it. But there are too many signs that they just decided to leave."

"But you know they didn't," Robin said intensely, staring at Graham. "It just doesn't make any sense, does it? How could they think that is normal?"

"I guess the police see a lot of odd things. They do see cases where people just walk away from their lives. You've seen enough cases like that on the news, right? Someone is found twenty or thirty years later. Their family all thought they must have been killed or kidnapped because they just disappeared and never came home one day. But really... they just decided to start a new life. Or sometimes they find out that they got hit on the head or had amnesia or something like that and couldn't remember who they were or where they lived."

"It can't happen *that* often."

"But it does happen."

"But that's not what happened here, or there wouldn't be any note. No one had amnesia. Both of them couldn't get amnesia and not know how to get back home."

Graham looked around. No one else was around or paying any attention to them. It was still early, and people had already gone to work or were just getting ready to leave. No one cared about the guys taking boxes out to the truck.

"I found something else."

Ian and Robin both spoke at once. "What?"

"Ashley's journal."

"She left her journal behind?" Robin again shook his head. "A girl wouldn't just forget to take her journal with her. Not only would she not want to lose it, but she wouldn't want someone else reading it."

"Well, in this case, maybe she did want someone else reading it."

They both stared at Graham, eyes questioning.

Graham lifted the last couple of boxes in the load onto the truck. "Do you have to go? Or do you have some more time this morning?"

"We're not leaving yet, man," Ian said. "Tell us what you found."

"I can do better than that. Come on back upstairs."

They walked as a group back up to their floor.

"I can't invite anyone into the apartment, so we can meet in yours." Graham motioned to Ian and Robin's door. "Just give me a minute to grab it."

Ian made a little squeal of excitement. "I'll get the coffee on."

# CHAPTER
# FIFTEEN

Graham returned to Ashley and Ethan's apartment and took a minute to grab the journal and look around to see how many more trips it would take to get everything down to the truck and whether he would need to take more than one trip in the truck. It looked like he would be able to take everything in one load, which was ideal.

He locked up again and went over to the neighboring apartment. Ian was waiting at the door to usher him in. He eyed the nondescript journal in Graham's hand eagerly.

"Can we see it?" he asked immediately when Graham sat at the table and picked up one of the mugs of fragrant coffee.

Graham opened the journal. He took a sip of the coffee, which was scalding hot, but reassuringly grounding. Reading the journal had put him into an odd headspace. It felt good to know that he was fully there, in Ian's and Robin's apartment, on the same wavelength and timeline.

He found his place and started to read aloud.

I heard footsteps again last night. I keep telling myself that it is just people moving around in the other apartments. You always hear other people when you are living so close together like this.

Once, when I woke up, I knew Ethan wasn't in bed with me. I thought he must have just gotten up to use the bathroom, but I waited for him to return, and he took so long that I eventually fell back asleep. I don't know what time he came back to bed. When I asked him about it in the morning, he couldn't remember being up. I guess he could be walking in his sleep. Or he might just not remember that he was up at all. Everybody does that, right? You are so close to being asleep that you just can't remember whether you really got up or just thought it or dreamed it? I need to stop worrying about little things that don't matter.

I wish I could explain all of the rest away. Even though I check the locks on the door every night, I still feel like someone has been in the apartment. Maybe it is the lack of sleep or the noises in the night. I feel out of sorts and like someone is watching me all the time.

When I got home from work today, my picture of me and my brother in Disneyland had fallen off the shelf and was on the floor. Like there had been an earthquake or something. But we don't get earthquakes here. And if we feel one that happened somewhere far away, it is just a little vibration, not enough to knock a picture off a shelf. The glass in the front was broken. It didn't look like it had just cracked when it fell on the floor. It looked to me like someone had smashed it on purpose.

I asked Ethan what had happened to it, and he just looked at it and shook his head and said he didn't have any idea. He said it must have just fallen down. And maybe it did, but...

If that was all, I could convince myself that it was just my imagination getting away from me. One thing happens and then you start seeing things differently, interpreting them with a different lens. But when I showered after work and got out to dry off, something was written on the mirror in the steam.

Ian made a little noise that sounded like "Eep!" His eyes were wide and round. Between the two of them—Ian and Robin—he was definitely the one who was more emotionally involved in the reading.

"What did it say?" Ian demanded. He leaned forward. "You can't just stop there!"

"She doesn't report what it said," Graham advised them. "Just this."

If anything happens to me, please let my parents know.

# CHAPTER
## SIXTEEN

Ian freaked out. Graham was glad, because that was precisely what he wanted to do, but he had been holding himself back, keeping his reaction calm, carefully schooling his emotions to keep from exploding. But Ian's near-hysterical exclamations over the journal entries were strangely comforting.

Robin stepped behind his partner and gave him a squeeze. "Just calm down, Ian. It's okay. This isn't anything. It doesn't prove anything. Hearing footsteps? Broken picture glass? Even the writing in the fog on the mirror... that's nothing. If you write a message once in the condensation, the oils in your finger stay on the mirror and keep the condensation from collecting there. The message could have been written at any time, not necessarily while she was in the shower."

"She was being *stalked*," Ian insisted. "Why does everybody insist on looking at this logically? The girl was scared; you have to look at it *emotionally*."

"Well... you've got that covered," Robin told him dryly.

"Do you think she ever would have written that in her journal if she wasn't terrified? '*If anything happens to me*?'"

"I'm not saying she wasn't scared," Robin admitted. "I'm just saying anyone could have written on her mirror any time. It didn't mean someone was in the bathroom with her when she showered. It doesn't mean that it was a ghost."

"I don't think it was a ghost," Ian snapped, his hysteria coming down a notch.

"Then what do you think?"

"I think that... someone was threatening her. Or trying to drive her crazy. Maybe that weirdo husband of hers. Maybe he was gaslighting her."

"Why would he do that?"

"Why does anyone do it? Because they are narcissistic. Because they can. Because they like making everyone around them just as crazy as they are."

"Okay... but Ethan wasn't like that. He was quiet and shy. He barely spoke to anyone but her. He loved her, so why would he want to scare her?"

"She said that he was out of bed. So *he* was the one doing all of these things. Setting up all of these scenarios to scare her and make her think someone was stalking her."

Robin flashed a look at Graham, evaluating his response, before trying to address his partner's concerns.

"You met Ethan. Can you really see him doing that?"

Ian calmed down a little, his voice lower and more relaxed. "No. I can't. But what other explanation is there?"

"Maybe he was keeping watch. Making sure no one could come into the apartment at night."

"Well..." Ian nodded slowly. "That could be. But then, why tell her he hadn't been up at night?"

"Because he didn't want to make her think there was a serious threat."

"But he knew there was."

Robin nodded slowly. "If he was getting up at night to watch for an intruder... then yes. Ethan thought they were being harassed as well. He was just trying to look tough in front of Ashley. Pretend that he wasn't getting scared too."

Ian took a deep breath in and let it out. "But whatever was

written on that mirror... it was enough to make Ashley think there was a real threat to their safety."

"Maybe they did leave voluntarily," Graham suggested. "Maybe they were both afraid, and the only way to escape this sicko, to make sure he didn't do anything to harm them, was to run away. Just leave and not tell anyone where they were going so no one could follow them."

"Is that what you think happened?" Ian asked.

Graham shook his head. "I don't know. I think we should call her parents."

"We?" Ian repeated.

"I was the one who went to the police. I think someone else should call her parents. You guys know Ashley and Ethan; I don't. They would rather hear from someone who knew them than some stranger clearing out their apartment."

"You're just trying to get out of doing it yourself."

Graham nodded. "Yeah. I am," he agreed. "So, do you want to give them a call?"

"Shouldn't the police do that? They're the ones that make notifications of this kind of thing. Of deaths and disappearances. I didn't sign up for that."

"The police won't do anything yet. Maybe if we can get her parents involved—get them to say they are concerned that something happened to Ashley—then the police will pay more attention."

"Do you think they would?" Ian asked skeptically.

Graham and Robin both nodded. Ian looked at Robin and opened his mouth.

"No," Robin interrupted. "I'm not talking to her mother."

Ian was definitely the more social of the two. From what Graham had seen, Robin preferred the "strong and silent" supporting role.

"Oh..." Ian bit his knuckle anxiously. "You don't know how hard this is going to be. Her poor parents. How would you like to get a phone call out of nowhere telling you that something had happened to your daughter?"

"It would suck," Graham agreed. "But it would be better than nobody noticing or caring. Sooner or later, they will realize she is missing, and something might have happened to her. Sooner is better."

Ian made several other distressed noises, but he pulled out his phone. "You'd better give me the number before I lose my nerve. The more I think about how hard it will be and what I am going to say, the harder it will be to even make the call."

# CHAPTER
## SEVENTEEN

Graham waited until Ian's phone number pad was up on the screen and then read out the number with a 305 area code.

Ian shifted anxiously. "Should I put it on speaker? So we can all hear them?"

Robin and Graham didn't answer. Graham worried it might be too overwhelming for Ashley's parents to talk to them all at once. But it might be difficult for Ian to know what to say or to recount their reaction to the news afterward.

The ringing sounded over the speaker, and then an answer, sounding strained and a little too high-pitched.

"Hello? Ash?"

Ian was startled. He cleared his throat and swallowed.

"No, this isn't Ash," the woman's voice said, dropping in disappointment. "Who is calling?"

"Mrs. Carter? My name is Ian. I'm Ashley's next-door neighbor."

"Do you know what's happened to her? Where is she? Did she lose her phone?"

"Uh... we don't know. We're trying to figure out what happened to her. When was the last time you talked to her?"

"Sunday. We had our usual chat. But she hasn't responded to any emails or text messages, and I tried calling her... but the message just keeps saying she is out of the calling area. I was hoping she just lost her phone... dropped it in the sink or something and hasn't had time to get a new one or to let me know her number changed." Mrs. Carter's voice was hopeful and breaking at the same time.

"We haven't seen her since then either," Ian told her. "The landlord said that she abandoned her apartment and hired someone to clean it out."

"Abandoned it? It's only been a few days; how could he say that? Does he know where she is?"

"No. She left a note and her keys. Both of them. Her husband, too. They are both gone, and left both sets of keys behind."

"I tried to get Ethan. There is no answer on his phone either."

"We tried to get the police to look into it, but they won't because she left a note and her keys. Or because someone did. They don't believe that... something might have happened to her. They say that she just left voluntarily."

"Give me the detective's name and I'll tell him. There is no way that Ash just left on her own. I know that. My husband said I am overreacting, that she would get a new phone and call me, and we would laugh over how I panicked over her being out of touch for a few days."

"I'll get the name and number for you," Ian promised, clearly deciding not to let Mrs. Carter know that she was on speakerphone and there were two other men listening in on the call. Probably a good call on Ian's part. That might be overwhelming to her.

Mrs. Carter was sobbing. She called out a few times for her husband, but Graham didn't hear him join the call.

"Mrs. Carter, did you know that... Ashley was being stalked or harassed by someone?"

A long sniffle from Mrs. Carter and a few more sobs before

she spoke. "She mentioned some of the things that had happened... but she didn't know for sure that anyone was actually doing all of those things, or whether it was just... noises in the apartment... from other tenants or as it settled... Houses can make strange noises, and so can other people and their hobbies. We joked around a little about her poltergeist. But I knew she was concerned about it. She didn't think that it was a ghost or something supernatural."

"No," Ian agreed. "She wouldn't think that. Do you think... do you know if she had any suspicions about who it might be?"

"No, I don't. It wasn't like she had broken someone's heart or was a celebrity or something. Why would anyone start stalking her?"

Ian shrugged helplessly. "I don't know. I don't know of anyone here who would do something like that. But... people do. You can't tell by looking at someone whether they are mentally ill, whether they might... do something like that."

"Do you think he did something to hurt her? Do you think that she's..." Mrs. Carter broke off, sobbing again.

This time, Graham could hear someone talking quietly to her in the background, comforting her.

"Is it the police?" a male voice inquired gruffly. "Who is this?"

"No, we are neighbors of Ashley's. That's all. We live next door. We were worried, so we decided to get in contact with you. We hoped... that she would have told you where she was going."

"What do you mean, where she was going?"

"If she left voluntarily, maybe to get away from this guy who was stalking her. I figured she would have let you know. If she planned to go."

There were a few murmured exchanges between Mr. and Mrs. Carter as he got up to speed on the call.

"Why aren't the police on this?" Ashley's father questioned after a moment. "They should be all over this."

"They didn't think there was any evidence that something had happened to her. They said she had just walked away."

"Well, that is ridiculous. My daughter didn't just walk away. And where is her husband? What does he say?"

"He is missing too, Mr. Carter. They left—or disappeared—together."

"Give me the information for this police officer, and I will light a fire under him."

Graham passed Detective Joiner's business card across the table to Ian, and he read the information off to Mr. Carter.

"Good. If you hear anything, please call back. You have the number."

Ian pointed to the journal and mouthed words at Graham. He couldn't tell what Ian was trying to say, but shook his head. It didn't seem like the right time to tell Ashley's parents about the journal and everything that Ashley had written about. They hadn't asked how Ian had gotten their phone number, and they were going to talk to Joiner, so it was probably best to just leave it at that.

Mr. Carter said an abrupt goodbye and hung up. He was, Graham hoped, going to call Joiner and tear a strip off of him. Hopefully, Mr. Carter could "light a fire under" Joiner and get him to at least open a file on the missing couple.

Graham would give it a while, and then call Joiner about the journal and how it provided confirmation that Ashley and Ethan had, in fact, been in danger and there was at least some evidence that they might have come to harm. He just hoped that wouldn't convince Joiner that the two of them had fled under cover of darkness to escape their stalker, and there was no need to pursue an investigation and possibly lead the stalker right back to them.

# CHAPTER
## EIGHTEEN

A shley slept restlessly. She felt like she was moving around every thirty seconds, trying to find a more comfortable position and a deeper phase of sleep.

It was strange. She would have thought that her captor reducing the amount of whatever drug he had given her and leaving her unbound would be a good thing and would calm her body down and let her sleep more soundly, but that was not the case. After being tied into one position for days on end, she felt like she was going to fall off the edge of the world every time she moved freely. She kept jumping and bracing herself, trying to keep herself from falling off the bed, even though she was nowhere near the edge of the mattress.

The drug that had previously kept her asleep or close to it most of the time had been reduced, so instead of fighting to stay awake when he was gone, she was restless and constantly vigilant, unable to calm down and relax. Instead of being bound in the living room as she had been to start with, she was locked in the bedroom.

She had been unable to explore it thoroughly. Every time she sat up or got off the bed, he was there, watching her, telling her to go back to sleep, to stay where he had left her. He seemed a little calmer. She hoped it was a good sign, the fact that he had moved her to the bedroom and let her have a little more freedom of movement. Maybe eventually, he would give her enough freedom that she could get out of there.

There was a window, but it was always dark, and she was afraid it was boarded over and, therefore, not a way for her to get out of the room. Her captor had put locks on the bedroom door, installing strong bolts so that no one could get out of the room without a key. She had watched him test the strength of the door and the frame, pounding his shoulder into it to make sure that she would not be able to break through by force. She knew that the only way to get out of the room was with the key. And only one person had a key.

His eyes were dark and haunted. She had searched for some sign of empathy or humanity in those depths, and just got lost in them. There was nothing there. No responding tug to her pleas. Like he was far, far away.

Ashley fell into a restless dream. In it, she was with her beloved Ethan in their cozy little apartment. Everything was well. No more terrifying messages, unease over someone else being in the apartment and moving things around. Everything was perfect, with just the two of them, safe and sound, keeping each other company. When she watched a game on TV, he sat close to her, drawing in his sketchbook, intent on the page.

But then it began. She heard a scratching noise. What was it? A key in the lock? A rat or some other vermin? Ashley looked around, trying to identify it. She tried to turn her attention back to the game, but it was impossible. She was sure someone else was there or trying to get in.

"Ethan?" she whispered, trying to get his attention. "Do you hear that? What is it?"

He did not respond, lost in his drawing.

"Please," Ashley whispered. "There is something in the apartment. Can't you hear it?"

Words whispered back to her, but she couldn't understand

them. The wind was blowing cold through a gap in the window, whistling and making her arms goosebump and the hair on the back of her neck tickle.

"Ethan?"

She turned her head slowly to look at him, and instead of seeing Ethan's reassuring expression or his face in repose as he worked on the drawing, there was a faceless mask.

A black balaclava, with dark glittering eyes behind the eyeholes and disembodied lips in a mouth hole. Ashley shrieked in terror.

She scared herself awake, her own screams ringing in her ears, her hands clutching the bedding with talon-like curved fingers.

And he was there. Shouting at her and berating her. He slapped and punched her, trying to make her be quiet, hitting her again and again. There was blood in her mouth, tears or blood running down her face, every place on her body where he had touched her the last few days throbbing with every beat of her heart.

"I'm sorry. I'm sorry," she slurred, trying to protect herself by keeping her chin tucked and her hands in front of her face to ward off the blows. "Shh, shh, I'm sorry."

"There is no Ethan here!" he shouted. "The only people here are you and me!" He punctuated *you* and *me* with a hard finger drilling into her chest. "Ethan is gone! Never say his name again! You are loyal to *me*. To *me* only." He grabbed her by the shoulders and shook her, rattling Ashley's teeth. "Do you understand me?"

"Yes, yes. I'm sorry. It was a dream. It was just a dream; I didn't mean to."

"*He* is *dead*. Do you understand? Dead! You will never see him again!"

"No. I understand. Please. Please don't hurt me anymore. Please."

He stopped shaking her and stared into her face, wary, searching for something. She tried to look as compliant and devoted as she could. She didn't care if she died, but she cared if he kept beating and terrorizing her. She just wanted peace.

He pushed her away, back into the soft mattress and blankets. Ashley covered her face and closed her eyes. She breathed slowly, trying to relax him and entrain his breath to hers as if trying to calm a fractious baby. Nice slow breaths. Help him to feel the air flowing in and out, keeping him calm and focused. "It's okay," she whispered. "Everything is okay."

He sat down on the other side of the bed. He did not reach for her, did not try to get close to her or to touch her. He just sat there on the edge at first, and then pushed himself gradually over until his entire body was on the bed, and then shuffled back until he sat where the pillow should be, his back to the headboard, knees drawn up to his chest, and the pillow clutched in front of him, a barrier to the rest of the world.

What did he have to be afraid of? He was the monster here, not Ashley. She wasn't going to attack him.

But he reminded her of the abused children she had seen in shelters and group homes. Walling off the rest of the world. Afraid to trust anyone, no matter how soft or safe they seemed.

He looked so much like a child that she whispered to him, reassured him as if that was exactly what he was. And deep down under all of the other layers, that was probably exactly what he was. An abused, terrified child.

"It's okay," she assured him, "everything will be all right. No one is going to hurt you here. You're safe."

He breathed raggedly. He wasn't looking at her, but she knew by the tension in his body that he was listening to her.

"Tell me your name," Ashley coaxed. "What can I call you?"

He breathed in jerkily, out a little more smoothly. His body still all edges and prickles, afraid to let her get too close to him. Afraid that she too would break her word, would break the tentative peace between them.

She would do anything to keep him in this state instead of the raging, incoherent monster that he turned into at the slightest

provocation. Most of the time, she didn't have any idea what had triggered him.

He sat beside her, his back pressed to the wall and the pillow a shield between them, shaking and listening.

"Nicholas," he said finally. "My name is Nicholas."

# CHAPTER
# NINETEEN

Graham took the boxes from the apartment to his warehouse and unloaded them. Sadness weighed on him as he unloaded the boxes and sorted them into piles according to where they would be taken next. He had done everything he could to convince Marcel and the police that Ashley and Ethan might have been the victims of foul play, and they had not listened. Hopefully, when he took the journal to Detective Joiner, he would be convinced and would start the search for the missing newlyweds. It was terrible to think of them out there, suffering at the hands of some psychopath or already dead, while everyone went on with their lives and forgot all about them.

Before going to the police station again, Graham laid the journal on top of one of the boxes. The good quality lay-flat binding ensured that it stayed open, so that he didn't have to hold it down at the same time as he positioned his phone over it and snapped pictures of the pages. If the clues to what had happened to Ashley and Ethan lay within those pages, he wouldn't lose them by handing the book over to the police. With the photos saved to his phone, he could continue to read and study the journal and somehow figure out what had happened to Ashley and Ethan.

Somehow.

~

Detective Joiner did not appear to be in a good mood when Graham was allowed in to see him. He scowled at Graham, shook his head, and eventually took him back to the same interview room to talk to him again.

"You have been causing trouble for me," he accused.

"Me? No," Graham insisted. He had come with the journal to give Joiner the additional evidence he needed for his case. He hadn't been telling people that the Bleeding Hearts Valley cops were incompetent, which was something he was considering; he had not been the one to call Ashley's parents, even if he had provided Ian with the phone number to do so, and had given them the phone number for Detective Joiner so that they would be talking to the right person. But those were just helpful little things that Graham had done for him. He had not been working against Joiner.

"Yeah? I hadn't heard anything about Ashley Carter and Ethan Quick before, and now I am getting phone calls about them? That was just coincidental? Now everybody is suddenly concerned about them being missing?"

"I don't know anything about that," Graham assured him, which wasn't entirely true, but would have to do for the moment. Sometimes, one had to... get creative with the truth to get the correct results. "I came back with more information for you. I know you said there wasn't enough when I came here yesterday, but when I returned to the job, I found something that I thought you would want to see."

"Oh, is that so? You just *happened* to find something at the job site?" Joiner repeated sarcastically.

"The job needs to be finished in time to rent it out again next month, so I don't have very long," Graham explained. "I had to

go right back to it, especially after losing time talking to you yesterday."

"Yeah?"

"So..." Graham decided to go on with the story, even if Joiner wasn't asking for it at this point. "I stripped the bed and was flipping the mattress when I came across Ashley's journal."

"You know for sure that it was hers? Not his? Not from some previous tenant?"

Some previous tenant would have left it there? And it had not been discovered for months?

"She talks about Ethan, so yes, I know it is hers."

"You've read it?" Joiner demanded.

"Not all of it. But enough to be sure that something was going on with that couple, and it wasn't good."

"What does that mean? They've been fighting?"

"I'm sure if you talk to her neighbors, you'll find that they did a good amount of... *talking* from time to time. But what was in this journal that couldn't be corroborated by anyone else, was that Ashley thought they were being stalked or harassed. Someone was moving things around in the apartment while they were out. Strange noises at night. Precious things that were moved or missing."

Joiner opened his mouth to comment.

"Something written in the steam on the bathroom mirror," Graham provided.

Joiner closed his mouth and thought about it. "What was written?"

"She didn't say what it was. I haven't cleaned the bathroom yet. You might be able to see what it was, if she didn't clean it off. But I expect... she probably did. You know that the oils in your finger when you write a word on the mirror—"

"Stay on the glass and don't get fogged over again," Joiner finished. "Sure I know that. But you don't know what was written?"

"No. I know that it upset her. You can find it in here." Graham took out the book and laid it on the table.

"I suppose you got your fingerprints all over that."

"Uh... yeah, I guess I did."

"Not that it matters. If it was Ashley's journal, then those are the fingerprints we are going to find on it. Not the prints of some... psycho stalker."

"I don't think he found the journal, or it wouldn't have still been there, would it?"

"Probably not. Maybe he read it and left it there. It's something a stalker might do to get his jollies. I don't imagine it was too hard to find. Under the mattress, that's one of the first places you would look for something like that."

"Well, it wasn't right at the edge. I missed it the first time I checked. It was pushed all the way to the middle, so I didn't see it until I lifted up the mattress to flip it."

Joiner grunted and didn't make any comment on that. "Well, thank you for this," he said briskly. "I'll have a look at it. Who do I talk to if I want to look at the apartment? You or the landlord?"

"Uh, Marcel, I guess. I don't have permission to let anyone else in. Best to keep everything regular. Make sure you've got all of your ducks in a row so that no evidence can be excluded."

"You're an expert on that, are you?"

Graham shook his head. "I watch as much TV as the next guy."

"Not the best source of information on police procedure and legalities."

"Nope. I'll just leave all of that stuff to you. All I did was bring you information."

"And you haven't touched anything else at the apartment."

Graham's mouth went dry. "Well... yes. I thought I explained that. I was there to clean it out. To remove all of Ashley's and Ethan's possessions."

"Then exactly what do you expect me to find out by looking at the apartment?"

"Uh... I don't know. I didn't say anything about it. That was your idea."

"You were the one who brought up me looking at the mirror."

"Well, yes. Because I know I haven't cleaned it yet. But I will if you don't want to see it. I planned to sanitize the bathroom, vacuum and wash the floors, and touch up the paint today. So that it will be ready for Marcel tomorrow."

"You do all that?"

Graham nodded. "People appreciate it when you go the extra mile. When they walk into a room or home you have cleaned and everything is fresh and clean..." He shrugged. "It gives people something to remember the next time they need a job done. Or a friend does, and they give you a referral."

Joiner shook his head slowly. It seemed like he was disapproving rather than impressed by Graham's work ethic and efforts to impress his client.

"I'll send someone over to fingerprint the mirror," he said, "see if we can get anything off of it. I don't know what the chances are, but if someone used his ungloved fingertip to write on it, we have a chance of getting a print. If Ashley didn't immediately wipe the mirror, which I suspect would be anyone's reaction."

Graham let out his breath. He was relieved that Joiner was opening an investigation and was seemingly open to the idea that something might have happened to Ashley and Ethan. But Joiner was probably right. They probably wouldn't be able to get anything helpful from the mirror. The only prints on it would be Ashley's and Ethan's. She would have wiped the offending words off.

"You've already hauled all of their stuff to the dump?" Joiner demanded.

"No, no. I've sorted and boxed it and it is in my warehouse. I didn't want to... I normally would have started to process it already, but I was worried about something having happened to them and about there being evidence... I didn't want to take the chance."

"We might want to take a look at it. You said there were passports?"

"Yes."

"Don't destroy those. Bring them to me when you have a few minutes. Anything else you think might prove that they didn't leave voluntarily...?"

"Their wedding album and pictures. Medications. Jewelry."

"Prescription medications?"

"Yes."

"What for?"

"I didn't really..." Graham thought back. He tried to picture the labels that he had barely glanced at. "Uh... I don't remember. I should have taken a picture or written them down. But... one of them was for... Dilantin? Yeah, I think Dilantin."

"For epilepsy?" Joiner swore. "Which one of them was on that?"

"I think it was Ashley. I should have paid more attention. They're at the warehouse, too, so I can grab them when I am there next."

"I can call the pharmacy, too," Joiner advised. "See whether the prescription was transferred to another pharmacy, somewhere else. If they left voluntarily, and then she realized she didn't have her meds, she would have had to get them right away."

"They won't give you that information without a warrant, will they?"

Joiner blinked at him. "You think I don't know how to do my job, Mr. Hall?"

"No, sorry."

"There were more prescriptions than that? What else?"

"I think there were three bottles."

"All for Ashley?"

"I don't think so. I think it was a mix between the two of them. But I don't remember what else was there. Maybe an antidepressant or something? I didn't look them up, and I didn't know what they were all for. I was trying not to invade their privacy. I mean, I was going through all of their stuff, all of their private stuff, but I didn't want to... cross the line."

"You read her journal."

"Part of it," Graham admitted. "I admit I was curious. But I also wanted to see whether it was anything that you would want. If it was just... I don't know... weather and plans to meet her mother, then you wouldn't care about that. If it didn't give any clue that something was going on..."

Joiner gave a sardonic smile. As if he knew that Graham would have read it anyway. It didn't matter whether he thought it would help figure out what had happened to her or not. Who could ignore a journal that fell serendipitously into their hands?

Graham shifted uncomfortably. Despite their padding, the chairs were not conducive to long conversations.

"So you'll send a fingerprint guy. Does that mean I shouldn't touch anything else in the apartment, or can I go ahead with the other rooms and just leave the mirror alone?"

"You can do the rest. It isn't much good to me if you've already cleaned everything else out. Unless there is a big blood-stain or bleach marks or some sign of violence, which I have to assume you would have told me about."

"No, nothing else that was suspicious. And I can let Marcel know that he can get renters looking at it tomorrow? Your guy will have collected the fingerprints by then?"

"Yeah, he'll get over there today."

# CHAPTER
# TWENTY

G raham headed back to the apartment to finish his final cleanup and prep for Marcel. The sky was overcast, making it look like late evening rather than morning. Before calling Marcel to report, he looked the apartment over to catalog everything he still had to do. He would need to take his lights for any painting that needed to be done. The overhead bulbs would not be enough on a day like this.

"Graham?" Marcel demanded, obviously identifying him by his number. "What the hell? You reported Ashley and Ethan missing? I told you, they just took off. You're going to make it impossible for me to rent that apartment!"

"No," Graham protested. "I'll have it all ready for you by tonight. And the police said they would just stop by for fingerprints sometime today, after they got your permission. They're not going to hold it as a crime scene. You'll be able to start touring potential renters through there tomorrow."

"You think people are going to want to rent it if they think there was a multiple murder there? Or a kidnapping? Way to make people feel safe!"

"Uh..." Graham was immediately defensive and embarrassed that he hadn't considered this possibility. "I don't know how anyone would know about it. The police *just* opened their investigation. All they're going to do at the apartment is take fingerprints. They aren't convinced that anything happened to Ashley and Ethan."

"News spreads fast in a town like this. You let off a bombshell like that and think that it won't spread? It's going to be all over town."

"I'm sorry. But I do think something happened to them, I couldn't just not say anything."

Marcel muttered something Graham didn't catch and probably didn't want to know.

"Maybe you'll get lucky," Graham said. "Maybe the listing will get more attention because of the possibility that something happened there, and you'll find a renter because of the publicity."

"No one wants to rent an apartment where someone was kidnapped or murdered."

Graham swallowed and tried to come up with a response to this, but couldn't think of anything positive to say.

"I'll be here finishing everything up today. Do you want to stop by around six or seven to look at it? Make sure everything is done up to your standards?"

Marcel grunted irritably, as though Graham's invitation were an inconvenience. "I suppose."

After finishing the call with Marcel, Graham got to work. He had a good amount to do before Marcel got there, and he didn't know what time the officer or evidence tech would be there to collect fingerprints, at which point he would be able to finish cleaning up the bathroom. If he got everything else done before that, then once the evidence was collected, he could do a final sanitization and touch-ups. And then he would be finished with the job. Other than having to deal with the boxes sitting in his warehouse.

By the time six o'clock rolled around, Graham was packing up his equipment. The tech had been unable to pull any good prints from the mirror and was not interested in anything else in the bathroom, such as the faucets or toilet flush handle, that might have fingerprints on them. The only thing they knew for sure that the stalker had touched was the mirror. Everything else would likely have been wiped out by Ashley's and Ethan's regular use of the facilities.

Marcel's key turned in the door, and he let himself in. He looked just as greasy and unkempt as he had the day he had let Graham in. And on top of that, he was irritated about how things had turned out rather than happy about getting the apartment cleaned, refreshed, and ready to rent.

"Hey, good timing," Graham said, forcing good cheer in the face of Marcel's disapproval. "I was just getting ready to go."

Marcel looked around the apartment, and the heavy look of displeasure faded. He walked around, checking the fridge, cupboards, and then each of the other rooms. Graham stood back, waiting, looking at his handiwork. It was fresh and bright and clean, smelling of cleaning chemicals and fresh paint.

"It looks good," Marcel admitted grudgingly. "Better than it did before I rented it to them."

Graham smiled. "I aim to please."

"Well, you did the job you said you would. This is very well done. If you had just kept your mouth shut about them being missing..."

"Sorry. I really had to, though. With their passports and jewelry and everything here. Ashley's epilepsy medication and her journal..."

"Her journal?" Marcel repeated sharply.

"Yes." Graham studied Marcel's face for any tells. "She had written about how someone was... stalking her. Coming into the apartment at night or while they were away and leaving nasty messages for her to find..."

"What?" Marcel's face paled. "What are you talking about?"

"Didn't she report it to you? I assumed that was why they had an additional lock on the door."

Marcel's eyes skittered around the apartment. Not evaluating how it looked this time.

"She might have said something. Asked if I'd been in here or if the maintenance guy had been by. But neither of us had been."

Ashley hadn't contacted the police about her stalker either. Or had she talked to them about it, and they had told her that she didn't have enough for them to act upon, as they had when Graham had tried to report the newlyweds missing? Graham could imagine the police trying to brush it off, telling Ashley she was imagining things or that they couldn't do anything if she didn't know who it was. To go by the attitude of the cop on reception and Detective Joiner, it seemed like the police department wasn't that interested in pursuing such minor issues.

"She was really scared," Graham told Marcel. "I'm surprised she didn't say anything more than that."

If the police and their landlord hadn't shown any sympathy to Ashley or offered any kind of increased security or help, Graham wouldn't have been surprised if she had started looking at other apartments or even moving out of town. But that wasn't what had happened. Something had happened to her before they could find somewhere safer to live.

"Well... it looks really good," Marcel said, refusing to comment any more on Ashley's stalker. "If I need something like this done again, I'll know who to call. As long as you aren't going to make police reports or spread rumors every time."

"Of course not," Graham agreed.

Unless more people disappeared from Marcel's buildings. Graham certainly wouldn't turn a blind eye to that.

Marcel fidgeted, then nodded, closing the conversation.

"Just leave your key here when you go. I'll transfer you the rest of your fee."

After he left, Graham assembled the rest of his equipment to take down to the truck. His hands were dirty, so he paid one last visit to the bathroom to wash up and gave the sink a final wipe-down.

His toe accidentally hit the kick-plate below the vanity as he leaned in. It not only sounded hollow, but also sounded like it had shifted, hitting the wall or something else. He knelt down and ran his fingers along the piece of wood, seeing if it would move.

It did, and he grasped at the edges of the piece with his finger-nail, prying the piece of wood out. Someone had removed the nails that were supposed to hold it in place, and it was just sitting in position, not fastened to the bottom of the vanity.

He shone his phone light under the vanity to see whether the wood had gotten wet and rotted away, or if perhaps a valve was located underneath to make it easy to shut off the water to the sink for repairs.

There was something under there.

# CHAPTER
# TWENTY-ONE

I t was a narrow space. Holding his hand flat, Graham slid it into the hole and pincered the package between two fingers. He tugged it out carefully, holding his breath.

Exactly why was he holding his breath? He didn't actually know. Did he think it was going to tear or explode? That it would be drugs or a murder weapon or something that would bring his world crashing down?

It was a book.

A hardcover black book inside a zip-seal plastic bag to protect it from dust and damp and whatever creepy crawlies thrived in the spaces between walls and floors.

Another diary? Were both Ashley and Ethan keeping diaries? Hiding them from one another?

He hesitated before opening the bag. Should he pass it on to Detective Joiner without even looking at it? He did not want to get fingerprints all over it. Graham held it gingerly by the corner to avoid contaminating it any further.

His phone started to ring a loud alarm, startling him so badly that he nearly dropped the book.

It was not one of his routine ringtones or alerts. He was so surprised by it that for a moment his brain didn't process what it was, and he just laughed at himself and tried to catch his breath and slow his rapidly beating heart. He reached for his phone with his other hand, but by the time he pulled it out, he realized what the alert was.

It meant that the burglar alarm at his warehouse had been tripped.

Chances were, it was just a squirrel or cat that had managed to get inside and run in front of the motion detector. It wouldn't be the first time. The first few days after Graham had installed the alarm, he had to run back to the warehouse multiple times as he adjusted the direction and sensitivity of the sensors to try to eliminate the false alarms, but still keep it sensitive enough that it would detect an actual burglar.

It was probably a false alarm. That was why he didn't have it hardwired to any security company or the police yet. Until he was sure he had it properly calibrated, he didn't want to pay someone to run over there every time it went off.

Graham returned the kickplate to its previous position. Chances were, no one would notice it. And if they did realize it was loose, they would just call Marcel to send his handyman over to fix it. Graham put the book into a bag of cleaning supplies, where it was least likely to be bumped around as he took the remainder of his gear down to the car.

He wasn't going to race back to the warehouse, discover that the alarm had been set off by an errant mouse, and then have to come back to the apartment to load up his gear and return to the warehouse again. It made more sense to take the extra few minutes to remove all of his possessions from the apartment and lock it up for the last time, leaving his keys there for Marcel.

He lugged everything down to the truck, threw it in the bed, and drove to the warehouse.

He was finished with Ashley's and Ethan's apartment. He felt a little sad to end the chapter without having discovered what happened to them. But he wasn't a cop. He was a junk removal specialist. Yes, he enjoyed solving the little mysteries that presented themselves at the sites he cleaned out, but that didn't make him a law enforcement officer or even a private investigator.

He was just the garbage man.

He couldn't see anything obviously out of place when he drove up to the warehouse. No strange vehicles were parked nearby, no patrolman investigating the report of a suspicious person lurking around the property. Everything seemed quiet.

But when he approached the door, he saw it was not shut flush with the frame, but slightly open. He stood outside looking at it, his heart pumping hard.

There was no damage to the doorframe that he could see without touching the door. It was entirely possible that it hadn't latched properly when he had left. So it popped back open again when the wind had picked up. An animal could have gotten in while it swung open and then been trapped inside.

That was probably it.

He used a rag to pull open the door so he wouldn't get his fingerprints over top of whatever was already there.

"Hello?"

Why did stupid TV heroes and heroines always call out when they entered the open door at a crime scene, as if the criminal would answer them and identify himself? Graham just felt the need to reach out and see whether someone was there legitimately. A friend who had stopped by and found the door unlocked. Never mind that he didn't have any friends who would just stop by to see him.

Maybe a customer who had seen an internet ad for the storefront. Or someone inquiring about his rates. Not everyone was comfortable using the internet or a phone. An older person or someone not computer literate might just stop by for a chat rather than trying to connect electronically.

"Anyone here?"

Of course there wasn't. The place was as quiet as a tomb. Graham listened for the sound of paws skittering on the ground or jumping off of something. There were lots of interesting things to investigate in the warehouse. He imagined that with the smells of so many different people and origins, it would be a fascinating place for an animal to explore.

He walked down an aisle and reached the stacks of boxes from Ashley's and Ethan's apartment. The neatly sorted and stacked towers had been tipped over, several of the boxes now lying on their sides or tops, the contents spilling out.

Just an animal? Now Graham wasn't so sure. A larger animal *could* have tipped the boxes over. But they hadn't been unstable. It wasn't something that he thought would happen accidentally.

"Anyone here?" Graham asked once more, more to fill the silent, waiting space than in expectation of an answer. He listened for the scuffing of a shoe or a furry body rubbing against a box or shelf.

He took a deep breath and walked around the warehouse, keeping his breathing steady and attention strictly focused.

In the end, it didn't take any special attention or intelligence to figure out what had happened. There were knocked-over or spilled-out goods on several aisles. And at the back of the warehouse, emblazoned across the inside of the big loading bay door, his visitor had spray painted, "Go home Hall," along with several other choice words that could not be used in polite company. Graham stood there looking at it for a long time, as if it might tell him a different story if he studied it for long enough.

There was no mistaking it—someone had broken in, tossing things around in a rage, and scrawled a pointed message that Graham could not miss.

*Go home.*

# CHAPTER
# TWENTY-TWO

Ashley huddled on the bed, feeling like a baby rabbit, nestled in the grass, waiting for the danger to pass. She had always found it strange that such a tiny, vulnerable creature would not run in the face of danger, but instead froze and stayed there, right out in the open.

She had a blanket pulled around her. She didn't know how long the musty, scratchy blanket had been stored in the house, who had used it last, and what kind of nasty vermin or pathogens it could be harboring. She just knew that she was cold and tired and needed to hold on to something for comfort. Every so often, the wind blew a patter of rain against the window, and she felt a chill.

Nicholas was on the bed with her. Ashley stayed frozen, afraid that any movement she made would wake him up, and then he would attack her, again venting his rage until he was too tired and weak to go on. That was when she should have retaliated and tried to hurt him and escape from that awful place. But by that point, she was way too exhausted, overwhelmed, and in pain herself to do anything to harm him.

And even if she had been able to fight back physically, she didn't know whether she would have been able to do anything to hurt him anyway. She was terrified of him and knew that her continued existence hinged on how he felt about her and treated her.

Another beating, and she might not survive.

If he took off again and didn't bring her any food or water for another day, she might not survive.

If he didn't like the look in her eye, she might not survive.

So she did everything she could to avoid bringing his wrath down on her again, even though, given the choice between living as she was and dying, logic dictated that death was better.

It was terrifying to look into Nicholas's glassy eyes and not see a spark of recognition or humanity. When he swung from the violent persona to the withdrawn, childlike one, she did what she could to connect with him, to make him see that she was a real person. Maybe even one who could help him.

She was, after all, a social worker. She knew many different programs, grants, therapies, and shelters that might be able to help someone in distress. And he was clearly in a bad place. She didn't think it was drugs. She had never seen him take any illicit drugs.

Schizophrenia? Bipolar? Some sort of dissociative disorder? She was not a psychologist, but she could recognize many of the disorders the men and women she dealt with were affected by.

If Nicholas would talk to her more, she might be able to put her finger on it. And might be able to start to move him in the right direction, to start to work on him and help him to see that there was a way out of the deep pit he found himself in.

Ashley coughed.

She had been trying to suppress the tickle. To swallow and to breathe deeply and to try to keep it from exploding out, but in the end, she couldn't keep it in any longer.

Nicholas convulsed on the bed beside her and brought his fists up in front of his face to protect himself from whatever it was that threatened him. His eyes flew open, and he stared at her with what looked like a combination of horror and rage.

"I'm sorry," Ashley whispered. She could barely speak after so many days of silence or crying. "I just coughed. I just... I just need a bit of water, that's all."

"Who are you, and what are you doing here?"

She stared into his eyes and saw no recognition.

"You brought me here. I'm Ashley. I'm... I'm..."

He sat up and looked around. Gradually, he seemed to recognize his surroundings, and his rigid body softened. Was this a safe space for him?

Or did he not have anywhere he felt comfortable and safe?

Ashley coughed again. Every time she did, her body hurt all over. All of the places he had hit or kicked her. All of the muscles that she held tense, unable to relax anymore. The way that she had been tied up the first few days. She couldn't breathe without her chest hurting. She wished that it would just end.

Tears started to flow down Ashley's face. She hadn't thought she was hydrated enough to cry anymore, but she was wrong.

She hurt so much and was so exhausted and overwhelmed by all that had happened.

"Please help me," she cried. She struggled to sit up. "I know you don't want to hurt me. Please, let me go. I won't tell anyone what happened. You can go... wherever you want to go. I won't stop you. I won't tell anyone it was you or how to find you. Please... you don't want to do this. I know you don't."

His eyes burned with an inner fire. He straightened his shoulders and held himself as straight and unyielding as a board.

"Women who stray have to be punished," he told her coldly. "You must be punished for what you did to me."

"I didn't do anything to you," she protested desperately. "I don't know what happened to you... but it wasn't my fault. I've always been faithful."

He didn't yield, shaking his head angrily.

"If someone betrayed you," Ashley said desperately, "can't you find it in your heart to forgive her? Didn't you ever make a mistake that you regretted later? Didn't you ever want someone to forgive you, even though you made a mistake that hurt them?"

"There must be justice! It isn't *just* to let someone get away with a crime. They must be punished."

"I didn't commit any crime. Who made you judge and jury? I haven't done anything wrong. Whoever accused me is wrong. I didn't do anything."

He backhanded her. Ashley fell to the mattress and covered her burning face.

"No, please!"

He didn't continue to hit her this time, but got off of the bed and went to the door. He unlocked it and let himself out, not looking back at her or saying anything.

Ashley lay there weeping, grateful for this one small mercy.

# CHAPTER
# TWENTY-THREE

Graham didn't think Detective Joiner would come to the warehouse when he reported the break-in. Joiner appeared to be close to retirement, senior in the department, not someone who would concern himself with the petty break-in of some junk dealer's warehouse.

Graham *did* tell him that the burglar had knocked over and broken open some of the boxes of items he had taken from Ashley's and Ethan's apartment. He couldn't prove that the break-in had anything to do with the disappearance of the newly-weds, but if there was any possibility that the two events were related, Graham thought it should be pointed out.

Joiner was apparently of the same mind. He pulled into one of Graham's parking slots in a dark, older model sedan and sat there for a moment before getting out of the car. Checking his onboard computer and signing himself out, Graham assumed. Then Joiner climbed slowly out of the car and looked Graham over.

Graham hadn't changed since Joiner had seen him last, so he didn't know why Joiner was giving him such a thorough appraisal. Graham looked exactly the same as the last time they had seen each other.

"Show me what happened," Joiner told Graham impatiently.

Graham stepped over to the door and positioned it as it had been when he had arrived after receiving the notification from the burglar alarm. Joiner looked around at the ground, but didn't find whatever he was looking for. He looked back at Graham.

"Probably used a crowbar or similar tool," he said. "This door isn't very secure. You can see there is a good gap between the door and the frame. All you need to do is put a tool here by the latch and pop it open. There is enough flexibility in the door and hinges that it can be popped open without even breaking the frame. You'll need someone to replace the door and frame for you if you want it to be less vulnerable."

Graham nodded. "Okay. Good to know."

"A lot of these old buildings are not maintained very well. Maybe get a security guy from the city to audit it for you. Find out where the other vulnerabilities are. There's not much point in having a burglar alarm if you don't make the building secure. You'll just keep arriving in time to lock the barn after the horse is gone."

Graham's cheeks warmed. "Yeah... by the time I got here, he was already gone. If he had been after valuables, he could have grabbed some high-value items and been long gone."

Joiner nodded. "And that's probably a good thing. Did you stop to think about what you would do if the burglar was still here? Were you just going to walk in there and ask him what he was doing? You obviously don't carry."

"Well... yeah. I didn't think it was going to be a burglar. I'm still trying to get the sensors set up so that I don't get false alarms triggered by a mouse or the wind."

"You need to take your security seriously," Joiner told him firmly. "Stop using half measures. Either don't bother to lock your door, or get the building properly secured."

"Yeah. Thanks. I will. I didn't think I was being that sloppy, but I guess I was."

Joiner nodded. He pulled the door open abruptly. "So let's have a look at what he got into, then."

He walked in ahead of Graham and started pacing up and down the aisles to see what had been touched. He stopped and looked at the boxes that had tumbled over, but didn't touch them. He ended his tour as Graham had, staring at the angry imprecations on the closed garage door.

"Somebody doesn't like you very much," he observed. He pulled out a small spiral notepad and made a few notations on it. "Is this the first time you've had any threats?"

"Well... it isn't exactly a threat. It says to go home, but it doesn't say what will happen if I don't 'go home.' Which I assume means getting out of town. Go back to where I came from. Even though Bleeding Hearts Valley *is* my home now."

"Are you going to nitpick about it or answer the question?"

"I haven't had any threats."

"Any phone calls with hangups? Anyone with road rage because you cut them off or stole their parking spot?"

Graham thought uncomfortably about several of the town's residents who had not been so happy with him since he moved into town, either because they perceived him as a competitor or didn't like how he had handled a job for them. People like Marty Ballantyne, who didn't like Graham knowing their secrets.

"I think... that this is related to Ashley's and Ethan's disappearance," he told Joiner. "The first thing you see when you enter the warehouse is those boxes that he knocked over. That tells me he was mad about something to do with the couple disappearing, or me asking questions about it." Graham thought of how angry Marcel had been that Graham had taken it to the police after Marcel had said it was nothing.

"Or it just happened to be the first thing within reach when he walked into the building," Joiner told him. "Don't have tunnel vision about these kids disappearing. Those boxes were not the only things he touched here. And he doesn't say anything about the case on that door."

"Well... no. That's true."

"Is there anything missing? Those boxes that are tipped over and spilled out—anything missing?"

"I don't think so." Graham started to walk back toward them, and Joiner tagged along. Graham looked at the boxes and read the handwritten tags as he righted them. "There wasn't anything valuable in these ones. Mostly just clothing and bedding."

"Where are the passports and jewelry?"

Graham moved boxes around to uncover the ones with the more intriguing items from the apartment. He dug out the passports and jewelry and handed them to Joiner. Joiner briefly looked at the passports before placing them in evidence bags. He examined the jewelry more closely, turning the pieces back and forth so that the light reflected off the facets.

"I'm not an expert, but those look valuable. Not just your Cracker Jack off-the-shelf pieces."

"I can't claim to be an expert either," Graham admitted. "Enough to say there is enough gold to make the larger pieces pretty heavy. I looked at the gems with a loupe and couldn't see any flaws, but I'm not a jeweler."

Joiner nodded and put each piece into a separate bag. He gathered everything together.

"Interesting person, your Ethan Quick," he commented.

Graham blinked at this comment and tried to unravel it. "He's not 'my' Ethan Quick. I've never even met the guy."

"Not a lot of people have."

"Uh... what does that mean?"

"It means that he doesn't have an established history. Not in this state, anyway. He has a valid passport and driver's license in this name, so it appears to be his legal name, but it's been changed at some point. He hasn't always been Ethan Quick."

"Do you know what it was changed from?"

"That's what we're trying to find out. No name change in this state, and we don't know yet what part of the country he came here from. We're looking into it. We'll find out his previous name sooner or later."

"Where was he living when he and Ashley met?"

"According to her parents, he was volunteering at the homeless shelter where she worked. But I wonder whether that is true or whether he was actually a resident of the shelter, and she didn't want to pass that information on to her parents."

"Because dating and marrying a homeless guy doesn't exactly go over well with the folks."

Joiner nodded, one corner of his mouth quirking up in amusement. "Exactly."

"So, does he even have a work history? Oh—" Graham remembered the detail he had learned from Ian and Robin. "Their neighbor across the hall said he was an unemployed artist. But the ones next door, Ian and Robin, they said that Ashley got him a job through her connections. And it was a really good opportunity. So it might have been an office job that allowed him to use his art skills commercially."

"They didn't have an employer name or place?"

"No. Sorry. Maybe they'll have remembered now, since they've had time to think about it."

Joiner cast an eye at the boxes. "Are there any tax records in there? Employment files? Resume or personal references?"

"I think it was all Ashley's files... but she had both of their passports, so maybe she had a file for his employment too, but I don't remember seeing anything like that."

Joiner made a face.

"You can take a look if you like," Graham offered.

Joiner sighed. "There is the issue of who those files actually belong to and who can give permission for us to look at them. Do they belong to you? To Ashley? To her next of kin? I can't take the chance of having evidence thrown out because we didn't have the proper consents to look at them."

"So even though I've got them, you can't look at them?"

"I'll have to apply for a warrant. Then I'm covered."

Graham looked at the boxes sitting there. It seemed ridiculous for Joiner not to be able to look at them. Graham had obtained them legally. He'd been able to give Joiner the journal, passports, and jewelry because they were evidence that a crime might have been committed. He had filed the missing person reports based on that evidence.

"What if I look at the files?"

Joiner shrugged and looked in the opposite direction. "I couldn't encourage you to do that. You would be acting as an agent to the police, which is the same thing as if I looked at them myself. If you come across something as part of your job that you feel relevant to the case, that is another thing. But I cannot be any part of a search of those files."

Graham nodded slowly. "With these boxes having been moved and opened by the burglar, I should probably do a quick check to ensure nothing is missing. They didn't get the jewelry, but you never know; they might have taken something else."

Joiner nodded. "I'll be in my car, getting the burglary report started. You let me know if you discover anything missing or tampered with."

Graham understood that Joiner did not want to be anywhere in the vicinity while Graham looked through the boxes. "Thanks. I appreciate you coming out here. Do you need to... take pictures before I touch the boxes? Or dust them for fingerprints or anything?"

"It looks like they were knocked down, not opened, so I don't expect to find any prints on the boxes." Joiner hooked his thumbs over his belt and looked around, considering. "If you find the can of spray paint he used on that door, it might have usable prints on it, if the burglar was not wearing gloves. Let me know if you find that. I'll take some pictures of the door, because that's the real crime we're concerned about here. As far as you know, nothing valuable has been stolen. But breaking and entering and making threats... that's something we take seriously around here."

"Okay. Thanks."

Joiner nodded and left the warehouse, whistling to himself. Graham looked at the box labels and searched a couple to find the paper files he had intended to recycle. He paged through them, hoping to find information on Ethan's employment, taxes, or change of name.

One out of three wasn't bad. At least it would give Joiner a direction to investigate. Graham pulled out his phone and called Ian.

"Graham," Ian greeted when he identified himself. "I didn't think we'd hear from you again, since you're finished next door."

"You might be getting a call from Detective Joiner, who is looking into Ashley's and Ethan's disappearance.'"

"Well... we'll help him out all we can."

"You might tell him that you've remembered where Ethan worked."

"That we remembered...? But we don't know where he worked."

"It was at Perennial Path Promotions. An ad agency. He did graphic design work for them."

Ian was silent for a moment, processing this. "And how did you find that out? How are we supposed to have found it out?"

"Someone must have told you. Ashley, probably, since Ethan didn't talk much. You said she was the one who lined up the job for him."

"Yeah, she was. So... I'm not going to have to swear that in court or something, am I? That Ashley told me?"

"This isn't about who told who. Joiner just needs to know where to go to ask people about Ethan. Did he give notice before they left? Did he tell them what trouble they were having or where they were going?"

"Well... okay. But if it comes down to who told me that... I'm going to have to say it came from you."

"Fine," Graham agreed, slightly irritated that Ian couldn't just lie about it. "I got it from one of Ashley's files. As long as you give it to the police, and there is no suggestion that they got it from the files themselves, we're good."

"Why?"

"Because that's how it must be," Graham insisted.

"Okay, okay," Ian agreed sullenly. "Fine. What's the name again?"

"Perennial Path Promotions."

Ian repeated it, maybe writing it down so he wouldn't forget it when the detective called.

"Thanks."

Graham hung up. He repacked the boxes and stacked them neatly so there could be no question of Joiner seeing the files when he didn't have the proper permission. He went to Joiner's car, where the detective hunched over his onboard computer, awkwardly typing away. He motioned Graham over to talk.

"I've looked through the boxes," Graham confirmed. "I don't see anything missing from them."

"Good. I'll come take those pictures of your new artwork."

Graham looked at him blankly.

"On your door," Joiner reminded him dryly.

"Oh. Right. The... little note."

Joiner chuckled and nodded.

"And you should talk to Ashley's neighbors, like I said. They might have remembered where Ethan worked, now that they've had a chance to think about it."

# CHAPTER
# TWENTY-FOUR

A shley knew that something was wrong before it happened. She could just feel it, hanging heavily in the air. Something was coming.

She didn't know why she had that feeling of dread; she couldn't think of anything worse that could happen to her. She might die, but it would be a relief not to suffer any further. Nicholas's behavior couldn't get much more erratic and violent. At this point, she had hit bottom and didn't see how things could get any worse.

But she still had that feeling in the pit of her stomach and the back of her brain. That foreknowledge that something terrible was going to happen, and she wouldn't be able to stop it.

She had one instant of clarity right before it happened, and she knew that she was about to have a seizure.

≈

Ashley's awakening was slow. She didn't know where she was or how she had gotten there. She couldn't remember where she had been before. Everything was muddled and stirred together in her brain.

She evaluated her body. That was the only thing familiar to her, so that was where she started. She was uncomfortable lying on the hard floor. Not only were her muscles flaccid from the violence of her convulsions, but she hurt all over. Not just the back of her head and the parts of her body that were in contact with the floor, but every part of her body felt bruised and beaten.

Her clothes were wet. She wanted to change. Was she alone? Was there anyone there to help her? She groaned and tried to roll over and get up, but couldn't.

Where was she? Nothing she could see from her position on the floor was familiar. She couldn't remember how she had gotten there.

Someone was shouting. At first, it sounded like a foreign language. She was too disoriented to make out their meaning. But eventually, she could understand the familiar man's voice.

"Stop it! Stop it! Have to find a way to make it stop! Mama! Please, Mama, stop!"

Ashley groaned. Who was that? And why was he calling her Mama?

"Ethan?" she murmured, unable to use her voice properly yet.

"No!" A face appeared over her. Haggard. Deep set, hollow eyes. A frantic expression. "Ethan is gone! Not Ethan! I'm the only one here. Nicholas."

"Nicholas?" Ashley repeated, confused. "Who are you?"

"Oh, oh, oh!" He tore at his hair. "You were..." He held himself rigid, vibrating, to mimic a seizure. "You were..."

"A seizure. I have epilepsy," Ashley told him. "I need my medication." She felt unstable. Like she had been off of her meds for days, and the seizures would keep coming. She tried to stay focused on Nicholas and on getting her memories back. "Can you help me?"

"Oh, no." He reached down a hand to help her to her feet. "Are you okay? You shouldn't get up."

Even with his hand, Ashley couldn't get up. She relaxed her body back to the floor. "I can't," she said softly. She closed her eyes and tried to go to sleep. Sometimes, it helped to sleep. But she was hurting too much and couldn't fall asleep there.

"I'm wet," she murmured to Nicholas. "Do you have my clothes?"

"Yes... your suitcase."

He walked away from her. Ashley heard his key turn in the lock, then the door close, and then the key turn again. She frowned, puzzling over where she was. She tried to make sense of the images around her. At first, she couldn't form a coherent picture. Shapes didn't coalesce into *things*. It was hard to sort it out.

She was in a bedroom, but she didn't recognize it. A hotel? Hospital? Was she visiting a friend? Nicholas or his mother?

The ceiling was a long way away from her, but looked dingy and stained. She blinked her eyes, not sure if it really was, or if she was not seeing clearly yet.

There were some thumps, and then the door opened and closed again. Nicholas thumped down two large suitcases.

"Your clothes."

"You need to help me."

He looked down at her, uncertain.

"Help me change," Ashley told him.

He tried to kneel down next to her, but it was difficult for him to fit in the space she was lying in, between the bed and the wall.

To begin with, he seemed fine with helping her. His fingers moved nimbly to unbuckle her belt and to open the button and the zipper. Pulling her pants off was difficult as the wet fabric clung to her. Nicholas looked at her after removing them, his face getting red.

"No," he shook his head. "I can't!"

"I need to get into dry clothes." Ashley's throat was sore, and her voice was hoarse. Her tongue hurt and tasted of blood. "Can someone else help?"

"Nobody else here."

"Then you need to help me."

"It's wet under you. You need to move."

Ashley lay there, trying to gain the strength and coordination necessary to move herself. But her energy reserves were too low.

"You need to help me move. I can't."

"On the bed. You should get back on the bed."

"Then help me."

His behavior was confusing. He was an adult, but his behavior was childlike. But whatever his challenges, she desperately needed his help. He looked strong enough to help her, even if he couldn't pick her up in his arms.

Ashley held her arms out. He was more helpful this time, not just giving her one tentative hand, but grasping her arms hard to pull her to her feet. Ashley couldn't stay up, but between them, they managed to turn her so the bed was behind her to fall back on. Ashley put her arms out to steady herself, afraid she was going to fall back off. But it didn't tip and dump her onto the floor again. She slid her thumbs under the waistband of her panties and tried to remove them.

"Help me," she ordered.

He covered his eyes with the back of his arm and reached out ineffectually with the other hand.

"Come on. Use both hands. Help me. You don't have to look, but help!"

He used both hands and looked away from her as he pulled them off, squinting his eyes shut. Ashley was too tired to do anything else for a few minutes. Eventually, Nicholas overcame his embarrassment enough to go through her suitcases to find her replacement clothes, and he brought them away and again went through the motions of looking away while he helped her dress, pulling the dry clothes on over clammy, cold skin. Ashley hugged herself.

"I need a blanket."

He covered her with a smelly, scratchy blanket. Ashley closed her eyes. She would sleep, and when she awoke again, she would feel better. Then she would know what to do next.

# CHAPTER
# TWENTY-FIVE

J oiner had called Perennial Path Promotions while he was still at the warehouse, within Graham's hearing, though he had not been invited to sit in on the call. It was a short call. It was obvious they were stonewalling him. Despite repeated questions from different angles, he wasn't getting anywhere. He hung up eventually, growling about their unhelpfulness. He looked up and saw Graham standing there, listening in.

"Ethan left the company," he told Graham. "They won't tell me anything about when he left or why or if he got something else after leaving the company. He probably has a case for wrongful termination against them, or they at least think he might litigate. So they are refusing to say anything."

So Ethan was an unemployed artist once more. Had Myrtle known about the termination? Or did she not know he had been working in the first place?

"When was he terminated?"

"They wouldn't give a date. Said they won't give me anything without a subpoena for the information, not even the last date he worked. What a pain in the neck."

"There wasn't anything in Ashley's file about him being terminated."

"Maybe he didn't tell her. It's not unheard-of for a terminated partner to keep leaving the house every day, even though he's got nowhere to go, because he can't bear to tell his wife he lost his job. He has to keep up the pretense for as long as possible. The same kind of guys end up killing their entire families. Family annihilators, they call them. They can't stand to disappoint their families, admit that they can't be the provider they're supposed to be, so they kill them instead."

Graham shivered, goosebumps standing up on his skin. "What makes you think Ethan is the kind who would do that?"

"How much of that journal did you read?"

"Not all of it. A few entries. Enough to see that Ashley was afraid of whoever was stalking her."

Joiner pursed his lips. "I'm not convinced there *was* someone stalking her."

"What? *Someone* was." Ashley had listed the things that kept happening, the intrusions on the privacy of their apartment, and, of course, the threatening message on the mirror. Graham felt violated and angry by the burglar who had broken into his warehouse, touched things, and written a message for him on the door. He couldn't imagine how much worse Ashley would have felt about those things happening in her own house. Repeatedly.

And that got him thinking about Marcel's access to the apartment and the possibility that he was letting himself in at night or other times when the stalker had managed to get in.

"I have to wonder about Ethan," Joiner said. "He had access to the apartment any time, night or day. There was never an actual break-in. No sign of who was actually gaslighting her. Not a glimpse of him, no footprints, hairs, or other signs of who the burglar was. What's to say it wasn't Ethan?"

"She would have known if it was Ethan."

"Would she?"

"She heard noises at night. He would have been in bed with her."

"There are a lot of noises at night in an apartment or old house. That wasn't necessarily related."

"She would have noticed that they only happened when Ethan was home and they had not been together."

"I've read through most of the entries in the journal. I don't see any of them that couldn't have been Ethan, if he'd been clever about it."

"How could he hide it from her? She would have known if he was lying to her about it. He could look her in the face and be surprised about what had happened while he was supposedly gone?"

"You're not a cop, so I'll give you a pass on that one. Yes, spouses lie to each other all the time. Many of them are very good at it. Extremely good, in fact. And a psychopath... they may have zero tells, because they don't feel any guilt about lying."

Graham couldn't believe that it was Ethan. Besides, the couple had disappeared together. Whatever had happened, it had happened to both of them.

"Mark my words," Joiner said with certainty. "When we sort this out, we're going to find out that Ethan was involved somehow, even if it was only peripherally."

Graham pondered this, shaking his head slowly. But Joiner was right. Graham wasn't a cop, and he didn't think like one.

"So... you think Ethan is an 'annihilator.' You think that he killed her and disappeared voluntarily? How would he do that?"

"Or killed himself too. We know that Ethan has changed his name before. What's to stop him from doing it again? By the time we track down his previous name, he may already have changed it again. And he doesn't even have to change it legally. He can drive into the city and start using another name, working for cash under the table at any one of a hundred businesses. No tax records, no ID required. Rent a room for cash, stay at a homeless shelter, or sleep rough. How easy do you think it is to find someone who just disappears through the cracks like that?"

And Ethan had a deep knowledge of the system. He had lived

on the street, lived at the Sixth Street Mission and then in their transitional housing. He knew how it all worked.

"So what *do* you do?" he asked.

"Just keep working the case. Track down his previous name or names and history. Find out what his past MO has been. Has he done this before? What kind of places has he worked? How far has he run before? A few miles? Across several states? Does he have any living relatives or anyone he keeps in touch with? If we're lucky, we'll track him down eventually. But without Ashley's body... what are we going to charge him with? There's no evidence right now that he's done anything to her."

"You can't charge him with murder if you don't even know if she's dead."

Joiner pointed at Graham, nodding. "Exactly."

# CHAPTER
# TWENTY-SIX

J oiner's words and suggestions of Ethan's complicity in Ashley's disappearance kept repeating in Graham's brain. He had planned to go on to his next cleanout job, but he was too distracted. Joiner would continue to work the case, but would he be able to find anything? Especially if he was only looking for Ethan, assuming that he had 'annihilated' his wife.

Graham didn't really plan out what he did next. He only looked up Perennial Path Promotions out of curiosity. Checking to see how close it was to the apartment. Had Ethan driven to work? Walked? Had he kept up the charade of going to work as Joiner had suggested, maybe sitting in a coffee shop nearby whiling away the time on his computer and phone until it was time for him to go home again?

Graham didn't really plan to go there to check it out, but before long, he found himself in the well-appointed reception area of the advertising company. It wasn't a big company, but it employed a number of people. The reception area was decorated in blues and grays, very soothing and professional-looking. All designed to assure clients that they were dealing with the right company.

Graham looked around, not sure why he was there or what he was going to do.

"Can I help you, sir?" the pert receptionist asked with a friendly smile.

"Well... I've started a new business recently, and I would like to have some promotional stuff developed. I mean, it's one thing to print off some business cards on my inkjet printer to hand out to people, but... I think I need more. A brochure, a website... an actual logo..."

She nodded her agreement. "Oh yes. So much more effective if you can present yourself in a professional light," she agreed.

"I wonder whether there is anyone who can talk to me right now. Just throw some ideas around, get an idea of whether I can even afford you." Graham chuckled. "I'm just getting it off the ground, so I need the 'starter pack' rather than the 'deluxe' package. You know?"

He wasn't really expecting that someone would be able to see him right away. They would ask him to make an appointment and come back in a day or two. And in that time... the longer it took to find Ashley, the lower the chances were that she would still be alive when they eventually found her or Ethan.

"Let me see if anyone is available," the receptionist told him with a smile. "Why don't you have a seat for a minute, and I'll see what I can do for you?"

Graham nodded and sat down to look at the array of glossy brochures, cards, and folders that had been left out for customers to peruse.

A few minutes later, a young-looking man with a prematurely receding hairline stood before him with his hand out to shake.

"Jerrold Pole," he introduced himself. "I understand you would like an initial consult?"

"That would be great," Graham agreed. "I don't want to take too much of your time." He looked at his watch. "You guys are probably knocking off for the day soon. I was just hoping for a few minutes..."

"Sure, no trouble. Let's grab a meeting room and see if we can be of any service to you."

"Thanks, I appreciate it."

Graham followed Jerrold to a small meeting room, which was also finished in the gray and blue color scheme, with business packages designed for other companies mounted and framed on the wall for examination.

"This is great," Graham said, looking at a few displayed branding kits. "Really nice. Just so you know... I'm just starting out here, so I don't have much to bring to the table. This would just be a little commission."

"No problem," Jerrold told him with a smile. "We have all kinds of clients, from sole operators to multi-million-dollar companies and everything in between. Why don't you have a seat and tell me about what you do?"

Graham pulled out one of his self-designed and printed business cards, which looked embarrassingly amateur compared to the other offerings displayed around him.

Jerrold looked at the card. "Oh, I *love* the name!" he gushed. "Hall it Away! Very clever. We could do a lot with this."

Graham felt a bit better about that. "Really? I was afraid it was too... juvenile. Or dad-jokey. Or something."

"No, it's great, honestly. Something people will remember. And you're the only one who is going to use it. No one else would come up with the same idea."

"Well, they would have to be named Hall and be in the junk business," Graham agreed. Chances that he would have any competition on the name were pretty low. The fact that it would always be unique was a big draw. Besides the fact that he was actually proud of the wordplay.

"Exactly," Jerrold agreed. "I can already envision a number of opportunities for this brand. Nice bright yellow or orange colors, with a guy in a hard hat, high-vis vest, or dump truck. A chunky graphic that is nice and bold. A really good branding opportunity."

His ideas raised Graham's heart rate as he got excited about it. He could see it in his mind's eye too. The little graphic could be on his store sign, the side of his truck, and his business cards. He could also have a little price list rack card to hand out to people. Or a magnet to put on their fridge. A little die-cut yellow dump truck, of course.

"That would be really cool. How much would something like that cost?"

"Let me price it out for you," Jerrold told him. "The biggest chunk will be designing the graphic. But then it can be the basis for the rest of your advertising. You don't need to redo that every time you want a new piece of advertising or swag."

Before long, the workday had come to an end, and Graham could hear people leaving the office. He gathered the various pieces of paper and samples that Jerrold had given him.

"I should let you go. It sounds like everyone is heading out." Graham held out his hand and shook with Jerrold. He hung on a second longer. "Tell me, is there a watering hole nearby that you would recommend? Where do you guys like to go when the workday is done?"

Jerrold hesitated momentarily, then squeezed Graham's hand and let go. "Sure. Do you know Poison?"

Graham had been there a few times, so he nodded. "Yeah, I know the place. Usually later in the day when I get there. You guys hang out there much?"

"A drink or two after work, then we head for home. Not a long time, but... it's nice to relax for a few minutes before heading back to the wife... or whatever else you are facing at home."

"Would I be in the way if I went over now? Would that be a buzzkill?"

"Not at all," Jerrold assured him, slapping him on the shoulder. "We don't own the place. Always a lot of other people there, not just Perennials."

Graham snickered a bit at the thought of the employees of Perennial being the guys who were always there.

"I'll join you for a beer, then, if you don't mind me hanging out for a bit."

"Sure, of course."

~

One thing led to another, and after a couple of hints about Graham knowing of Ethan Quick, the Perennial employees brought up the fact that he had worked with them for a time.

"Really?" Graham asked. "He's not the kind of guy I would have pictured working there." He crossed his fingers that since Ethan was the quiet type and had only worked at the company for a few months, he was not the kind of guy they normally hired. Ashley had talked someone into it, and it hadn't worked out.

"You're not wrong," agreed Sharon, one of the women who had joined them for an after-work bull session. She was a brunette with long, sleek hair and a chunky build. "Ethan really didn't fit in. We did our best to make him feel like he belonged, but..." she trailed off.

"But he didn't," Jerrold said baldly. "Some people, it doesn't matter what you do, they'll always be outsiders. Ethan Quick... he's one of those guys. Doesn't fit in. Social outcast."

Graham grimaced. "He is a bit... awkward."

"A bit!" an older man guffawed. The employees had introduced themselves too quickly, and Graham wasn't sure he'd gotten them all right, but he thought the man's name was Ward.

The two women shushed him, looking around like they feared someone would overhear them.

"The guy was like a pair of mismatched socks," Ward insisted, not lowering his voice. "Basically useless. You couldn't take him into a meeting without him making everyone feel awkward. He might have been a good graphic designer, but he was always doing or saying the wrong thing."

"He couldn't help it." Sharon tried to smooth things over. "And he was improving. You just had to walk him through things and show him what to do or say. He was getting better."

"No, he wasn't," Ward snapped. "He was getting worse. Wasn't he, Jerrold?"

Jerrold hesitated, obviously not wanting to badmouth Ethan behind his back, but wanting to answer truthfully.

"He was having a lot of difficulties," he admitted. "I think... if things were getting worse at the office, it wasn't all Ethan's fault. I mean, the guy was awkward and could behave strangely sometimes, but he wasn't exactly treated like a valued employee, either. There was..." Jerrold licked his lips and glanced at Graham, "like, maybe, sometimes he was the butt of a joke, and not in a nice way. He didn't always get what was going on. He might have felt... I dunno... he might have felt bullied sometimes."

Everyone was silent for a moment. It was an ugly word, and even though Jerrold had tried to soften it, it was still a shock that he would admit that people had been bullying Ethan, who was awkward and different and needed help navigating the corporate culture.

"Was he?" Graham asked softly. "That's kind of rough."

"The guy was more than just awkward," Ward proclaimed. He ran a hand over his balding head. "He didn't know how to behave in a place like Perennial. He shouldn't have been hired in the first place. It was obvious that he didn't have what it took to be hired on his own merits. He wouldn't have lasted a week if Tony hadn't thought that he owed Ethan's wife something. As it was... things just kept getting worse and worse. The guy was a nutjob. Right?" He looked around at the circle of employees. "Call it what you like, but he was not stable. It's a good thing we got him out when we did."

"Why is that?" Graham prompted.

"I mean, before he ended up going postal and bringing an Uzi to work or something. Just because someone gets ribbed a little, that doesn't warrant violent retaliation."

"Did he retaliate?" Graham wanted to know. "What did he do?"

"He didn't do anything," Sharon said sharply. "He was asked to leave. And he left. And that was the end of it."

"Why was he asked to leave? Because he didn't fit in?"

Sharon glared at the other employees. "Because the company didn't want to deal with a lawsuit for the stuff that was happening."

"He was fired because he was being bullied?"

"He wasn't fired," Jerrold objected. "Like Sharon said, he was just... invited to leave. Management knew Ethan wasn't working out, but he was going to stick with it because of Ashley. They just told him... that he didn't need to. That if he wasn't happy, he should leave."

"And it was a good thing he did leave before he went postal," Ward maintained stubbornly.

"It's not a failure if you don't fit with the corporate culture." Sharon shot another look at Ward, warning him to shut up. "It doesn't mean he wasn't a good artist or designer. Just that Ethan didn't... he wasn't like the rest of us. He really didn't fit there. Square peg in a round hole. There's no point in pretending he is round when he isn't."

Everyone was silent for what seemed like a long time, before ordering more drinks and changing topics. No one wanted to say anything else about Ethan.

Graham wondered what they would say if they knew he was missing. Would they say, "good riddance," or would they be concerned about what might have happened to him and the possibility that they had contributed to his disappearance?

If Ethan *had* left voluntarily, it was quite likely because of these people. He had failed at the job that his wife had arranged for him.

Even with whatever hold she had exercised over Tony, Ethan hadn't been able to cut it.

# CHAPTER
# TWENTY-SEVEN

"You did what?" Joiner demanded.

Graham pulled the phone away from his ear for a moment at Joiner's loud response, then replaced it.

"I just... had a consultation with Perennial Path Promotions," Graham explained slowly, trying to make it sound like he had not done anything that might have interfered with Joiner's investigation. "I need some help with branding and getting some promotional pieces done for my company. So I had an initial consultation—which was really good—and then went for drinks with them at the end of the day. And... Ethan's name came up."

"It came up, did it?" Joiner's voice was a growl. "Are you seriously going to tell me you were not the first to mention his name?"

"No, I don't think I was..." Graham said. "But, I might have encouraged them to talk about him."

"You can't do that."

"Why not? I don't work for you. I'm just letting you know... that Ethan's name came up when I went for drinks with them after work."

"And what did they have to say about him?"

"I knew you had not been able to get anywhere with them,"

Graham pointed out. "And if you got a subpoena, the only thing they would tell you was hiring and termination date. They wouldn't tell you anything about how he fit in—or didn't. They didn't want any trouble. That's why they asked him to leave in the first place."

"Why they asked him to leave?" Joiner repeated. "Tell me what you found out."

Graham settled into his easy chair, the most comfortable seat in the house, and did his best to give Joiner all the information he had picked up at the session with the Perennial employees. When he had repeated everything he could remember, Joiner was silent.

"What do you think?" Graham asked when he couldn't stand the silence any longer.

"The poor sap. Being bullied because he is a misfit, and instead of trying to address the corporate culture of bullying, management decides the best solution is for him to leave. Good-bye; next time, don't get bullied."

"That's not exactly how they put it, but you've got the idea. That's how it felt to me, too. Not only were they kicking Ethan when he was down, but they were pushing him down and then kicking him."

"Nice guys. He should have been glad that he got out of that place. But I don't imagine that was how he felt about it."

"No. Especially if Ashley had pulled strings to get him in there to begin with. He can't even succeed when she paves the way for him."

"There isn't anything in her journal about him being fired or leaving Perennial."

"So you think he didn't tell her."

"Pretty sure. And the timing suggests that things were getting worse at home around the time he left the company. He was home during the day," Joiner said, thinking the idea through. "Ashley didn't think he was, so she thought someone had been there while they were both out. That explains her feelings about things being moved or someone having been in the apartment."

"Some of them," Graham admitted. "But it wasn't just a matter of him being home during the day when she didn't realize he was. There was no reason for him to be doing weird stuff like turning the chairs around backward or writing nasty messages to her on the mirror. Either he was doing more than just hanging out there during the day, or someone else was trying to upset Ashley. Do you still think it was Ethan? It couldn't be someone else doing those things?"

"I'm not set on it being Ethan, but it seems like more and more of a possibility. Did you know he was also arrested for public intoxication and disorderly conduct during that period? After he was terminated. Or 'asked to leave.'"

Graham took a deep breath. That wasn't good. "What happened?"

"His blood alcohol came back at zero. They decided to drop the charges. He was warned to watch himself and stay away from the strip."

"Stay away from the strip? What did he do?"

"He apparently objected to the ladies being on the stroll. Was yelling and harassing them."

Graham rubbed his eyes, thinking about that. Graham's coworkers had seen him as being not just awkward, but potentially violent or litigious. If Joiner was correct, he might have been gaslighting Ashley. And yelling at prostitutes. He wasn't coming off as being the most stable person.

"Just because Ethan has had these problems... it doesn't mean he is responsible for Ashley's disappearance. It doesn't mean that he killed her and went off and started a new life somewhere else," Graham reminded Joiner. If Joiner only looked at Ethan, he would be convinced that Ethan was the culprit and might miss other important facts that would lead him to the real kidnapper, if Ethan had been a victim rather than the perpetrator.

"Of course not," Joiner agreed, sounding irritated. "Trust me, Ethan is not the only one we are looking at. I will follow up on all the leads. Ethan is just the most promising right now. Whoever he is."

"You haven't been able to trace him yet?"

"No. Working on it, but it isn't like you can just type his name into a database and it will pop up his previous name. You have to know where he was living when he changed it, or to make other connections. It's not like what you see on *FBI* on the TV, where they have every database imaginable at their fingertips."

"What about his fingerprints?"

"None of the unknowns we have collected has given us an identity."

"That means he hasn't been convicted of anything before?"

"No. Not if any of the fingerprints we have recovered have been his."

Graham had to assume that he had recovered fingerprints from the passports or jewelry, or maybe from the bathroom surfaces at the apartment. Ethan's must have been included in those collected. It was reassuring to know that Ethan did not have a criminal history. Maybe Joiner was wrong, and Ethan hadn't been involved in Ashley's disappearance, but had been a victim of someone who had broken into the apartment.

Or *accessed* it, because the door and locks had not been broken.

"Have you looked into Marcel?" he asked tentatively. "I mean... I don't want to make any trouble for him, but he comes off as a bit... uh... suspicious, don't you think? And he was the one person we know had a key to the apartment, so he *could* have been accessing it while they were both gone, or while they slept. He could make it look like they had just taken off after he... did whatever he did to them."

"We have not overlooked him," Joiner confirmed. "We are fully aware of anyone who had keys to the apartment or might have been given access by either Marcel or Ashley and Ethan. They might have given a spare key to a neighbor who came in to check on things while they were away. Or if the locks had not been rekeyed for Ashley and Ethan, anyone who had the keys from the previous tenants."

What had been a very limited set of suspects was growing. Marcel, the neighbors, family or friends who might have been given keys, the building handyman, family and friends of the previous tenants, maybe several of them.

"Of course," Joiner continued, "the locks could also have been picked. They aren't anything complicated. Or if only the handle was locked and not the bolts, it could have been popped open like the one at your warehouse, without it being obvious. Or a bump key used. You think the locks on your door keep you safe, but it is only an illusion."

"Great." Graham shifted uncomfortably. He looked toward his own door. He had locked the handle when he returned home. He hadn't locked the bolt, though he always did before bed. As long as he remembered. As long as he didn't fall asleep in his chair, not even getting to bed.

He knew the police said that you should always lock your doors, even when you were at home during the day, to protect yourself against burglars and home invaders. But that had always seemed like overkill. He didn't like to feel like a prisoner in his own home. He didn't like to lock himself in except when he turned out the lights to go to bed.

"Your Marcel does have a few complaints against him," Joiner advised. "You're not wrong to be a little suspicious looking at him. But so far, we don't have any indications that he was involved."

"Does he have an alibi?"

"For what time? For what day? We don't even know for sure what day Ashley and Ethan went missing. Going by other people's recollections of when they saw them is not reliable. Memories are fallible. People attach a memory to a certain event, day, or time, and get it wrong. Realize that it was a different day altogether. We know Ashley didn't show up at work on the

Monday, but Friday afternoon through Monday morning is too long of a period for people to establish alibis."

So Marcel didn't have an alibi. Of course not. If he was doing his job properly, he would be around the building regularly, talking to his tenants, seeing to repairs, collecting rent, supervising move-ins or move-outs. Being a reliable landlord would put him on the scene.

"What kind of complaints?" Graham asked. "When you say that Marcel had complaints against him..."

"Why would I share that information with a civilian?" Joiner challenged. "I think you're too involved in this case as it is. If I were to share complaints with you that were untrue, I could be charged with slander. Besides which, they don't mean anything. He's never been convicted of anything criminal. Any landlord who has been in business for a few years is going to have complaints made against him. It's the nature of the business. You're demanding money from people who may be having financial problems. You have a key to their apartments. They resent you."

"Marcel doesn't have any convictions?"

"He doesn't have any criminal convictions," Joiner corrected.

Which sounded like he did have some misdemeanors on his record. But were they traffic violations? Assault? Stalking?

"Rest assured that we are looking at everyone," Joiner said. "And that includes you."

# CHAPTER
# TWENTY-EIGHT

Graham's mouth went dry. He cleared his throat.
"What?"

"You're Johnny-on-the-spot. You're all concerned about what happened to the happy couple and want to ensure a missing person report is filed. There are plenty of criminals in the world who bask in the attention. Firebugs who light fires and involve themselves with the arson investigation. Serial killers who announce their kills to the police to make sure they connect them together and recognize how smart the killer is. Reporting a crime does not guarantee that you were not the perpetrator. Many times, the person who reports a crime was involved themselves. They think reporting it will clear them of suspicion. But it doesn't."

Graham cleared his throat again. He knew he was innocent. He hadn't even met Ashley and Ethan. He hadn't had anything to do with them until Marcel had asked him to do the cleanout. He had done the right thing by reporting them missing, even if Marcel had been against it.

But Graham had never thought it would draw the detective's attention to him as a suspect. He had never thought that reporting the disappearance would shine a spotlight on him.

"I didn't have anything to do with their disappearance," he objected shakily. "I never even met either of them."

"You're staying awfully close to the investigation. Most normal people will report a missing person and then let the police handle it without involving themselves further. At least when it is someone they claim was a stranger. In fact... reporting a stranger missing is, in itself... pretty odd behavior."

"What would you expect me to do? Just ignore that they had left their passports and valuables when they supposedly abandoned the apartment?"

In his mind's eye, he could see Joiner shrugging. "Most people... would have just done the job and stayed out of it. Or packed the passports and valuables into a separate box in case they sent back for them later."

"And disposed of all of the rest of their possessions? When something might have happened to them?" Graham demanded in disbelief.

"Most people would not have gotten involved," Joiner maintained. "And forgive me for mentioning it, but there are certain parallels between you and Ethan."

Graham jumped out of his chair, alarmed, but there was no one to fight, no one to run from. Joiner stayed on the other end of the phone, out of his reach. Graham paced across the room. "What are you talking about?" he demanded.

"You're a newcomer to Bleeding Hearts Valley."

"Being a newcomer doesn't make me guilty of something."

"No need to be so defensive, Mr. Hall," Joiner's voice was indulgent. "I didn't say that you were guilty of something. Just that there are certain *parallels* between Ethan's life and yours. You were both new to town. You came here from..."

Graham didn't fill in the information. He didn't need Joiner digging into his former life.

"Let's just say out east," Joiner said smoothly. "And you lived quite a different life there, didn't you? Cut all your ties and moved out to the boonies to escape your troubles?"

"You don't know anything about it."

"At least you were easier to trace than Ethan. You could take a page from his book. A name change makes things a lot more difficult for the police. Even more so if you can get your social security number changed at the same time."

Graham paced across his living room and back again. He had felt comfortable and safe there. He had cut his ties with his previous life and everyone who had been a part of it. He had not thought that anyone would be able to trace him back to his old life.

He had not gone through the bother of a legal name change. Hall was a common enough name. He had thought that going by his middle name instead of his first name would be enough to obscure the trail. He didn't meet any of the qualifications required to change his SSN. He had considered it briefly, but reading through the limited set of circumstances where the government would grant a new SSN and the hoops one would have to jump through to get it done, Graham had decided there was no point in applying. The average person was not able to access the SSN database. As long as he kept his number and former identity to himself, no one in his new life would be able to trace him back to his origins.

He hadn't counted on law enforcement taking an interest in him. Even when he had gone to the police station to report the missing couple, he had not thought that they would dig into his background. He wasn't the one who was missing. He didn't know them or have anything to do with their disappearance.

"I don't know what you think you found out about me," he told Joiner, trying to keep his voice calm and even, "but there are no parallels between my life and Ethan's. And I never met him."

"You both decided there were things in your lives that you wanted to leave behind. You didn't want anyone to know who you were. You wanted to erase your past. Right?"

Graham couldn't talk about what he had done without explaining why he had done it and why he'd wanted to leave that life behind. Joiner already knew more than Graham wanted him to.

"I haven't done anything wrong," he pointed out. "All I did was move from one part of the country to another. People do that all the time. There is nothing suspicious or illegal about it."

"There were charges made against you. Domestic abuse. Stalking."

"Those charges were dropped. They were spurious. An ex who couldn't get over a breakup."

"She didn't want to break up with you, so she said you were abusive? What kind of sense does that make? And stalking her? Why would she take out a restraining order against you if she wanted to get back together with you?"

"I can't explain the twisted logic," Graham said helplessly. He hadn't understood it himself. If Candice wanted him back, why would she make accusations against him? Why would she pretend he was a dangerous stalker? Did she think that reverse psychology would work on him? That if she pushed him away, he would want her back?

He hadn't fought the restraining order. He had denied the domestic abuse charges, but he had let the restraining order stand, assuming it would work out in his favor. She would stay away from him and leave him alone.

It hadn't turned out that way.

"Look, she was crazy. She wasn't ready to break it off, so she went a little nuts. I was going through my own thing..."

"I will be reaching out to the cops who charged you. So if there is anything you want to say first, now would be the time."

"I didn't do anything to Candice," Graham insisted, trying not to raise his voice. It wouldn't do him any good to show Joiner his temper. "There is no connection between her charges and what happened to Ashley and Ethan. I can't believe you even found those charges," he fumed. "Once they are dropped, you shouldn't be able to search them. They shouldn't be on my record. I didn't do anything, and they knew it. That was why they were dropped."

"Then that's what they will tell me, right?"

Graham's stomach tied in a knot. He had not enjoyed his interaction with the cops back east. So far, Joiner had been pretty open and understanding, willing to talk to Graham and listen to what he had to say. It had been a whole different story when Graham's girlfriend—ex-girlfriend—had accused him of beating on her and stalking her after she had dumped him.

The cops had not been friendly and indulgent then.

Weren't cops taught how to tell when someone really was being abused? How she would behave? How she would be afraid of him? It didn't make any sense that she would be the one yelling at him and calling the cops on him. She would be too afraid.

"The cops who laid those charges..." Graham rubbed his head, which was now pulsing with pain, "they didn't listen to anything I said. So... no, they aren't going to have good things to say about me. Why would they? They thought that I was abusive. But I swear, that wasn't how it was."

"I'll find out what evidence there was against you."

"Just her word. That's all."

"Uh-huh."

"Look, I was going through a difficult time. It wasn't just her. It was everything. And I didn't handle it very well. But I never did anything to hurt Candice. I never did any of the things that she said I did."

"What were you going through? Maybe I could understand it better if you were more clear. These vague references don't do anything to help you."

"I don't feel like telling you my whole story," Graham said tightly. "You're right; I came out here to escape all of that and leave it behind me. A fresh start. A new life. I don't want to have to relive it all, and I don't want people around here to..." He stopped, unsure how to finish the sentence without sounding like he was guilty of something.

When he was *not*.

"What don't you want people in Bleeding Hearts Valley to know about you?"

"I don't want them to know anything about me," Graham said lamely. "I want them to meet me and to like or dislike me based on what they see, on the person I am now. Not who I was back then."

"And who were you?"

Graham rolled his eyes and shook his head, dramatic movements that Joiner couldn't see. Was the man dense? Did he not understand anything that Graham was trying to tell him?

"I don't want to bring that part of my life here. I left it all behind. It's over. It's in the past."

"What kind of a person were you? Why do you want to leave that behind?"

"What kind of a guy do you think I am? What have *you* seen? I'm working an honest job, running my own business. I do it well. You saw how clean the apartment was, everything I took out of there and how it is all organized to dispose of it. And you saw that I'm trying to do the right thing. I thought someone might be hurt and a crime might have been committed, so I went to the police. Twice. Does that sound like someone who was involved in whatever happened?"

Joiner scoffed. "Like I said, I'm familiar with serial killers who taunt the police and firefighters investigating the fires that they themselves started. It isn't outside of my experience that someone who kidnapped or killed a couple would go to the police to make sure they were aware of it."

"Well, I wouldn't. I'm not crazy. I'm not violent. I don't hurt people."

"I'll be in touch with your friends out east."

Graham thought he meant the cops when he said "your

friends," but he wasn't sure. He didn't want Joiner talking to the people who had been his friends. Or his family.

"I don't want people to know where I moved," he warned Joiner. "I don't want anyone trying to contact me. If you tell people where I am..."

"What will you do, Mr. Hall? Sue me for defamation? Kill me? Tell my friends lies about me?"

Graham shook his head. "Just keep my private life private. I haven't done anything wrong." He drilled a knuckle into the knotted muscles in his head, which were now pounding with pain. "Just goes to show you what happens when you try to be a good guy and do the right thing," he complained. "I should have just minded my own business and not cared about what might have happened to Ashley and Ethan."

He wanted to whip his phone across the house and watch it shatter into a million pieces. But he didn't have the energy to do that or replace it. So he just touched the End button, which was thoroughly unsatisfying.

But at least he was left in silence, and Joiner did not try to call him back.

# CHAPTER
# TWENTY-NINE

Graham wished he could return to the frame of mind he had been in before beginning Marcel's apartment cleanout. He had been calm, happy with his work and with what he was accomplishing. He loved to take rooms and houses from a state of chaos, piled with the accumulated junk of decades, and to turn them back into livable spaces, clean and freshly painted and inviting. He enjoyed figuring out what he could get money for and what had to go to the dump or hazardous materials. He loved the crazy things he found in some houses. And putting people like Marty Ballantyne in their place.

Now he couldn't sleep. He couldn't eat. He couldn't stop thinking about the missing couple, no matter how hard he wanted to put it behind him.

The police were on the case. They would take care of it. If there were anything to be discovered, they would find it. He should be able to put it behind him.

But Ashley and Ethan had been missing for over a week. They were bound to be dead.

But people had said the same thing about Elizabeth Smart. They had said the same thing about other girls and women who had disappeared, who had been gone for years. But some men kept the women they took, hidden from sight in secret rooms. If Ashley Carter was still alive, Graham wanted her to be found and rescued.

And if Ethan Quick was still alive, he wanted him found, too. Even though he had never met the man, he felt a kinship with him now. Here was another man who had been misjudged. Someone who was being vilified just because he fit a profile. Husband of a woman who had disappeared. A man who had changed his name and must, therefore, have done terrible things.

There wasn't a shred of evidence that Ethan had done anything.

Graham couldn't stand to be at home. He had no brainpower to go to work and get started on the next cleanout. So he went for a walk. He didn't plan to go anywhere in particular. Just to take some time to clear his head. The fresh, crisp air would be good for him. It would clear his head. The exertion would exorcise his demons. He would be able to focus when he got back.

But something was wrong.

Graham was uneasy. He felt like he was being watched. He looked around for any sign of Joiner or a patrol car. Were they keeping an eye on him? Seeing if he would bolt?

Did Joiner really think that Graham could be involved in Ashley's and Ethan's disappearance? It was crazy. He would never have hurt Candice. No matter how badly she had hurt him, he would never have retaliated.

He looked around once more and started walking, moving as quickly as he could. A power walk. Candice would not have been able to keep up with him, as fit and athletic as she was. Graham could move. He could really tear up the sidewalk when he got going. He left joggers in the dust.

The neighborhood was still new to him. He hadn't walked much since moving to Bleeding Hearts Valley. It was an attractive little town. It had its poorer neighborhoods, but for the most part, it was clean and neat, and people seemed to be happy in their own little lives. The trees were all budded out in fresh green.

Early flowers were popping up in gardens, and annuals were being planted. The air was sweet and fresh and birds trilled in the trees.

After fifteen minutes he stripped off his hoodie, too hot for his amount of activity. He should have known just to wear a t-shirt.

A car pulled up to the stop sign that he was approaching. Irritated, he motioned for it to go through. He wanted it out of the way when he crossed, not sitting there idling, waiting for him to get across the intersection.

The doors of the car opened. Graham's eyes were drawn to the men who stepped out. Tall, strapping young men. But the most striking thing about them was not their muscular appearance or how they were dressed. It was the black balaclavas that they wore over their faces.

It was a crisp day, but certainly not one that demanded knit hats, even for someone who had immigrated from a warmer country. The only reason for them to be wearing them was to keep him from seeing their faces. Graham turned the other way, looking for the best direction to run.

He wasn't a sprinter, had never done well in track and field at school, but if his life depended on it...

He ran as fast as he could. Faster than those joggers. Faster even than some of the cyclists who had passed him on their early morning commutes.

But there were a lot of things that were faster than he was.

# CHAPTER
## THIRTY

A shley wasn't sure how long she had been drifting. Falling asleep, dreaming restlessly and moving around, and waking up again. Lying there unable to go back to sleep, but unable to comprehend where she was and why she should get up. She thought she'd had a run of seizures. It was a long time since that had happened. She was always very diligent in taking her medication, and that kept the seizures at bay. Most of the time. She still had a few sneak through, but they weren't as severe as when she was off her medication, and she didn't have repeated seizures like she used to when she was a kid.

Like she was having now.

Her meds must have stopped working. That happened sometimes.

Gradually she was able to properly catalog her surroundings. But she still wasn't sure where she was or why she was there. Was it some sort of game? A vacation? Role playing? It didn't make any sense. Why would she be in the dingy little house, in that one room?

She tried to travel back through time, to figure out the last thing she remembered and work her way back from there.

She had been working. Though things were disrupted at

home, work was going quite well. Some of the men she'd been working with were really making progress. She loved to see them going from living on the streets and having no way to support themselves to being independent, with housing and a job and maybe making contact with family members or old friends. Or making new friends.

Often, things did not go so well. She would work so hard at helping someone, and they would push her away, refuse to trust her, retreating to some situation that felt safe and familiar to them, even though they were putting themselves in danger. They returned to what they knew. It took a lot of willpower and practice to form new habits and beliefs. Some people were able to do it, and others just could not seem to find it within themselves.

Sometimes things looked good for a while, and then they fell off the wagon, went back to the streets, reverted to old habits and old friends.

The director of the shelter had complimented Ashley, told her she was doing a really good job. She had been excited about the promotion and bump in pay and could hardly wait to get home and tell Ethan about it.

Ethan.

Ashley frowned and tried to focus on him. To remember what had happened when she had gotten home. He would have been proud of her progress. He always told her what a great job she was doing and how amazed he was to be with someone like her.

Ethan's past was shadowy. She understood he didn't want to discuss it or dwell on the past. Things had been rough for him as a child, and he wanted to leave that life behind. She could understand that.

When she had first met him at the shelter, she had been impressed with how hard he pushed himself. She knew he was doing everything he could to move forward in his life and leave all of the sadness and tragedy behind him.

She had been especially impressed at his kindness toward

others and his ability to reach the children. He seemed to have a knack for communicating with them, even the ones who were the most hurt and scared.

She had seen that vulnerability in him, as well. She knew that too many women partnered with men they wanted to fix. That wasn't what she was doing. She was already impressed by him. She didn't need to change him. She just wanted to nurture the kindness and vulnerability she saw in him. She wanted to pair his strengths and weaknesses with hers, so they were shoring each other up.

Ethan would be excited about her work successes. He would be happy that she was going to get the promotion.

Ashley tossed and turned restlessly, trying to remember how things had gone when she got home and how happy Ethan had been about it. He must have been impressed and given her a big hug to congratulate her.

He must have.

Nicholas unlocked the door and came into the room. He sat down on the edge of the bed next to her, staring into her face, his dark eyes intense.

"Are you hungry?"

Ashley nodded. Her stomach had been growling for a while. Sometimes, when she woke up after a seizure, she was starving. Other times, she was nauseated and could barely look at food.

"I have these." He presented her with some fries in a plastic bowl. She couldn't smell them, which told her they were not fresh. But who was she to judge what food he could or could not get for her? She took one of the shriveled fries. Not only was it cold, but it was as hard as a rock. Ashley looked at his face, trying to understand if this was some kind of joke. Was she supposed to laugh? Pretend to eat them voraciously? Push them away with a groan and tell him that she was full?

Ashley chewed on one fry. It was almost too hard for her teeth, but she managed to grind it down. He hadn't given her any water, and Ashley couldn't swallow it, it was so dry. Nicholas kept staring at her. She took another fry. "Do you have any more water?"

He considered this, then shook his head.

"I can get you some more," he offered finally. "But it will be from the tap. I don't know if it is good for drinking."

"I need water. I don't care where it comes from."

"Okay." He let himself out of the room and locked the door again behind him. She had asked him why she was there and why the door had to be locked, and he had told her that was what he was supposed to do. He wasn't allowed to let her out. And Ashley was still too confused and foggy brained to understand why, and whether it made any sense.

She stared down at her arms while she waited for Nicholas to return with the water. Her throat was so dry, and the fry was just a dry paste in her mouth. She wanted to swallow it and she wanted to spit it out.

There were bruises up and down her arms. The way she felt, she suspected the rest of her body was mottled with them as well. What had happened? Had it been because of her seizures? Had she fallen down? Maybe down a flight of stairs? She shook her head, trying to understand it.

It seemed like a long time before Nicholas returned. She had been drifting off even though she was sitting up. She didn't want to lie down and choke on the fry before she had a chance to swallow it.

Nicholas handed her one of the water bottles he had refilled from the tap. It was cloudy, but she didn't care. She took it from him and greedily swallowed several large gulps of water that nearly made her choke. But that was just because of the french fries. She guzzled water until her stomach hurt, and then she figured she'd better stop, or she would throw up. She did not want to do that.

"Where are my meds?" she asked Nicholas. "I need my Dilantin."

"I don't know. I don't want to take any meds. They make me feel bad."

"But I need mine. I don't have a choice whether to take them or not. I need to take them to stop the seizures."

He stuck his lip out stubbornly.

"Please. You don't want me to keep having seizures, do you? They are dangerous. I can't think straight when I keep seizing. You need to get them for me."

"I don't have them."

"Aren't they in my suitcase? I wouldn't have left without packing them."

"No."

"Then I need to see a doctor to get a prescription and a new bottle. I can't go on like this."

"No! You can't see a doctor. You can't go anywhere. You have to stay here."

"Why do I have to stay here?" Ashley demanded. "I need a doctor. Either one needs to come here, or I need to go see one."

"No."

"Yes," Ashley told him forcefully. Her voice cracked, she was so insistent. "I need to get to a doctor now!"

He punched her in the mouth. Pain bloomed, and a spurt of saliva and blood washed her mouth. Nicholas's face twisted into a mask of rage. No longer looking vulnerable and haunted, but like a monster. "No! No, no, no!" each "no" was punctuated by another blow. "You can't leave here. Ever!"

Ashley covered her face and tried to shield herself from further abuse. "Please, you don't understand. If I can't get out of here, I'm going to die. Is that what you want?"

His dark eyes burned into her, pure hate and rage radiating from him. "You have to be punished. You must be punished for what you did."

"I didn't do anything."

"You did!"

He started calling her names. Even more than the punches to

the mouth and nose, his words brought tears to her eyes. She knew they were undeserved. She had always followed the rules. She would never have done the things he accused her of. Never.

"Please, please," she begged. "It isn't true. You know it isn't true."

# CHAPTER
# THIRTY-ONE

Everything was chaos.

Graham couldn't tell what had happened. He had been running, and then he was not. It was like the whole world had exploded around him.

He was on the ground and knew he had skinned several surfaces; they burned like the dickens. There were shouts and pain and screams.

When the sirens arrived, he thought they would split his head right open. When they were right on top of him, they sounded like a herd of screaming cats. He would have covered his ears, but he couldn't seem to control any part of his body properly, and could only feel himself shouting nonsense and writhing on the ground. What had happened? What was going on?

"It's okay," one of the people who arrived put a hand on his shoulder and pressed him down. "We're here to help you. We're going to take good care of you, okay? Can you tell me your name?"

He couldn't control his tongue to answer properly. He was just crying and shouting, trying to understand what had happened.

"Did you see who shot you?"

*What?*

He grabbed one of the hands tending to him, holding it tightly and trying to rewind, to understand what they had just said.

*Shot?*

"It's okay," the calm voice reassured him again. "It looks like a clean entry wound. At the hospital, they'll make sure it hasn't hit anything vital."

Hands probed his back, chest, and belly.

"Minimal blood loss," someone observed. "Unless he's bleeding into the thoracic cavity, I don't think any arteries were hit."

"It's okay, Mr. Hall," the calm voice told him. "You're going to be okay. Everything is looking good."

There were more sirens. Graham squirmed, trying to escape them. More slamming doors, voices, questions, angry and urgent.

"Any eyewitnesses?" one of them barked. "Who saw what happened?"

"No one saw anything until after the shots were fired."

"Someone must have seen something."

"They just heard the shots and the screaming."

Graham tried to get up and demand an accounting of what had happened, start to finish. Hands pressed him down.

"Just lie still, Mr. Hall. You don't want to make your injuries any worse. Let us finish evaluating you, and then we will move you when it is time. You just lie back and let us do our job."

"Hall?" the demanding voice questioned sharply.

"That's what his identification says. Maxwell Graham Hall."

He tried to tell them to call him Graham, but still couldn't master himself.

"Okay, Mr. Hall. We're going to move you. I just want you to relax and let us do our job. Don't try to get up or help. Just stay nice and relaxed. We're going to lie you on your stomach, all right?"

Graham braced himself for an explosion of pain as they

picked him up and put him on a gurney. But even though he knew he was hurt—shot, if he was to believe what they were telling him—his body wasn't getting those messages to his brain. He was incapacitated, but felt removed from his body as the emergency responders moved him around.

Eventually, he was face down on a gurney, a couple of straps pulled across him to keep him from turning over or rolling off, and the gurney was moved to the ambulance, which bounced and jounced around like it was going to tip over. He would no longer be able to believe those TV shows that portrayed delicate medical procedures being performed inside a moving ambulance. They'd be just as likely to slice an artery or someone's throat going over a pothole as to save a life.

It was quieter in the ambulance with only two people watching him, monitoring his condition, and repeating in a calming voice that they would be at Valleyview South Hospital soon, and the doctors would patch him up.

"I was shot?" Graham asked, and although he was able to speak this time, the words came out sounding mushy and slurred.

"Yes, do you remember what happened?"

"Why?" He'd intended to ask why anyone would do something like that, but it was way too many syllables, and he stopped at one.

"I'm sure the police will get that all sorted out for you. You are lucky. Your injuries appear to be minor."

# CHAPTER
# THIRTY-TWO

A t the hospital, Graham couldn't keep track of the various people who leaned over him to look at the gunshot wound or to ask him questions. They seemed to be endless, and yet the same questions were repeated over and over again. Everyone wanted to know what had happened, and Graham had no idea. It had all happened so fast.

"How are you doing, Mr. Hall?" A slim black nurse with short purple hair touched Graham gently, taking his pulse at his wrist even though he was already hooked up to a machine to monitor his vital signs. Her touch was warm and reassuring.

"When can I go home?"

She chuckled. "Not for some time, I'm afraid. We need to see how much damage that bullet did and get you all stitched up. Wouldn't want you to go home and bleed all over the place. Your wife would not like that."

"Not married."

"Oh, your girlfriend then. Even if it's just you, you wouldn't want to wake up dead tomorrow, would you?"

He tried to work that one out logically, but couldn't figure out how to argue with her. She patted him on the shoulder. "The doctor is on his way. We're going to get you lined up for surgery, and they can take out the bullet and repair any damage. Do you have any allergies? Have you ever had general anesthetic?"

"No... once, but I don't remember it. I was just a kid. My appendix."

"No complications?"

"No... don't think so."

"Good. There will be a lot more people asking you questions, but you're doing great. Can you tell me your date of birth?"

Graham stumbled over it, grasping at wisps of memory until he could pull together the information and give it to her. She nodded and checked it against what was on her clipboard.

"Great! Is there anyone we can call? Do you have a friend or relative who should be here?"

"No. It's just me."

"No one? A coworker? Friend? The neighbor who watches your dog for you?"

"Don't have a dog."

"Now, what do you have against dogs?" she teased. "It can be awfully nice to have a warm body to lay down on your toes at the end of the day."

He tried to laugh, but his body stiffened and didn't want him to jiggle that way. He murmured something to her about cats that probably didn't make sense.

"I'm tired. Can I go to sleep?"

On TV, they always tried to keep the injured person awake with shouts of "Stay with me, look into my eyes!" But things were apparently not that dire with Graham. The nurse patted him again on the shoulder.

"You go right ahead, honey. Close your eyes and get what rest you can. They won't let you sleep for long, with all of their poking and questions. But you get what you can."

"Okay. Goin' to sleep."

~

The timeline was disjointed, and Graham had a hard time following what they told him about what was going to happen next and how serious his condition was. But eventually, before the end of the day, they were finished working on him and he was in a regular room, with a curtain drawn between him and whoever he was sharing it with.

"Mr. Hall."

Graham startled, realizing he had been drifting along, half awake and half asleep. When he opened his eyes, he saw Detective Joiner sitting in a chair beside him, close to eye level.

"Oh... hi."

"Well, this is an interesting development, isn't it?" Joiner asked.

"What?"

"Do you often get shot? Or is this because you have been poking around about Ashley's and Ethan's disappearance?"

"Oh." Graham had not drawn a connecting line between the two. "I don't know."

"What did they say to you? Did you get a good look at the person who shot you?"

Graham was face-down on the bed. He turned his head to look at the bandaged area on his flank. It still didn't hurt, but the bandage felt bulky and warm, and he swam through a heaviness that he thought was probably painkillers in his IV bag or the aftereffects of the general anesthetic.

"Behind me," he pointed out. "Didn't see."

"You must have seen something. You were just walking along the street, and a shot rang out?"

Graham remembered the noise of the gunshot. It hadn't been as loud as he would have expected. Then, the punch to his back and falling. He shook his head slowly.

"Yeah... I was running away, and they just shot me."

"Running away? Who were you running away from?"

"I... don't know." He strained to remember more. The memory was far away, buried under cotton wool. "A car... men..."

What had scared him so much that he had started running without even knowing who they were or what their purpose was? Had they said something to him? Yelled at him?

"Men. More than one?"

"More... four of them? Three?"

"What did they look like? Can you describe the men or the car?"

"Dark car... didn't really notice it. The men... they were wearing masks."

"What kind of masks? Halloween masks?"

"No. Ski masks. Knit... caps. What do you call..."

"Balaclavas?"

"Yeah. Right."

"Three or four men in balaclavas? What can you tell me about them? Skin color? Eye color?"

"Don't know. I just ran."

"Can't blame you. I would, too."

Graham doubted that. And even if he did, Joiner would undoubtedly get a complete description of the men despite their masks. Maybe not their faces, but their build and skin color, their other clothing.

"Maybe... not blue jeans."

"Not blue jeans. What kind of pants were they wearing, then? Suit pants? Sweats?"

"Suit... tall... not brawny."

"Slim or fat?"

"Slim."

"Four tall, slim men in dress pants and balaclavas." Joiner considered this. "Sounds like mob. But I would expect them to be better shots. And they would be really clear about why they were shooting you."

Graham grunted.

"You're sure they didn't say anything to you?"

"No. All jumbled. But I don't think so."

"First, your warehouse gets broken into, and nothing is

stolen, and then you are shot. Is this normal for you? Maybe something that connects with your former life? Who are you hiding from?"

"I'm not."

Not the way that Joiner was thinking. There were lots of things to hide from and a lot of ways to hide. He wasn't hiding from some mob connection in his past.

"Your business here in Bleeding Hearts Valley. You're a garbage man. You haul junk. I wouldn't expect that to be a hazardous job."

"No. Gotta watch out for bats and mouse droppings."

"Mouse droppings?" Joiner repeated, frowning.

"Hantavirus."

"Ah. But not people coming after you, trying to steal your garbage."

"No." Again, Graham tried to chuckle, but his body did not appreciate jerking movements, and it came out as a piggish grunt instead of a laugh.

"Then is it related to Ashley's disappearance? Or to them running away?"

"Don't know," Graham insisted. "Maybe. But... I haven't found anything."

"You've found plenty. You found the journal and a number of items that indicate they didn't leave voluntarily. If Ashley and Ethan were kidnapped by someone else, then you are the one responsible for figuring out that it was not just a run-of-the-mill apartment abandonment."

"Smart of me," Graham groaned.

"I haven't found any connection between either of them and any criminal enterprise, but maybe it is time to dig more deeply into that possibility."

"You think... this was to stop me from finding out who did it?"

"Maybe you are closer to the truth than you thought. Who have you talked to that you haven't told me about? What do you know that you either didn't think was important enough to tell me or have tried to keep quiet? It's not the time to hide anything. Your life is at stake here. They didn't succeed in killing you the first time; they could come back."

"No. I don't know anything else. I've told you everything." Graham sighed, impatient with himself and his slowed-down thought processes. "Maybe they think I know something, but I don't."

"It's possible. You could have unknowingly asked the right question—or the wrong question—and stirred up a hornet's nest. Who have you talked to most recently about it?"

"Aside from you... the guys at Perennial." Graham tried to think of how that might be significant. What had he learned about Ethan from his coworkers? What had he learned about the company that might be suspicious if he looked at it a little differently? Had they revealed anything that they might later regret having said?

"Can't think of anything... Just the bullying. Treating Ethan like crap, then asking him to leave."

Joiner stared off into space, thinking about it. "What if he went back there... and there was a fight. He took a gun with him. Or one of them had a gun. But why wouldn't they just report it if he came back at them all aggressive... and it doesn't account for Ashley, what happened to her?"

"They could have gone back together."

Ashley was his initial "in" with the company. Maybe she wanted to talk to the man she had leaned on the first time. Ask him why he had let Ethan be treated that way.

"And then someone got rid of both of them?" Joiner shook his head. "No, that doesn't seem likely. Perennial... You had a consultation with them? What did you think of them as a company? Did they seem aboveboard? You get the feeling that there was anything shady going on?"

"No, just... normal. Lots of samples. Had good design ideas."

"Why was Ethan bullied?"

"He... was different. Awkward. Misfit."

"And that's how they treat everyone who is a little different?"

"Maybe. Some places... bad corporate culture."

Joiner nodded his agreement. "But that doesn't connect up in any way to a kidnapping."

Graham closed his eyes, thinking about it, but couldn't find any scenario where it made sense for one of the Perennial people to have done something to Ashley and Ethan.

"Who else have you talked to about the disappearance?" Joiner asked. "You talking about it at the bar? Where people could overhear?"

"No. Went out for drinks... never mentioned them disappearing."

"Who else, then?"

"Ian and Robin." Graham moved his hand slowly to the back of his head and scratched. "And Marcel, but you already..."

"Yeah, I'm already looking into him. I don't see what motive he would have had to make them disappear. I mean, if he was going to do that, why wouldn't he take their valuables instead of leaving them in the apartment? He could have sold the jewelry in the city. If everyone thought that Ashley and Ethan had taken off on their own, they wouldn't think anything of the jewelry being missing. It was stranger that they were there. They weren't hard to find, were they?"

"No." Graham licked dry lips. "Easy to find. Her dresser drawer." He opened his eyes and saw a cup on the side table.

"That water?"

Joiner picked up the cup and held it with the straw in front of Graham's mouth. He sipped and relaxed again.

"Think I'll go to sleep now."

"Okay." Joiner stood up. "You know how to reach me if you think of anything else. I'd love to know what's going on here."

"You an' me both," Graham agreed.

Joiner wasn't the one who had drawn the short straw. Graham did not enjoy being someone's target.

# CHAPTER
# THIRTY-THREE

Graham was still in the hospital the next day when Ian and Robin paid him a visit. By then, he was starting to feel the aftereffects of being shot. He didn't know whether they had decreased the dose of his painkillers or whether his body was just catching up and letting him know what had happened. He had expected to feel pain after being shot, but he hadn't expected so many places to hurt.

Not just his back, where the bullet hole was, but all of the muscles in his torso. Bruises and areas scraped raw on his hands, knees, and chin where he had landed on the pavement after being shot. His head and neck. Everything seemed to have taken a beating with just that one shot.

But he was glad for the company. He didn't want Ian and Robin to go away because he was in pain. He wanted them to distract him and take his mind off of the pain.

"Hey," Ian greeted. "Look who I found! Mr. Graham Hall, junk hauler extraordinaire! You're looking a little *down in the dumps* there, Mr. Hall."

"Ha ha." Graham tried to readjust his position so that it was easier to see the two men, but he did not want to turn over to lie on his back, aggravating the wound. "How are you guys?"

"Better than you," Ian contributed. He sat in one chair, and Robin dragged another over from the other curtained area. Ian shook his head. "They shot you in the back? What kind of a coward does that?"

Graham wasn't sure he would have preferred to be shot in the face or heart. Being shot in the back was awkward, but at least he had survived.

"Never saw it coming," he said. "Don't understand why they did it."

"You didn't see the shooter at all?"

"I saw them get out of a car that pulled up to me. They had masks on. I ran."

"Quick thinking. Sounds like maybe you'd better start carrying."

"A gun?"

Graham could think of about a hundred ways that could have gone wrong, and he would have been a lot worse off. Maybe dead. Confronting the men when he was outnumbered four to one, potentially all of them armed. Even if he had managed to get a shot off at them, even a lucky shot that injured or killed one of them, things would probably have ended up much more dire for him. And even if he survived without worse injuries than he had now, he would have ended up with another man's death on his conscience. Not something he wanted to have to deal with.

"A gun," Robin agreed, surprising Graham. He had assumed that Robin would remain silent on the topic, as he did on most others, or that he would be a pacifist despite his tough look. "If you're going to be wandering around isolated areas, you should have a way to protect yourself."

Graham shook his head. "I could never shoot someone."

"What about a bear or other wild animal? We still get them in town from time to time, especially late at night or early morning before traffic gets heavy enough to scare them off."

"What would it take to stop a bear?" Graham objected. "That

would take more than a handgun, wouldn't it? You expect me to go out for a walk carrying a shotgun?"

"Might discourage predators," Robin said darkly.

He was obviously not talking about the wild animals. A bear wouldn't know the difference between Graham carrying a stick or a shotgun.

He didn't say anything, and there were a few awkward minutes of silence.

"So, we wanted to know whether you had made any more progress on finding out what happened to Ashley and Ethan," Ian offered, leaning forward and keeping his voice low and confidential. "Have you gotten any closer to figuring it out?"

Graham couldn't believe that Ian or Robin could have had anything to do with the young couple's disappearance. But how many times had he been wrong about the culprit on a TV murder mystery? People could look and act harmless and yet have terrible secrets.

"I haven't found out anything," he told Ian firmly. "I just turned it over to the police. They are the ones investigating it now, not me."

"Have *they* found anything?" Ian gave a shudder of delight. "I would *love* to have an inside view on a murder investigation. Or whatever this is," he added hurriedly. "Of course, no one is saying they are dead."

But Graham was worried. Even if it had been a kidnapping, what were the chances that Ashley was still alive? There had been no ransom demand as far as he knew. Ashley's parents had not known about her disappearance until Ian had called them. No one had reached out to them.

There was another period of silence. Graham didn't know what he was supposed to be talking about, but it was clear that he was not living up to their expectations as a host.

"Hey, what's this?" Ian asked, picking something up from Graham's side table. Several pieces of paper stapled together and folded.

P.D. WORKMAN

"I don't know." Graham tried to turn his head further to look, but strained his neck.

A bill? His menu choices? No one had said anything to him about it.

"It's a search warrant," Ian said breathlessly, his eyes scanning back and forth. "Were you served this by the police?"

Graham turned onto his side and tried to take it from Ian, but the other man was not relinquishing it. He read out the address. "Is that your house? No, your warehouse," he said, reading further.

"They're searching my warehouse?" Graham demanded.

He couldn't remember anyone mentioning the search warrant before that. They had to actually give it to him, didn't they? Not just leave it in his hospital room. But he'd been on general anesthetic and painkillers. None of his recollections of the past day were very reliable.

"Yes, they're searching your warehouse," another voice contributed, and Graham looked over to the doorway to see Joiner standing there. "And you and I need to talk."

# CHAPTER
# THIRTY-FOUR

A shley moved from one position to another slowly and painfully, and then back to her original position again. She felt fevered, like when she'd had chicken pox as a child and suffered through several sweaty, restless, uncomfortable nights.

Her mind kept going back to that day.

The day she had talked to the director about her promotion, and had gone home bubbling over with excitement about the prospect, eager to tell Ethan the good news.

She relived the sequence repeatedly, never getting to the part where she told him about it and saw the smile on his face.

Until finally, her brain was able to break through the barrier, to unlock the memory and play it back to her like a movie.

~

Ethan was already home from work, busy with his laptop at the table. He hunched over it in a position that was bound to give him stiffness and pain later and eventually lead to a hunchback. As the thought crossed her mind, Ashley automatically straightened as if her mother had pulled on a string. She did *not* tell Ethan to pay better attention to his posture. She was not his mother. He could make his own decisions in life without Ashley mothering him.

He looked at her sourly, but Ashley knew he would be delighted to hear her news. She bent down to him and kissed him on the cheek. Then she bounced over to the fridge to find herself a celebratory drink. She found some cranberry juice. It would do.

"I had the best news today," she told him, unable to hold it in any longer. "You know how they have been looking for a new supervisor over the men's program? They advertised for it and everything?"

Ethan grunted. He could barely seem to tear his eyes away from the laptop to listen to her.

"The director called me into his office this afternoon to say I got it! I didn't think I had any chance! There are so many people out there who are so much more qualified."

"Then how did you get it?" Ethan demanded, his face pale and his deep-set eyes dark.

"Because they know my work. They've seen what I can do. They know that I can run the program. I already know the men. It won't be a difficult transition for me. And I'll be supervising other case workers. Showing them how to use their tools to keep the residents progressing. I mean, not all of them will; there are always setbacks, but I've been having great success with them, and the director said that had been noticed."

"You like him?" Ethan demanded.

Ashley was momentarily thrown. "The director? Well... yes, of course I do. He's very kind and really knows his stuff. He's been there for so many years, spearheading the program and—"

"You're sleeping with him!" Ethan accused.

"What?" Ashley was floored.

"That's how you got the job when other people were more qualified. You've been sleeping with him. That's how you got the promotion."

"No! How could you say such a thing, Ethan?"

"While I was working my butt off at Perennial and not

getting anywhere. Being bullied and excluded and told that it just hadn't worked out! I didn't 'fit in'! I did everything I could, everything they wanted me to, and people just kept... they just kept pushing me. Until I couldn't stand it anymore!"

"What?" Ashley sputtered weakly. "What are you talking about? They are bullying you? Why haven't you said anything about it before this?"

"They are horrible people. Monsters. They just want to hurt everyone. They didn't want me to be there."

"Did you... get fired?"

It was awful to think he had been fired the same day she had been promoted. What kind of a horrible coincidence was that?

"They told me I had to leave," Ethan snapped. "Told me that I wasn't any good and was causing too many internal problems and that I should just go home and not come back."

"They said that today? I'm so sorry, Ethan, I didn't know. How horrible. And then I come home—"

"Today?" Ethan repeated. "No, weeks ago! I quit weeks ago and you didn't even notice. What kind of a caseworker are you?"

"Well... not your caseworker. Why didn't you tell me?"

"You should have known." He stood up and shouted at her. "How could you not know what was happening? You sent me there. You are the one who put me into that horrible place."

"No, I was just... I was just trying to help you out, Ethan. To help you get a position where you could use your art instead of just being a gopher or doing industrial work. I thought you would enjoy it more."

"You were wrong! They were horrible monsters!" His voice was breaking. "They ripped out my soul!"

"Ethan... Ethan, baby, I'm so sorry. You should have told me what was going on. I could have helped you. We could have done some role-playing and worked out some scripts to help—"

"I didn't need your help. I didn't need you at all."

"I just... I'm just trying to help."

"You think you're helping by sticking me in a place like that?

You said you would never do that. You promised me." His voice rose to a shriek, and Ashley was worried about the neighbors banging on the wall or calling the police. "You said you'd never make me go anywhere they would hurt me. Anywhere I didn't want to go."

"But I meant... yes, you're right, I did. That's why you should have told me. I don't know if you don't tell me, Ethan. We could have talked about it. Figured out what to do." She held out her hands in a calming gesture. "But you sorted it out yourself. So, good for you. You figured out that it was bad for you, and you got out. And you never have to go back there again. I'm so glad you did that."

He looked confused, frowning and looking at her with his brows drawn down.

"You did good, Ethan," Ashley repeated. She held out her arms to him, and he tentatively accepted her embrace. "You took care of it yourself," Ashley repeated. "I know that couldn't have been easy. I'm glad you told me about it now. We can sit down and figure out your next step when you're feeling up to it." She smiled at him. "Tonight, we'll just relax, and maybe tomorrow, we can talk about what you want to do next."

He held her, rocking slightly side to side in a gentle sway. His body gradually relaxed, letting go of the tension.

# CHAPTER
# THIRTY-FIVE

I an and Robin excused themselves, looking uncomfortable and curious at the same time. They left slowly, maybe hoping to hear something of what Joiner had to say before they were all the way out of the room or out of earshot. But Joiner waited after their voices faded away. He looked out the door and down the hall, then walked over to Graham's bed and stood there looking down at him.

"Sit down," Graham said irritably, not happy to have to turn over to look up at Joiner towering over him. "I can't see you up there."

Joiner stayed for a moment longer to emphasize the power he had over Graham, then settled into the guest chair vacated by Ian.

"You searched my warehouse?" Graham demanded. "Don't you have to give me notice of that?"

"You already knew I was getting a warrant for Ashley's files. And I gave you the warrant yesterday. Put it into your hand."

Graham looked at the side table and shook his head. "I don't remember. There isn't anything in the law about me having to be conscious when you do it?"

Joiner grinned and leaned back in his chair. "It's kind of nice not to have you arguing with me about it. Not like you would change my mind about the search anyway. Once the warrant was issued, I was searching it as soon as I could, whether you liked it or not."

"I don't remember anything about the warrant," Graham insisted.

"Maybe not. But I did give it to you and you were awake at the time. It's not my fault if you don't remember."

"You knew I'd been under anesthesia," Graham complained. "There has to be a rule about that."

"You don't have any questions about what I found there?"

Graham frowned. He stopped to think about it. What could Joiner have found that Graham hadn't told him about already?

"What?"

"Interesting little place you've got there."

"Did you search everything? Or just the boxes of stuff I took out of the apartment?" Graham tried to think of whether there was anything in the warehouse that might make Joiner suspicious about his other activities. He didn't think there was anything that would look strange. It was just a warehouse of stuff that needed to be sold, repurposed, or recycled.

"Mostly the boxes. A few other places that looked like they might have stuff that was taken out of the apartment."

Graham shook his head. "It was all in the boxes."

"Was it?" Joiner shifted in his seat and lifted a soft-sided brief-case onto his lap. He unzipped it and pulled out an evidence bag that contained a hardback black notebook. Graham stared at it for a minute before he remembered. The book he had found hidden under the bathroom vanity.

"Oh! I found that after your evidence guy finished in the bathroom. He missed it!"

"Exactly how did he miss it?"

Graham described the hiding place behind the kickplate on the vanity. "That's why it was in a plastic bag. They wanted to protect it from dirt or damp."

"And why didn't you bring it to me?"

"I completely forgot!" Graham shook his head. "That was when I got the alarm at the warehouse. I shoved it in with my cleaning stuff and got to the warehouse as fast as I could. I forgot with everything that happened... I would have brought it to you once I found it or remembered I had it." He swore, amazed that he would forget something that was seemingly so memorable.

"I didn't even take it out of the bag to look at it. What's inside? Can I look?"

"This is evidence. You can't touch it."

Graham tried to hold back his disappointment. Of course Joiner wouldn't let him handle evidence. What made Graham think that he would?

"Was it another journal?"

But why would Ashley have another journal? An older one? A secret one? Was she so worried that whoever was harassing her would find the journal that she had kept another one in a different hiding place? Hoping that one or the other would be found if something happened to her?

If she feared for her life, why hadn't she ever gone to the police?

"Not a journal," Joiner told him. "A sketchbook."

"Oh! It was Ethan's, then?" It made sense that he would pick a different hiding place from his wife. Did he know she had a journal? Did she know that he had a sketchbook? He could picture them at opposite ends of the apartment, both scribbling away covertly, with no idea that the other was doing the same thing. Except that Ethan's was in pictures, and Ashley's was written.

"I thought it might be yours to begin with," Joiner told him. "You never said you had found it at the apartment, and it was separate from the rest of the junk from the apartment. There's some pretty disturbing stuff in there, and with your history..."

"I don't have a *disturbing* history. I have... a history. You said you were going to talk to the cops out there. What did they tell you?"

"Well, they *did* say that your ex was stalking you, and not the other way around. That she kept following you, then calling the cops and saying you had shown up there to confront her, breaking the restraining order. But eventually, they figured it out."

It had taken them long enough. Graham had gone through the humiliation of multiple arrests and several nights in jail before they realized that Candice was the obsessed stalker.

"But that doesn't mean you didn't entertain violent fantasies about her," Joiner pointed out. "I certainly might have if a woman did that to me."

"Violent fantasies?" Graham cast another look at the sketchbook.

"Once we pulled prints from the book, it was obvious it was his, not yours."

Graham had never even taken it out of the plastic bag. His prints would not be on the journal itself.

Joiner pulled an iPad from his briefcase and returned the sketchpad to it. With a few presses and swipes, he brought something up on the screen on the iPad and handed it to Graham. Still lying stomach down, Graham placed the iPad flat on the mattress and swiped the pages across one at a time. The iPad was only an inch or so smaller than the sketchpad, so the pictures were almost full-size.

There was lots of contrast. Lots of charcoal darkness against white paper. From his limited experience with such media, Graham knew that Ethan would have had to be extremely careful to keep the charcoal from smearing, never allowing his hand to touch the paper. And when each page was finished, he would need to spray it with fixative to keep it from transferring to the facing page or smearing with the movement of the pages within the book.

Nightmarish figures filled the first few pages. Monstrous faces peeking in the window, lurking in the shadows, hiding over people's shoulders. He recognized Ashley's face in a couple of the pictures, looking distressed as she was tormented with demons.

Had Ethan been gaslighting her, then? Wanting to see her distress, to capture those pictures of her fear? There were some more normal sketches. Idyllic mountain and pastoral scenes. Maybe something he had been working on for Perennial? Or as he came out of a depressive episode?

"Some nicer stuff in here," Graham observed as he paged through them.

"For a few pages."

Then the twisted, disturbing pictures returned. Not all of them included Ashley, but other faces were repeated over several pages. Someone else from Ethan's life? Or something from his nightmares? At least he didn't see any Perennial employees in the pictures. He was glad not to find pictures of any of them bleeding and gory. Maybe he had bought into Ward's comments on Ethan "going postal" more than he had realized.

But as he swiped through the photos, there were more and more graphic depictions of violence, and more than one of them included Ashley as the victim being tortured. Eventually, Graham came to the end of the pictures and slowly handed the iPad back to Joiner.

He didn't have any desire to look back through them a second time.

"Thoughts?" Joiner asked after a period of silence.

"Disturbing is a good description."

Joiner nodded. "Yeah. I've asked a psychologist to look at them and to tell me what he can about what they might mean."

Graham lowered his head and massaged his forehead and temples. He felt like he had the worst ever hangover.

"Like whether he fantasized about hurting Ashley or was worried about someone else hurting her. Her stalker, maybe."

"Exactly. Was he a danger to her or not? From this... it certainly looks like it."

"Was he... on anything? Legal, I mean. Prescriptions. At least one of those bottles I picked up must have been his."

"I can't divulge private medical information."

"Have you found out his former name? Or his history?"

Joiner weighed his answer. So he had, Graham assumed, made progress on that front.

"He had changed his name from John Brown." Joiner sighed. "And as you can well imagine, there are more than a few John Browns in the country."

# CHAPTER
# THIRTY-SIX

Graham's injury was not severe, as he had been reassured several times, and after keeping an eye on him for a couple of days, the doctor told him that he could go home.

"Just don't do anything too strenuous," he advised. "Make sure you give that wound some time to heal. And please, try to avoid getting shot again."

Graham rolled his eyes. "I'm not planning to get shot again."

"Did you plan on it the first time?"

Graham wasn't sure what to say about that.

He was going to have to be careful. He wasn't sure who had attacked him the first time. Had it been someone connected with Ethan or even Ethan himself? Had it been about something completely different? Or had it been random? Some kind of gang thing, maybe. Did gangs still do that? Initiate members by having them kill some innocent bystander?

Graham didn't plan to get a gun like Robin had suggested. He didn't like the idea of carrying one with him. He handled guns from time to time when he came across them in his cleanouts. He wasn't wholly opposed to the idea of guns. When they were necessary for hunting or protection. But he hadn't trained with a firearm and could see a dozen different ways that things could go bad if he started carrying a gun without having been properly trained with it. Or if he wasn't committed to killing whoever attacked him. If he wasn't going to use it or was hoping to only use it to threaten someone, then what was the point?

Instead, he resolved to be more careful and aware of his surroundings. He wouldn't wander the streets alone until he was sure that whoever had shot him the first time was actually gone. When he was at his warehouse or at home, he would lock and bolt the doors. He would be extra alert and aware of what was happening around him.

Hopefully, that would be enough. Graham didn't relish the idea of getting shot a second time. He would try to convince himself that it had just been a random thing. It was like he felt after having a car accident. He would resolve never to drive again, wanting to avoid the possibility of ever being in another wreck. But within a few days, it would become too inconvenient, and he would get back behind the wheel to run a few errands. Before long, he was driving just as much as before and had completely forgotten his fears about having another accident.

He had not learned much more from Joiner about Ethan and his life before he had changed his name. Not because he was trying to keep Graham from finding out the truth—though Graham was sure he would do whatever he could to preserve his case and not give Graham information he deemed vital to solving it—but because he really didn't have anything. Ethan Quick of Bleeding Heart Valley had previously been John Brown of Kentucky, and before that...? Who knew? There were hundreds, probably thousands of John Browns across the country. Maybe only exceeded by the number of John Smiths.

Graham would leave Joiner to his investigation. It was not Graham's job. He would go back to junk removal, a job he was good at and that allowed him to relax at the end of the day.

He had to go into the city to see what he could get for some jewelry recovered during another cleanout. Samuel Davidson had a good reputation as a jewelry dealer. He would sort through what Graham had and determine what was good, what was junk, and what were really outstanding pieces that should go to auction to bring in the best price. Graham had used him several times since starting his junk removal business, and Samuel had always been invaluable. Graham never got the feeling that Samuel was trying to scam him. He had never seen any of the "fair" pieces end up in auctions after selling them to Samuel.

There was nothing too exciting in the lot that he brought Samuel this time. He hadn't expected there to be. But there had been a couple of good pieces that Samuel had been willing to buy. The rest could go to one of the pawn shops down the street.

That was when Graham had spotted the Sixth Street Mission. The name had a familiar ring, and it only took him a minute to figure out why. It was the shelter Ashley Carter had worked at.

That was interesting, but he wasn't a cop. Joiner was investigating Ashley's and Ethan's disappearance, and he was the one who would be following up on all of the leads.

But when Graham came out of the pawnshop, he stopped and looked at the shelter again. He was there. It wouldn't hurt anything for him to stop in and make a few casual inquiries.

He really shouldn't go poking his nose where it wasn't wanted.

Especially not after being shot.

But that had been in Bleeding Hearts Valley. Obviously, whoever had it out for him—or had picked him as a random victim—lived in Bleeding Hearts Valley. Not in the city.

The front door to the mission was not unlocked. Graham was surprised. He thought that kind of place remain unlocked all day so that people could come and go and access their stuff. And they would need meals, phone access, counseling, and whatever other services the shelter offered.

There was a doorbell beside the door with a little notice beside it to please be patient and wait after ringing. Graham hesitated once more. Should he just walk away? It didn't really make much sense to leave when he was right there. He might as well take advantage of his proximity.

Graham rang the doorbell. Now he was committed. He wasn't going to ring the bell and then ditch. He would talk to whoever came to the door. If they sent him on his way, he would go.

Despite the sign, he was tempted to ring the bell again when no one answered after a minute or two. Maybe it hadn't worked the first time? Maybe he hadn't pushed it hard enough, or no one had heard it.

# CHAPTER
## THIRTY-SEVEN

He was just reaching out to push it again when the door opened.

"Don't ring it again!" the woman told him. "Can't you read?"

"I just wasn't sure if it worked the first time..." Graham's face heated in embarrassment.

"It works. You just have to wait. It takes time to get to the door and there is a lot going on." She looked Graham up and down. "Now, what do you need? You'd better not be selling Bibles door to door."

Bibles?

"Uh, no, ma'am. I wanted to talk to someone about one of your employees here."

She scowled. "What employee? Who are you?"

"Ashley Carter." Graham didn't answer the second part of the question, unsure how to introduce himself or explain his interest in Ashley's disappearance, since it didn't really have anything to do with him.

"Ashley." The woman put her hand on the door frame, considering. Then she nodded and stepped back, motioning him inside. "We talked to that police officer on the phone."

"Detective Joiner?"

"Yes, that was it. So sad. I can't understand how a girl like Ashley could just go missing like that. He seemed to think she had just taken off, but that doesn't make sense. Why would she do that? Things were going really well for her here."

Graham followed the woman through several different hallways. The place smelled like bodies and stale smoke. It must have absorbed the smell over the years; he was sure they wouldn't allow smoking inside the building in today's environment.

The woman led Graham to an office and poked her head in.

"Mike, can you talk to someone? He's asking about Ashley."

"Come in, come in."

The woman motioned Graham in ahead of her. The name beside the door was Michael O'Neil. Graham entered and looked around.

The office had been cobbled together with odds and ends of furniture, none of which went together. A dark desk, a blond bookcase, a rosewood credenza, and metal file drawers. There was a comfortable mess, lots of piles of paper. A busy place.

"Mike O'Neil," the man introduced himself, standing up to reach out a hand to Graham, then deciding that the distance was too far with the desk between them and sat down, motioning for Graham to take a chair, which was stacked with files.

The woman approached and efficiently moved the files out of the way, and Graham sat down carefully, heedful of the injury caused by the bullet.

"I'll leave you to it, then," the woman said and left the office.

"So what can I do for you?" Mike asked in a friendly tone of voice. There was a slight frown line between his brows. "You're asking about Ashley?"

"Yes. I guess you already talked to Detective Joiner, so you know she is missing."

"I couldn't believe it. And he thought that she had just taken off. Dumped her job here and her apartment and left everything behind to start a new life?" Mike shook his head. "That doesn't make any sense."

"I know," Graham agreed. "I'm sure it does happen, but Ashley seemed happy here..."

"I thought so." The man leaned forward on his desk. "She just got a promotion to a job that was really good for her and would have done wonders for her career. She was excited about it. Why would she leave?"

"She got a promotion?"

"I told that to the detective. She had just been placed over the men's program. It was a very responsible position. She would have been supervising other case workers. Making programming decisions. Reporting to the board. It was a big deal; I'm convinced she would have been great at it. So why would she just disappear?"

"It doesn't make any sense," Graham agreed. "I'm worried about what happened to her. And to Ethan."

He watched Mike carefully for his reaction to Ethan's name. Did he know the man? Or had he just heard about him through Ashley's casual comments?

"Ethan, too," Mike agreed, the frown deepening.

"He seemed like... he had been through a lot. Wouldn't you say?"

"Yes, of course," Mike agreed. "I've been the director here for ten years. I knew Ethan before Ashley did."

"Someone said that he volunteered here," Graham recalled.

"He did some volunteer work," Mike agreed. "It was his way of giving back. And hopefully, a way to build work experience so he could get a good job. It's hard to build a resume coming from the circumstances Ethan did."

"Because he had been homeless?" Graham guessed, trying to make it sound like a foregone conclusion. Of course Ethan had been homeless. That was why he was associated with the shelter.

Mike nodded slowly. "Ethan had been through some difficulties. But he was in transitional housing, and hoped that by building up experience by volunteering, he could get something better. There is so little money to be had in day labor and entry-level retail jobs or food services. It's hard to make any kind of living doing that. If Ethan wanted to be fully independent, he needed other training and opportunities."

Graham nodded. That all made sense.

"How did he do at that?"

"He was diligent. He was smart. He could do whatever you showed him, as long as you took the time to walk him through it a step at a time, give him pointers, let him practice a few times. He could keep up with most of the work that we gave him. He was a big help."

"And then Ashley started working for you."

"Yes. A very bright and promising young lady. She had all of the training and background experience needed to start as a case worker. She had good instincts. She was empathetic and made connections with the men. Her numbers were great. She was helping men to progress, some who we had previously been unable to do much for."

"Really? That's great. Good for her."

"She earned that promotion. I was excited about her taking up a supervisory position. If she could help the other case workers to achieve similar success rates..."

"And Ashley met Ethan here? At the shelter?"

"Yes. A bit of a whirlwind romance. I hadn't expected it. I don't think anyone had, much less either of them!" Mike smiled reminiscently.

"Was Ethan on meds when he was here?"

"Well... yes, of course."

"And he was stable? They seemed to be working for him?"

"Mostly, yes. He did have the occasional setback, sometimes didn't renew his prescriptions in time and ended up with a day or two not covered. Those days... it was a lot more difficult to work with him. He was less focused and easily distracted. More...

emotional. But we would get him back on track, and he would be back to normal after a day or two."

"You didn't worry about him being violent? About anything happening to Ashley?"

"No. She knew about his history. She recognized if he was off his meds."

"His history?"

Mike shrugged. "That he had been bounced around a lot. That he needed support and stability."

"He wasn't violent?"

"No. I never knew him to be. He was trying hard to be..." Mike grimaced, trying to come up with the right words. "For lack of a better term, to be normal. He wanted good relationships, a good home and job, all of those things. And he was willing to work for it. He went through lots of counseling and support groups. He was eager to be trained in whatever we could teach him."

Graham was reassured. "And you had no qualms about him and Ashley getting married and moving in together?"

"It wasn't my place to tell her what to do or what was best for the two of them. She knew Ethan as well as any of us did. And I know how good she was at working with people. I had no doubt that she would be just as good for Ethan as she was for the other men she worked with."

# THIRTY-EIGHT

"What was Ethan's background? You knew that he had changed his name?"

Mike frowned. "Changed his name? Why would he do that?"

"I don't know. I assumed it had something to do with his history. He wanted to distance himself from it. Start a new life."

"Well, I didn't know he had changed his name, but that doesn't make any difference. A lot of our men have gone by several different names. You're right; it is a way to get a fresh start. A signal to yourself that you are a new person, not to be burdened by the past."

Graham understood the sentiment and had done the same thing himself. Not a full name change, but he now went by his middle name rather than Maxwell or any of his nicknames.

"So, what was his background? Did he have family or friends around here?"

"From what I understand, he ended up homeless because of... his illness. It is not uncommon, unfortunately. They get to be more than their families can handle. The family may not understand they have an illness or how to deal with it. Or they may not be willing to accept help or try medication. Or it takes a while to find the right medication, and in the meantime, they are out on the street, or a younger sibling needs to be protected, whatever."

"So he did have family here."

"I... don't know. He didn't talk about them. But that is not unusual if they are trying to make a break with the past. Men are sometimes embarrassed about what happened to them, even though much of it was out of their control and not the result of their own choices."

"So you didn't know anything about him. How long was he here?"

"About a year before Ashley came on the scene. And she has been here for... almost two. So I guess I knew Ethan for three years or so."

"And the only problem was that he had trouble focusing if he was off his meds? Like ADHD?"

"Not ADHD, no. Really, Mr. Hall, I can't tell you specifics about Ethan's diagnoses or medication. I am stretching the bounds of propriety telling you what I have. But I want to help."

"I know, I know. I'm sorry. I shouldn't be pushing you for more information," Graham agreed. The director's shoulders relaxed. Graham looked for another way to approach the couple's disappearance. While he was focused on Ethan and his emotional health, there was no reason to believe that Ethan had anything to do with it, other than the high percentage of spouses who were implicated in their partners' deaths or disappearances. Ashley worked in an environment where she was exposed to individuals who were outliers. Men who could have been dangerous.

"You said that Ashley had done wonders with the men. Were there any... less satisfactory outcomes? Where the client became violent or got too close to her? Didn't know where to draw the line at a professional relationship?"

Mike rubbed his chin. "Again, an area where I cannot say much. The men's medical issues are private and cannot be shared."

"All you're doing is telling me whether she had any personal problems with any of them."

"There were a couple of cases where we... needed to intervene. Where we had to have someone transferred to another program or to take steps to protect the staff. As you can imagine, that happens sometimes. We do deal with a transient and sometimes volatile population."

"Was there anyone in particular? That you think could have been involved in Ashley's disappearance? You know that if you think someone is going to harm another person, you *do* have to report that. It's one of the privacy exceptions."

"I think I know the law better than you do," Mike pointed out.

"Yeah. So... was there anyone?"

"We recently had to transfer a resident to another shelter when he became... too interested in her. But he has not been back. I haven't heard about any more issues."

"And she would have told you if he was harassing her?"

"Of course. We can't deal with it if she doesn't tell us."

"Did she tell you that she thought someone was stalking her? Getting into her apartment while she was gone or even while she was home. Moving things around. Writing a disturbing message on the mirror."

Mike's eyes widened. He shook his head. "No. She didn't mention it to me. Did she suspect Ben? She should have told me."

"She didn't say who she suspected. She didn't report it to the police, either. Maybe she didn't think it was anything to do with work. I mean... would this Ben have followed her back to Bleeding Hearts Valley? Does he have a way to get around?"

"There are always ways to get around... but it would have been difficult for him to follow her or track her down there. She might have checked into it discreetly on her own... called the shelter to see if he was still there. If she knew he was in the city when these things were happening, then he couldn't have been in Bleeding Hearts Valley."

"Right. Maybe I should follow up on that. Where was he transferred to?" Graham took out his phone to make a note.

"Listen," Mike said slowly, "this is all a little bit irregular, isn't it? Shouldn't I be communicating with the detective? He is the one who called me."

"I'll pass it on to him. Or you can. Either way."

"I'd feel a lot better communicating with him. You haven't shown me any kind of ID. What is your standing in this case?"

"Nothing official," Graham admitted. "Just helping the police out with their inquiries."

It might have sounded good, but Mike recognized hogwash when he heard it.

"Yeah, then I really can't tell you any more. I have probably said too much as it is. I want to help Ashley and Ethan as much as I can. But this feels like... we don't have anything that indicates Ben was involved. Or anyone else Ashley had contact with at the shelter. You'll need to conduct your inquiries elsewhere."

Graham nodded affably. "Fine," he agreed. Mike was absolutely right, of course. Graham shouldn't even be asking questions. But he couldn't get the picture of the young couple out of his mind. And the violent pictures from Ethan's sketchpad. The director might think that Ethan had no violent tendencies, but didn't the sketchpad prove that he did? Would he have been drawing pictures of his wife or other women getting hurt if he didn't have those violent thoughts in his mind?

He stood up to indicate to Mike that he heard him and was not going to try to pry confidential information out of him.

"Would you let Detective Joiner know if you think of anything that might have any bearing on the situation? Like this man who was interested in her? Even if it is only a tentative connection... you never know when it might be an important lead."

Mike stood up as well, indicating the interview was over. But the expression on his face suggested that he still had something else to say. Graham paused, waiting.

"There is one other thing," Mike said slowly. "I don't know how it might be related, but... as you say... we don't know what might or might not be relevant."

Graham nodded encouragingly.

"There was a man here a few weeks ago. He was looking for Ethan."

Graham was still, thinking this over. "Did he say who he was? And why he wanted him?"

"No... he said it was personal. He said he was family. I don't remember what, for sure. Like a cousin or an uncle. He said he knew Ethan had been here and was hoping we had a forwarding address, so that he could send him something."

Graham felt a chill. "Send him what?"

"He didn't say. A memento or something like that. I didn't exactly get the best vibe from him, and I didn't know if Ethan was in contact with anyone from his family, so I was... unhelpful. I told him that if he wanted to get something to Ethan, he could leave it with me and I would do my best to track him down and give it to him."

"But that wasn't good enough for him."

"Would it have been good enough for you, if you had some family memento you wanted to give him?"

"No... I would be afraid that you would lose it or not be able to find him. That it wouldn't go past this office."

Mike nodded. "He was of the same opinion. So he didn't give it to me, whatever it was. If there really *was* something he wanted to give to Ethan."

Graham thought of the sketchpad. Was it possible that it had come from someone else rather than being drawn in by Ethan? Maybe this mysterious man was Ashley's stalker and had wanted to give Ethan the pictures of her to get an emotional response from him. And for whatever reason, Ethan had hidden it rather than turning it over to the police.

But that seemed unlikely and Graham discounted it immediately. If Ethan had received an implied threat like that, he would surely have taken it to the police, even if there was something in his past that he did not want to reveal.

Sometimes, protecting the ones you loved came at a price.

# THIRTY-NINE

G raham had not made it back to Bleeding Hearts Valley before his phone began to ring. Checking the caller ID, he saw that it was Detective Joiner.

Mike had clearly called Joiner to tell him about Graham's visit. Graham wasn't really in the mood to be drilled on why he had gone to the shelter or how he was not the one who was supposed to be investigating the case.

Besides, Joiner had already had his kick at the cat. He had been to the shelter before Graham, or at least had called them, to ask about Ashley and Ethan. Was it Graham's fault if he hadn't asked all the right questions and turned up exactly the same information as Graham?

And Graham had told Mike to call Detective Joiner with any information he thought the police should have, so why was Joiner getting on Graham's case? He had behaved responsibly and tried to ensure that all the information got to the right place.

He let the call go to voicemail. Hopefully, Joiner would vent to the recording and Graham would not have to talk to him.

It wasn't that far from the city to Bleeding Hearts Valley. It wouldn't be difficult even for a homeless man. He could have hitched a ride, jumped into someone's pickup truck, taken a ride share, or traveled with a friend with a car.

And once in Bleeding Hearts Valley, how would Ben find Ashley? Just hanging around asking questions? Watching for her on Main Street? Or checking in at the popular restaurants?

He had probably learned things about Ashley in their conversations before he became a problem. She probably told him things about her interests or activities. That was how you got close to people. You told them a little about you, and they reciprocated by telling you things about themselves. A relationship of trust was developed. And you built on that foundation.

What things would Ashley have told Ben about herself? Of course she wouldn't give him her address, but she probably would have told him what town she lived in, not thinking that he would ever try to find her there.

If it had been Graham, he would have gone to St. Francis, the homeless shelter in Bleeding Hearts Valley, and asked about her there. See if she ever did any volunteer work there. It was a cause she believed in, and she was very empathetic.

Rather than going directly back to his warehouse, Graham diverted to St. Francis.

He had arrived at the Sixth Street Mission during a quiet part of the day, but as he arrived at St. Francis, it was obvious that they were gearing up for dinner. Lots of people getting the food cooked and set up. Homeless people lined up outside to get in when they opened the doors.

Graham reconsidered. He should probably come back later, when things were not so crazy. It would be difficult to talk to anyone while dinner was being served.

But he was there. The worst they could do was tell him it wasn't a good time and to come back later. Maybe with an appointment.

He drove around the building to find the best place for access. He obviously couldn't pass by everyone queuing up for dinner to knock on the front door to be let in. That was a good way to get lynched.

But in the back, he found an open door where clouds of steam escaped the kitchen, and a couple of people visited outside, taking a break. Graham pulled his truck over and approached the workers. Volunteers, probably. They quieted and watched him approach, dropping their cigarettes and grinding them out. Probably breaking by-laws by smoking too close to the building and the food.

"Hall it Away?" the man with a white cap read the words on the side of the truck in a mocking voice. "You think you're going to get in to take anything away here? These people know how to put junk to good use."

"I'm not here to haul anything away," Graham assured him. "I was hoping to talk to someone for a few minutes."

"About what? Business opportunities?"

"No, I'm looking for a man who might have been by here in the past few weeks. A homeless guy named Ben who came over from the city."

They exchanged looks, then shook their heads.

"What do you need to ask after people for? This isn't your own personal information center."

Graham made a calming motion with his hands, wondering if they would take everything he said the wrong way. Maybe they were hungry, getting angry working and waiting around for the food. Hangry.

"Sorry, I think we got off on the wrong foot," he offered. "I didn't mean to start something. I'm just hoping for a little bit of help for a couple who might be in trouble."

"If they're in trouble, they can come to the front door like anyone else. And they'll be served just like anyone else."

"They can't exactly do that, they're missing."

The younger of the two men softened a little. He nodded, looking concerned, and lit a fresh cigarette. "Missing? How do you think you're going to help them coming here?"

"I heard that Ben was looking for them. And that he might have come here. I wanted to find out... whether he was able to find anything out about her."

"Why? You think that he caused trouble for her?"

"I was told that he was looking for her... that he might have caused some trouble in the past. I want to find out if he was able to figure out where she lived. If he showed up at her place..."

They looked at each other again, consulting with each other. Eventually, they seemed to come to a decision.

"You want to talk to Miss Beth. She is the one who would be on top of something like that. She knows who comes here and what they need."

"Is she here? That would be really helpful.'"

"Come in here, stay close," the taller man ordered, and led Graham into the kitchen.

It was even busier than Graham had imagined. They must have been feeding an army. He had no idea that so many people in Bleeding Hearts Valley were in need of a hot meal provided by St. Francis.

There were shouts back and forth across the room, which seemed to be utter chaos to Graham, but must have been organized in some way. If they pulled off a dinner like this every night, they must have had a system that worked.

"Busy place," the volunteer leading Graham told him. "Every night."

"It's mind-boggling."

"For someone new, I imagine it is," he agreed. "Stick close, now."

He weaved his way between counters and workers with ease. Graham found himself running into people, causing roadblocks, and generally being a nuisance.

Eventually, they were through the kitchen, and just as at the mission, Graham was led to an office space to meet the person in charge.

The gray-haired woman at the desk looked up at the interruption. She looked over them.

"Yes, can I be of some help?"

"Guy asking questions," the volunteer said, indicating Graham. "You can deal with him."

He left the office, heading back to the kitchen, Graham assumed. Miss Beth pushed her glasses up on her head.

"You've arrived at a rather busy time," she observed.

"I'm sorry. I probably should have come back another time."

"Well, you're here now. What do you need?"

"My name is Graham Hall. I'm looking for a homeless man who might have come here from the city. I don't know his last name, but his first name was Ben. And he was looking for a local named Ashley. Ashley Carter."

"Who told you this?"

"Well... no one has put all the pieces together that way. But I'm hoping it all fits together, and you might know who I'm talking about."

"I don't think so. That doesn't sound like anyone who has been here lately. When would this have been?"

"A few weeks ago. I can't get much closer than that."

"Well, I can ask around, but I don't think we've done an intake on anyone named Ben in the last few months."

"He might not have been registered, just stopped by to see if you had any information on where to find Ashley. Maybe to see if she volunteered here."

"Ashley?"

"Ashley Carter."

Miss Beth frowned, a crease appearing between her brows. "Ashley Carter," she repeated. "Is she a social worker?"

"Yes. She works in the city, but I thought she might volunteer here sometimes."

"And why are you looking for her?"

"I'm not looking for her—well, I am, but not here. I'm

looking for someone who might have had contact with her a couple of weeks ago, before she disappeared."

"She disappeared?" Miss Beth frowned. "What happened?"

"I can't go into too much detail, but she and her husband disappeared from their apartment. The landlord thought they had just taken off, but it turns out... well, it looks like that might not be what happened. Someone might have had something to do with it."

"This Ben?"

"Yes. Well, there is no indication that he did. But I'd like to pursue all of the leads, and Ben is one of them. He was... obsessed with Ashley. And then she disappeared. I'm leaving stuff out, of course. But if you could help me, I'd appreciate it."

"You are some kind of friend of Ashley's?"

"No, I didn't find out about this until after it happened. But let's say... I'm a concerned party."

Miss Beth didn't look reassured, and Graham couldn't blame her. It was a convoluted story and he didn't have any standing to investigate Ashley's disappearance.

"I don't think anyone called Ben has made inquiries after Ashley. I'm sorry, that is all I can tell you for sure. We don't keep records of every inquiry that is made."

Graham nodded. "Does Ashley do any work for you? Volunteering, I mean? I know she works at the Sixth Street Mission in the city. But I thought maybe she helped out here sometimes, too."

"No, she doesn't."

"Oh. Okay."

Graham stood there for a minute, reviewing his case and trying to think of whether there was another approach that might yield fruit.

He could walk around as the homeless people were being fed and ask them if they knew Ben. But that would undoubtedly be frowned upon. Even if he waited until they left the dinner hall, canvassing them probably broke the rules.

# CHAPTER
# FORTY

"Is there anything else?" Miss Beth asked, clearly expecting Graham to leave.

"No... well, there is... one more thing."

"What is it?"

"Ashley's husband, Ethan. He didn't ever volunteer here or stay here either, did he?"

"Ethan? No." There was a tightening of the woman's lips, and she frowned at the papers on the desk before her. "Ethan. Someone else was asking about Ethan."

Graham was still. He said nothing, waiting to see if Miss Beth could dredge up the memory. It wasn't likely to be a real clue in the missing person case, but he knew from the financial field that information could pop up in the strangest places. The shelter was a part of Ashley's and Ethan's community, both geographically and as a cause they were concerned with. If someone had been asking about Ethan, it was just possible that it could be Ethan Quick.

Miss Beth moved some papers around her desk and pulled out a notebook. She flipped through the pink pages, and Graham saw that it was not a notebook, but a message book, and that each message written down made a carbonless copy, so Miss Beth could take a message, tear out the slip to give to the person who was to follow up on the call, and still retain a copy logging the call.

Miss Beth looked carefully through the messages, going back farther and farther. Eventually, she stopped.

"Yes, I thought so. Someone was inquiring about an Ethan a couple of weeks ago. Would that be the same man?"

"Was it for Ethan Quick? Who was calling? What did he say?" Graham asked eagerly.

"Yes, Ethan Quick." She touched the place in her message logs. "He said he was a family member. He wondered whether Ethan was staying here or whether we knew where he was."

"But you didn't tell him anything?"

"No, I didn't have anything to tell him. I knew we didn't have anyone by that name staying here. He could have been here under another name. But the fact is, I would never tell a caller the person they were looking for was staying here. It is a matter of privacy and safety. People who are living on the street are often there because of violence in the home or in the neighborhood. It might be a wife fleeing her husband or a kid trying to break off from a gang. You just never know."

"Right, of course. But in this case, you didn't even know who Ethan was."

"No. And he didn't mention Ashley."

"Did he leave his name and number in case Ethan showed up?"

She nodded, but didn't immediately offer it to Graham.

"He said he was a family member. That he was trying to reach Ethan, who had called him recently."

"To give him something? A memento?"

"Yes." Her brows went up in surprise. "How on earth did you know that?"

"He showed up at the Sixth Street Mission too. Same message. That he had something to give to Ethan."

"What is this thing?"

"No idea. He didn't tell Mike. I take it he didn't tell you, either?"

"No. I thought it was probably a ruse. People will use all kinds of stories to get me to divulge whether the person they are looking for is staying here."

Graham imagined people made up all kinds of stories to get the information they wanted. Or to try to talk their way out of something. Some of them could be quite creative.

"If this man left his name and phone number, I would like to get them. If there is any possibility that he has information on Ethan and where he is now…"

"Since he was looking for Ethan, I would say you are probably out of luck."

"Unless he managed to find him. But he might still have background information on Ethan that could be valuable. If he is a family member, he might know things about Ethan that would help us figure out what happened to him."

"I can't give information like that out to just anyone."

"Could you call Detective Joiner and give it to him?"

"Police detective?"

"Yes."

She nodded slowly, her gray curls bouncing. "Yes, I suppose I could pass it along to him. Do you have his contact information?"

"Sure." Graham dug out his phone to retrieve Joiner's phone number. She tapped a button on her desk phone, and it emitted a low dial tone. She tapped the number into the phone as Graham gave it to her. Then it started to ring.

"Detective Joiner," the cop announced when he picked it up.

"Detective Joiner? What agency are you with?" Miss Beth questioned.

"Bleeding Hearts Valley police department, ma'am. What can I do for you?"

"I have a young man here asking questions about Ashley and Ethan Quick…"

"That darn Graham Hall?" Joiner snapped. "Who are you, ma'am? Is he harassing you?"

"No, not at all. He had some questions and thought that I had information that might be helpful to you."

"Oh?" Joiner sounded mollified. "What's that?"

"I work at St. Francis homeless shelter. Mr. Hall came here asking about Ashley and Ethan. And I don't know anything about them or where they are, but another man was asking about Ethan a couple of weeks ago, and Mr. Hall thought that you might find this information useful."

"Okay," Joiner said, "I would be interested in anything you could tell me about that."

"He said he was Ethan's uncle. I don't know whether that is true, but you can take it with a grain of salt. He said his name was Bernard Brown."

"Brown," Joiner repeated.

With a thrill, Graham remembered Ethan's former name was John Brown.

"Did you get any other information from him?" Joiner asked.

"He left a phone number, in case I found out anything about Ethan and wanted to get in touch."

Miss Beth read off the number. Graham tried to be covert about tapping it into his phone as she read it aloud. Joiner would call Bernard Brown, but it wouldn't hurt for Graham to have his information too. As he had demonstrated, he might be able to get information that the police were not. People didn't always like talking to the police. If Graham could take the man out for drinks, who knew what he might be able to get from him?

"Is Mr. Hall there now?"

"Yes. You are on speaker phone."

"Hall, what the hell are you doing? You think you're a cop or private investigator? Why are you pursuing this instead of running your own dang business?"

"I am... I just happened to be close by, so I thought I would check in... ask a few questions."

"You're just upsetting people. You don't have any right to ask questions—"

"Miss Beth isn't upset, are you?" Graham asked her, and she shook her head. "And I don't think Mike was either. They both had information to share. I told them to talk to you. That benefits your investigation, so I don't understand the problem."

"You need to keep your nose out of it. You will end up tainting witnesses or scaring the culprit off."

"I got you information you didn't have," Graham pointed out.

"Yes," Joiner admitted. "You did do that. Now, please stay out of police business and quit asking questions."

Graham looked at Miss Beth and shrugged. She gave him a little smile.

"Can I come talk to you?" Graham asked. "When you've had a chance to talk to this Bernard Brown?"

"I'm not giving you confidential information about this investigation."

"You could just give me some general information about who he is and why he wanted Ethan."

"No, I don't think so," Joiner snapped, and hung up the phone.

# CHAPTER
# FORTY-ONE

Graham had plenty to keep him busy for the rest of the day. The police case was intriguing, but it didn't bring him any money, and he needed to stay on top of his business if he wanted to run it profitably. Most small businesses failed within three years, and he'd not quite managed one so far. The initial interest in a new business around town was fading, and he had already contacted many of the people who needed work done. He needed to do more advertising and come up with campaigns that would keep people coming to him. Once he had acquired the clients, they would, hopefully, keep coming back to him. But not everyone needed ongoing junk removal services. They needed one job done, and that was it. They might not need him again for several years.

When he left his warehouse at the end of the day and retired to his living room with a warmed-up freezer dinner on his lap, he wondered what Joiner had learned from Uncle Bernard. Predictably, Joiner had not called Graham to inform him of the details of that call.

He had Bernard's number on his phone. What was to stop him from making a quick call to find out what Joiner already knew? He hadn't interfered with the police investigation. In fact, he had helped it along. He had supplied Joiner with information he didn't already have and helped put him in contact with Ethan's family, which seemed crucial if they were to figure out what had happened to the young couple.

He had the number on his phone. Right at his fingertips. What would it hurt to check in with him?

Graham resisted temptation for almost twenty minutes, which he considered an achievement. But then he broke down and tapped the number on his screen. The phone rang a few times, and then there was a voice on the other end.

"Yeah?"

"I'm looking for Bernard Brown."

"You got him."

"Uh... my name is Graham Hall. I guess you talked to Detective Joiner earlier today..."

"What? No, I didn't talk to any cop," Bernard growled. Then he added. "I did see a PD number on my caller ID. But I didn't have no reason to talk to the police."

"He was calling you about your nephew."

"What?"

"Ethan?"

"Ethan! How did you know I was looking for information about Ethan? Is he there?"

"No, I'm sorry. I'm looking for him too. But I'm hoping we can help each other. Pool our resources..."

"Are you a cop too?"

"No. Just... someone interested in what happened to Ethan and Ashley."

"Ashley. That's his girlfriend?"

"Wife, actually. They were newlyweds."

"Well, good for the kid. Never thought he would be interested in getting married. But you don't know where they are?"

"No, they've been missing for... about ten days now. I've been trying to find out what happened to them. I was the one who got the police involved."

"I can't say I'm happy about *that*. But it is what it is. If something has happened to them, then I guess involving the police might be necessary. But it throws a wrench into my work."

"So... you didn't take Detective Joiner's call this afternoon?" Graham confirmed.

"No."

"Well... he probably won't be happy with me talking to you, then. Do you want to call him to talk to him before me?"

"Why would I want to talk to a cop?"

"He is in charge of the missing persons investigation."

"Cops aren't going to be able to find him. That kid's been avoiding the police as long as he's been alive. He knows how to fly under the radar."

The hairs on Graham's neck stood up. "He's been avoiding the police? Why?"

"For that, you'd have to know his whole history. We don't need to go through all of that. What do you know? About him disappearing?"

"Well... nothing that is very helpful. He and Ashley dropped off the map about ten days ago. They left a note saying 'I'm sorry' at their apartment, with both sets of apartment keys. Took a couple of suitcases of stuff with them, and abandoned everything else—including passports, jewelry, sentimental stuff."

"Yeah, that sounds like John. Ethan, I mean."

"What do you mean it sounds like him? It makes sense to you that he would abandon everything at the apartment and take off?"

"It wouldn't be the first time. He's been running for a long time."

If it was normal for Ethan to run away and leave everything else behind, that didn't bode well for the missing person case. Once Joiner heard that, he would just go back to saying that Ethan and Ashley were voluntarily missing and there wasn't anything the police could do about it.

"What is he running away from?"

"From himself. From everything that scares him. I'm not a psychologist. They could tell me all about John's problems, but they could never tell me what to do about them. How helpful is it to tell someone their kid is damaged, but not what to do about it? How to raise him, how to discipline him? If a kid is acting out because of what's happened to him, you can't exactly erase that, can you?"

Graham settled into his easy chair and reached for a notepad to scribble things down as they spoke.

"You raised him?"

Bernard made a noise that was halfway between a cough and a snort. "Lots of people tried to raise that boy. In the end, there wasn't anything anyone could do for him."

"It sounds like there is quite a long story here. You're his uncle?"

"Uncle Boots," Bernard confirmed.

"Boots?"

"That's what I go by. Bernard. Boots."

"Uh... okay. Boots. I talked to Miss Beth at St Francis, the shelter in Bleeding Hearts Valley. That's how I got your name. You had called her looking for Ethan. And you were at the shelter in the city. Both times, you said you had something to give him."

There was silence for a moment. "Uh-yuh. That would be right."

"What is it you're trying to give him? And why now?" If Boots had tried to raise Ethan when he was a young boy, what had made him reach out now, years later, to pass a memento along to him?

"That's between me and the boy. But he'd called me. So I thought it would be a good time. Maybe help him out."

"He called you? What about?"

"Didn't say, exactly. Sounded paranoid. I figured he was off his meds. Thought maybe it would help if I followed up with him, gave him something to anchor him to the past."

"Didn't you say he was trying to escape his past?"

Boots gave a little chuckle. "Sometimes what we want isn't the best thing for us. In John's case... I don't think he's ever dealt with it. Really worked through it. Maybe if he did, he wouldn't need to run away anymore."

"What happened in the past?"

"That's his own business. Don't know that I have the right to share any of it."

"He could be in danger. If something happened to him and Ashley..."

"If something happened to him, what does that have to do with his past? I don't think anything happened to him. He just took off. Ran away like he always does."

"So we should stop looking and just assume he is okay."

"Chances are, he'll show up again sooner or later."

"But what if something *has* happened?" Graham repeated. "You won't ever know it, because you aren't looking for him."

"I'm not looking for him?" Boots repeated.

Graham felt a warm flush in his cheeks. "I mean... I know you are looking for him. But you could have the help of the Bleeding Hearts Valley police department. And maybe the city and state cops. The more people looking for him, the better our chances are, right?"

"Better not to have all of those people looking for him and spooking him."

"Mr. Brown... I'm worried about Ashley. I understand that Ethan has run before, so you're not worried about him. But Ashley... she's different. She wasn't raised the same way. She has two parents who are very concerned about what has happened to her. She could be in danger. She was worried about what was going on before she disappeared."

"Worried about what?"

"She was worried that they were being stalked. That someone had been in their apartment who was trying to scare her."

Boots thought about that, saying nothing for what seemed

233

like a long time. "I'm still not keen on bringing the police in on this. Chances are, they're just fine."

"What if this stalker kidnapped them? There was a man at the shelter where Ashley worked who became obsessed with her. He was moved somewhere else, but he could still have come back, followed her, known where she lived. *He* could have taken Ashley and Ethan, tried to make it look like they left voluntarily."

"You know this?"

"No... it's just speculation. Until we actually find a witness, someone who has seen them, we have no idea. But she *did* have someone stalking her. And there was this guy at the shelter."

"You really think they were kidnapped? Didn't just run away?" Boots sounded doubtful.

"I think they might have been. That's why we have been looking so hard for them. They could be in danger. Something might already have happened to them. If they really did just abandon everything and walk away... then wouldn't someone have seen them? Ashley would have called her parents to let them know she was okay..."

He remembered the note in her journal. *If anything happens to me, please let my parents know.*

"She was very close to her parents. She would have told them where she was so they wouldn't be afraid," he told Boots.

"John would have told her not to. To just keep under the radar."

"I can't see her doing it. I think she would have called them anyway. Maybe while Ethan—John—was out so he wouldn't know."

"Well, maybe you think she would," Boots acknowledged, "but *not* calling them doesn't prove she was kidnapped."

Graham had to concede the point. "How about this... what can you tell me about Ethan—or John—and how you became his guardian? If that's what you were."

Boots cleared his throat. Graham tried to build a picture of the man in his mind. His accent was what Graham would have called "hillbilly," and that, combined with the name "Boots," made it hard to see the man as anything other than a denim-overall-wearing hayseed or mountain man. Someone living in the backwoods in some insular community where he was related to everyone.

"John came to me after he was orphaned. Not right after, mind. A few other folks tried to look after him to start with, but they couldn't handle him. I said I would give it a try. He could come work the farm with me, and do his schoolwork in the evenings. He wouldn't have to deal with other people asking questions, bullies at school, or nothing."

"He was having problems with the other kids?"

"He didn't get along well with anyone. He'd been through a lot and he wasn't real social. Needed some time and some quiet. I had plenty of that at my place."

"So, how long did you have him?"

"Couple years. Then they came around saying he needed something else. Different experiences. Going back to school and getting to know people his age. Learning how to get along. Stuff he couldn't do if an old man was the only person he ever saw."

"How did he feel about that?"

"John didn't want to go. But it wasn't up to him or me. Family Services said he wasn't getting what he needed living with me, so the court said he had to go to someone else. They tried a couple of foster homes, group homes, institutions. He kept running. Until he aged out and they didn't have any jurisdiction over him anymore."

"But he kept in touch with you."

"My number hasn't changed. He knows how to get ahold of me. And he called me a couple of weeks ago. Scared. Worried. Bouncing around from one thing to another. Like I said, sounded like he was off his meds. I tried to talk to him, but it was pretty hard to connect with him over the phone. I decided to come out and see if I could talk to him face-to-face. But... I couldn't find him."

"Did you have his address? The apartment?"

"No. I knew the shelter he used to be at. Tried that one, and the one in Bleeding Hearts Valley. Called his phone a few times, but got no answer, just a disconnect message. Wasn't sure what to do. Figured... he'd show up again at some point. He always did. And he knows how to find me."

"You said he was orphaned?"

"Yep."

"What happened? Was it a car accident?"

"I don't think you need any details on that business."

*So, not a car accident.* Something more personal and tragic. Something that had scared Ethan and made him difficult to manage.

"And you wanted to give him something?"

"Yep." Boots didn't offer what it was. Graham knew that if he asked, Boots wouldn't tell him.

"Did he tell you about Ashley?"

"Sure. I heard about her. He was lucky to find her, someone who wouldn't be scared off by his problems. But I guess mebbe things didn't turn out the way he'd hoped. Someone like John—Ethan—he's stable for a while and then goes off track. Needs someone to anchor him and bring him back. I hoped Ashley could be that anchor."

And maybe she had been. But then something had happened. An external threat or an internal one? Had the couple been taken by Ben? By someone else they knew through the shelter or who had latched on to them for some reason? Or had Ethan been the problem? His behavior degrading until he had done something he regretted?

"Were you worried when you talked to him that he would hurt Ashley?"

"Nah, never crossed my mind."

"Did Ethan... draw when he lived with you?"

"Sure. Why?"

"We found a sketchpad at the apartment. It was filled with some pretty frightening stuff. Very violent images."

"Yeah, he's always done that. Psychologist said it's just his way of dealing with stuff."

"They didn't worry that he might hurt someone?"

"Those people are always trying to predict, to warn you what might happen down the road. But you can't tell what someone's going to do in the future. The future is still unwritten."

Graham cleared his throat uneasily. "Does that mean they *did* think that he might do something violent?"

"We lived on a farm, Mr. Hall. That boy never did one thing to hurt another living thing. Now, you watch all of this stuff on TV about serial killers; they'll tell you that those guys like to kill cats or other animals when they're little. They work their way up to hurting people. Well, John never hurt no cats."

# CHAPTER
# FORTY-TWO

G raham went back to work the next day, trying not to think about Ashley and Ethan, but also hoping that his subconscious mind would continue to work on the problem while he did other things and maybe it would come up with a solution that his conscious thought hadn't produced.

The cops who had searched the warehouse had not left everything as it had been, so it took Graham time to sort it all out the way he liked it again. He had a system. He liked being able to immediately put his hands on what he needed. It might not have been a system that worked for anyone else, but he understood it himself. He was just finishing when Joiner showed up. Graham wasn't sure how long Joiner was standing there watching before Graham noticed him.

"Sheesh," Graham complained. "Aren't you supposed to knock or ring the doorbell before you enter? You can't just come walking in here without announcing yourself."

"The door was open. I assumed that if you didn't want anyone to come back here, you would have locked the door. I didn't see any bell to ring."

Graham would have to get a bell put in if he was going to spend much time in the warehouse. There was a bell at the counter in the storefront, but it wasn't open right now, and Graham probably wouldn't have been able to hear it from where he was.

"Well, I just finished cleaning up after your search, so I hope you're not here thinking you can mess it up again."

"No, I looked at everything I wanted to last time I was in the building. Quite a little treasure hoard, isn't it?" Joiner looked around.

Graham couldn't help feeling a little flush of pleasure. He wasn't sure whether Joiner was sincere or sardonic, but Graham *was* proud of the treasure he had accumulated in the short time he had lived in Bleeding Hearts Valley.

Once, not so long ago, his treasure had been in things he couldn't see. Financial instruments that were supposed to keep their value, but were not always reliable. And suddenly, it could all evaporate as if it had never existed.

Now, he liked having things he could see. Physical things that retained their value, even years later. Some of them appreciated in value quite a bit. Others were just stable.

He liked to hold them in his hands, to touch them and feel their weight and solidity.

"I like it," he said neutrally.

"So, you wanna tell me what was up with your little excursion yesterday? You think you're the Hardy Boys all of a sudden, running around interviewing everyone without the benefit of law enforcement around?"

It could have been worse. He could have called Graham Nancy Drew.

"I just happened to be down the street from the mission, so I stopped in to see if I could figure anything out. I wasn't trying to investigate without you, just thought... I would take the opportunity since I was there."

"Uh-huh. And then came back to Bleeding Hearts Valley and visited St. Francis."

"I was just following up. Mike said that this homeless guy

named Ben had been obsessed with Ashley. So much so that they had moved him out of the shelter so that he couldn't bother her. Mike didn't think he would have followed her to Bleeding Hearts, that he couldn't have had anything to do with Ashley's disappearance. But I thought... I would just check to see whether he had been around St. Francis while he looked for her. Just to make sure that he hadn't."

"Ben."

"Yes. You can ask Mike about him. I told him to call you about Ben or if he had other information to pass on."

"Yeah, I got an earful, all right. About unofficial inquiries by private citizens that should have been addressed by the police."

"But you did talk to him. I just... *also* talked to him."

Joiner gave him a look. Graham had to laugh. His mother used to look at him like that and tell him he would grow up to be a great lawyer someday.

"Then there is this other guy," Joiner said. "Bernard Brown."

Graham nodded. "I guess... he didn't take your call or call you back."

Joiner raised an eyebrow. Graham shrugged uncomfortably.

"I thought... it wouldn't hurt anything if I called him after you had talked to him. Just to see if there was anything else I could get out of him that he didn't want to tell the police."

"Uh-huh."

"I thought that you would already have talked to him. Honestly."

"And I would have. If he had answered the phone."

"But he saw that you were calling from the police and didn't want to talk to you."

"Some people have an unfortunate aversion to talking to the police."

Graham could sympathize, after all that he had gone through with ex-girlfriend Candice. He wished that he had never met her. He really hadn't needed the education about the police that the experience had given him.

"Yeah. Well, he was an interesting guy. I'm not sure if I got anything of value from him. 'Boots' is the nickname he goes by, by the way."

"Boots. Yeah. I did a little bit of background on him. To try to tie in with Ethan's story. If we find this guy, it will be because we've built a good enough profile of him to understand how his mind works."

"Did the background turn up anything interesting?"

"I think you owe me a story before I tell you anything."

"He told me a little bit. But if I tell you that, you'll just tell me that your investigation is none of my business, and you won't tell me anything you found."

"Well, that would be correct. It isn't any of your business, and I don't share with civilians."

Graham folded his arms and waited to see if Joiner would relent and give him anything about what he had discovered.

"On paper, 'Boots' Brown is a corn farmer in Kentucky. Kind of an isolated area; doesn't have a lot to do with other people. Moonshiner. Don't know what other illegal businesses he might be involved in. No record of him having any dependents until Ethan—then eleven—shows up on his tax return."

"He said that Ethan was orphaned. Was passed around to several relatives before Boots took him in. He had behavioral problems. Sounds like things went pretty well with him living on the farm; he didn't have to get along with anyone but the old man."

Joiner frowned, looking at him, then nodded. "He was only there for a couple of years, and then he drops out of sight again."

"Yeah, Boots said that Family Services eventually pulled him out of the home. Figured it wasn't a good environment for him and that he needed to be in a foster home where he could be socialized. But that didn't work out so well. He kept running away. Foster homes, group homes, maybe some other institutions. Until he turned eighteen and wasn't their responsibility anymore."

"By which time he was probably on the streets," Joiner suggested.

"Yeah. Where eventually, he digs himself out, gets into the transitional program at the mission, and eventually meets Ashley."

"Not the most ideal childhood. That kind of beginning has produced a lot of cold-blooded killers."

"But Boots doesn't think Ethan is violent. He said that Ethan never did anything to hurt any of the farm animals while he lived there, and the behavioral experts always talk about them testing out cruelty on animals first and escalating from there."

"Might be he didn't start until after he was taken away from there. If it was the kind of place that he needed, he might have been fine while he was there. Then, getting torn away from the one safe place he had left in the world and getting passed around to strangers could certainly trigger violent behavior. Especially if he was abused in those homes. Kids who have been in that many different homes usually encounter predators in at least one of them."

Graham shook his head. He knew he was lucky to have grown up in a two-parent home and had all the stability and support he could have asked for from an early age. But not everyone was so lucky.

"This Boots struck you as honest and forthright?" Joiner asked. "He could have been lying to you. He might know very well that the kid was a predator from an early age. He might have been an abuser himself. There are not a lot of single men who would take in a young kid like that. Couples and some single women, but single men? He's a pretty rare breed. Unless he was happy to have a vulnerable kid under his roof for his own purposes."

Graham's stomach churned. "I don't know. He could have been lying, I guess. He certainly wasn't answering all of my questions. He wouldn't tell me anything about what had happened to Ethan's parents."

"I would like to know what happened to them," Joiner agreed, looking thoughtful. "Ethan's identity as John Brown does not go all the way back. It will take us back to the time that he spent with Boots. But before that? We end up with another black hole. What was his name before that, and who were his parents? Who else had Ethan been with before Boots took him? And since then. Accessing his Family Services file to see where he went or what issues he might have dealt with in those homes since then is not an easy matter. He apparently didn't just get transferred within the state, but across states as they found other people or programs to take him on. We would have to track down his records in each state and get a subpoena to get a copy, which, in my experience, might take months, if we're lucky."

"Months?"

Joiner shrugged heavily. "It is not a system built for easy access by the police. They prefer not to expose their mistakes and weaknesses to scrutiny."

But Ashley didn't have months. It might already be too late to do anything to save her. Graham brought his hand down on the counter in front of him in frustration. He paced, restless, trying to work out a solution.

"You said that finding Ethan would hinge on being able to get into his mind. Does any of this help?"

"Sure it helps." Joiner looked thoughtful. "It doesn't get us all the way there... but we can understand him a lot better with the background."

"And you think that he was voluntary? That he just took off? Convinced Ashley to go with him? Because he was a runaway from way back?"

"Could be. The chances of a stranger abduction are very low. Still a possibility, of course, but very low."

"If it was Ben, the guy who was obsessed with her, that would not be considered a stranger abduction."

"No, it wouldn't. It could have been him—or another homeless or mentally ill person who went through the shelter. She did put herself in a vulnerable position working with them. Not that I blame her if something happened to her. She was doing a great service, something that not a lot of people would do. She didn't deserve whatever it was that happened to her."

"But you don't think it was someone from the shelter."

"I don't. Look at the stuff she recorded in her journal. Stuff happening inside the apartment. Only a limited number of people could have pulled off that crap. And especially without being discovered. Then take a look at his sketchbook." Joiner held his palms up in appeal. "You can't tell me that stuff was produced by a healthy mind. Or by someone who was harmless. Those graphic depictions of violence... that doesn't bode well."

"Boots said that the psychologist said it was just John—Ethan —trying to work things out."

"I don't know about you, but I don't trust psychologists and their double-speak. It isn't a science where there are right and wrong answers. It is all just... people trying to guess what is in someone else's head. And trying to work *what* things out?" Joiner pointed at Graham. "Tell me what had happened in his past that had to be worked out through such violent imagery."

# FORTY-THREE

Ashley remembered waking up the next morning to Ethan packing a suitcase. She was immediately disoriented and alarmed. After his emotional outburst of the day before, she thought that she had managed to get him calmed down and in a good place so that they would be able to sort things out.

They would need help, of course. She wasn't a psychologist and didn't pretend to know how to care for Ethan after all he had been through in his life and the challenges that his mental health diagnoses posed. From the time she had first met him as a volunteer at the shelter, she had been warned that he had complex needs and could sometimes behave erratically. During the time they had dated and been married, she had certainly come up against some barriers and reactions she didn't understand.

But how *could* one person understand exactly what went on in another's mind? Weren't they all "complex cases"? Ashley had been lucky enough to grow up in a stable, two-parent home, and she still didn't understand her own reactions and motivations sometimes. She didn't know where some of her feelings of rebellion or hurt came from.

She didn't need to understand all of what Ethan was thinking or know about everything he had experienced to have empathy for him and be there to support him through times of trouble. All she needed was compassion and patience. She would stand by his side to give him a hand when he was willing to accept it.

But now, she wasn't sure whether something else had triggered him or he was still reacting to the loss of his job at Perennial and his surprise at Ashley being promoted.

It had to affect him, seeing her succeeding when he had failed. He was deeply disappointed over the Perennial job not working out. From the sound of it, he had been crushed by how he had been treated there. If he had only told her what had been going on at the time, she might have been able to help him to work through it. Maybe it could have been sorted out, and he wouldn't have had to lose the job. Maybe they could have gotten rid of the bad apple at Perennial and made a success of it.

But Ethan had kept it all to himself, burying his secret and the hurt for months. He had been out of work for weeks and she hadn't even known it. But it accounted for some of the stuff that had been going on. The fact that he had been there during the day when she had thought he was at work explained a lot.

And the rest... maybe there was a good reason for all the rest too. Maybe there had been a reason for him to move things around in the apartment, trying to recreate a different environment and work through something from his past. Or maybe he had just been bored and had not realized how it would affect her. The day that everything felt like it had been shifted a bit during the time she had been at work, maybe he had just been dusting, keeping the place nice while she was gone.

"Ethan, what are you doing?"

"We need to go. We can't stay here anymore."

"What?" Ashley propped herself up on her elbow, looking at him. She pulled the blanket snugly around her, trying to banish the cool air from touching her skin. "What are you talking about? Why can't we stay?"

"It isn't safe. We have to leave."

"Not safe?"

"No!" He threw clothes into the suitcase haphazardly. "We can't stay here. We need to go somewhere safe. Need to go home."

Ashley tried to slow everything down in her mind so she didn't feel rushed and say anything wrong. Ethan needed support, not an argument. If she dug too quickly for answers, he would push her out. Protect himself and his past and refuse to answer.

"Where is home?" she asked gently.

"He can't hurt you there. Nothing will hurt you there. I'll keep you safe."

"You always keep me safe," she affirmed. She liked that about him. How protective Ethan was of her. It made her feel cherished. Like he thought that she was valuable. A delicate piece of china or crystal.

Ethan paused for the slightest moment, looking at her. She tried to radiate back to him that feeling of love and protection so he would know he was safe with her too. She would protect him, and he would protect her.

"Get what you need," Ethan ordered. "We need to leave."

Ashley looked around, trying to figure out the best way to handle this new wrinkle. Go along with him and pack a bag? Stay firm and provide an anchor for him, to know that they couldn't just uproot themselves for no reason? Tell him that the apartment *was* safe and she would protect him?

She drew the blankets back and was immediately chilled. She reached for her housecoat and wrapped it around herself, but it didn't provide the same level of warmth and protection that the blankets had.

She would have liked to have snuggled in the blankets for another hour or two, but that was not to be. Ethan needed her help now.

"Are we going to be gone for long?" she asked.

"We can't stay here. It isn't safe."

"Okay. But what should I take? Enough for a few days? A week? What will it be like? What kind of clothes do I need?"

He looked at her with wide eyes, and she realized she had overwhelmed him with questions. Too much, too fast. Just keep it slow and find out the information gradually.

"Sorry. Show me what you're packing for yourself, and then I'll know what to do."

He made a helpless motion toward his suitcase. Ashley went over to it to straighten out the clothing he had thrown into it and to catalog what he was taking.

"No!" Ethan pushed her away. "Don't touch it."

"I just wanted to see—"

"No. Leave it alone."

"Okay." She held up her hands. "I'll leave it alone."

He withdrew and didn't touch her again. "Just get yours."

Ashley went to the closet and pulled out her suitcase. She set it on the bed next to his. It was empty and his was nearly full. Ethan ran his fingers through his hair. He curled his fingers around his short locks and pulled, eyes glistening with tears.

"It's okay, Ethan," she assured him. "We can work this out. How can I help?"

"Pack, just pack." He renewed his efforts.

Ashley tried to work things through in her mind. She could call the shelter. Let Mike know that she had a family emergency to deal with. They would need to cover for her for a few days, and then she would understand what Ethan needed and would be able to help him or find him the help he needed. It wouldn't hurt to take a spontaneous vacation. Once Ethan was away from there, he would tell her more about where he wanted to go. He had a safe place in mind, some "home" he wanted to return to.

It would be good. Ashley would learn more about Ethan's past, maybe about his family. He had shared little of his history with her. She knew it had been traumatic. Some of his mental health issues might be genetic, or he had a genetic predisposition to certain problems, but from what she had learned, those ACEs

—adverse childhood experiences—had pushed him well over the edge.

At least he had a safe place to go to. Someplace that, in his mind, would provide a safe haven. She might be able to meet family members who could tell her some of what he had suffered through in his life.

Ashley pulled a couple of outfits out of the closet and folded them carefully before putting them in her suitcase. She kept her movements slow and calm, hoping that would slow Ethan down as well, reassuring him that she was by his side no matter what. She would go into battle with him against whoever or whatever he was fighting.

# CHAPTER
# FORTY-FOUR

Constance Pennyman had called Graham earlier to tell him she had finished going through the maps and other papers he had saved from Mark Ballantyne's home office. They had not all been in very good shape, and when he first looked at them, Graham had not been sure whether they had any historical value. Even if they did, they were in such poor shape that he wasn't sure he would be able to get anything for them or whether any library or historical association would even be interested in them.

Constance showed up at the warehouse promptly at two o'clock. Graham looked the well-preserved woman over and invited her back to the large table he had cleared so that she could lay out the documents on a clean surface and not have to try to hold them up and juggle them while she told him about them. She carried a large artist's portfolio and a couple of tubes that would contain the larger-format papers.

She looked satisfied with the arrangements. She put down the portfolio first, unzipped it on three sides, and showed Graham each document. They had all been cleaned and pressed and restored as much as she had been able. Anything that was really valuable would have to go to an art restorer or other expert.

But from the start, her report was not what he had hoped it

would be. "None of this is very rare or very old. It was just not properly stored and aged quickly. I have compared the maps and documents with what is already at the library and historical society, and I have not been able to find anything unique. It is all duplicates of information that is already known and preserved. And the copies that we already have available are in much better shape."

"So this is basically crap."

She smiled and tried to put a better spin on it. "They have not been cared for very well. Maybe if they had been..."

"I should just cut my losses and recycle them. They're not good for anything but pulp."

"Pulp itself is still valuable..."

"In large quantities. Not a few maps like this," Graham flicked the corner of one of the sheets.

"No... well..." Constance looked at the pictures critically. "The maps are quite attractive, you know, even with the yellowing around the edges. They might have some value if made into art. Distress the edges, mount them, perhaps a little hand-inking over top. Frame them with a glass covering... You could end up with something that was very unique and attractive for display in a Bleeding Hearts Valley great room or study."

"Hmm." Graham studied them thoughtfully. "That's a possibility, I guess. I would have to make enough to cover the artist and the framing, but it would be a good conversation piece. And some of the other documents could be framed to make them into a set. A hand-painted map, distressed census page, and an old land deed with a big red seal all displayed together, that would be cool."

She nodded in agreement. "You see? You could still get more value out of them than you would just throwing them away."

Graham nodded. "Thanks for the ideas. Maybe I can recover something from these after all."

Constance nodded. "Thank you for the opportunity to look at them. Keep calling me with your finds, and sooner or later, we will find something amazing. You never know what treasure will turn up in someone else's trash."

Graham grinned. "That's why I'm in the business I am," he agreed. "You never know what you will dig up or how you can turn it into a profit."

Constance had *no* idea.

After she was gone, Graham spent some time looking over the currently worthless documents and maps. He was gradually learning his way around Bleeding Hearts Valley. Not that it was a big place, but there were always interesting finds tucked into corners and crescents he would never even know existed if he wasn't looking for them. And there were a lot of rural roads and properties around the town that he hadn't explored. The town had some interesting history.

And what kind of secrets did Moon Lake and First Moon Forest hide? He had already heard stories. Being a new implant in Bleeding Hearts Valley, Graham had been the recipient of plenty of crazy ghost stories and legends of things that had happened in the woods or been dumped in the lake. One day he would like to fund a dredging of the lake, just to see what sorts of treasures and terrors he could recover.

He could really scare the people who had thought that their secrets would remain forever drowned in the seemingly bottomless lake then. Considering the number of stories he had heard, such an action might cause a mass exodus as everyone who had used the lake as their dumping ground fled for parts unknown.

His eyes moved over the map, with its neighborhoods named after varieties of bleeding hearts flowers. Fringed, Gold Heart, Old Fashioned, Common. From what he understood, that was the doing of the wife of the original Bleeding Hearts Valley Mayor. It had probably seemed charming and quaint then, but Graham found it a bit weird and creepy now. Maybe that was just an outsider's viewpoint, and to everyone else, it seemed perfectly normal and logical. But Graham didn't like the idea of living in the middle of some old lady's garden. Some giant, hundred-year-old lady going potty over her flower children.

As he turned pages, he looked at the names of the owners and residents of seventy years before. Some of them he recognized. Ballantyne, Hanover, Price, Wilson, Pennyman. Others were too common to know whether the current residents were the progeny of those old families. Smith, Brown, Jones. And others he hadn't heard since he moved into town, old families that had perhaps died out or had only stayed for a few years and left when it became obvious that Bleeding Heart Valley was not going to be the next bustling hub of industry. Amundsen, Shufflebottom, Clampitt.

They certainly made an interesting little garden of posies. Bleeding Hearts. The name was supposed to be sweet and evocative of those beautiful stems of pink heart-shaped blooms. But bleeding hearts? It sounded more dark and gruesome to Graham's ear than pink and pretty. How many of them had bled to establish the town? How many to cover up their secrets?

Eventually, he rolled up the larger items and lay the others flat on a shelf. He would need to ask around for artists who might be interested in helping him with the project and still underappreciated enough that hiring them out wouldn't cost him an arm and a leg.

# CHAPTER
# FORTY-FIVE

After plenty of dusty, physical work, Graham was drained. The bullet wound in his back was causing more pain and fatigue than he had imagined it would. They had kept assuring him that it was a minor injury, so he had mostly ignored the doctor's advice not to do anything strenuous for a few weeks.

With no energy left to fend for himself, Graham headed over to the bar for a meal and something to dull the pain of his bullet wound and the surrounding muscles.

He should have listened better. He always had to find out for himself. His mother had despaired of how he always had to test her advice or demands rather than simply trusting and obeying her. Any other child would believe that you shouldn't jump into freezing water or off the roof. Or off the roof into freezing water. None of his siblings had found it necessary to test just how far they could push their high school teachers before getting suspended. But Graham knew where the line was because he had crossed it. It was right there.

He picked at the last few wings on his plate, and the busty young waitress stopped and hovered over him. "Need some more?" she offered.

"No, I think I'd better cut the wings off there," he admitted. "The beer, however, I could take another of those."

"You bet," she agreed. She grabbed his old glass and shimmied away.

Graham pushed the plate of bones away from him so she could take it when she returned with another beer.

"Are you sure you should be having another one?" a gravelly voice questioned as Graham sipped the head off of the freshly-pulled beer.

He turned his head and saw Detective Joiner. He looked like he was just starting out his evening. Graham nodded to the chair across from him. "You want to join me?"

Joiner lowered himself into the chair with a long sigh. "Some days are just too long," he complained.

Graham looked at his watch. "I hope you don't always work this late."

"No, I don't, or I might not still be alive," Joiner grumbled. "A person does need some time to relax and recreate now and then, or he'll just keel over one day."

He signaled to the waitress, who approached with a menu. Joiner shook his head. "BBQ sliders and some of those cheesy tots," he told her. "And bring me an Arnold Palmer."

"Be back in a shake," the waitress agreed, giving him a smile, and then she retreated again.

Joiner nodded at Graham's beer, bringing it up a second time. "It doesn't look like that is your first."

Graham looked at it, then at the table, which had been cleared of all empties. "What makes you think that?"

"You're looking a little... worse for wear."

"Oh." Graham ran his fingers through his hair, trying to straighten himself up. "That's just hard work. And maybe the aftereffects of being shot."

"That's right," Joiner said, looking surprised. "That was only a few days ago, but I had forgotten about it. You're moving around pretty good, so I haven't even thought about it since you got out of the hospital."

"Yeah. I thought I was good to go back to lifting and carrying, straightening out the warehouse and dealing with some old and new inventory. But..." Graham shifted from side to side and rolled his shoulders. "Apparently, the doc knew what he was talking about when he said to take it easy for a while."

"Bullets do more damage than you think," Joiner said. Then he chuckled at his own comment. "Well, that is... what I'm talking about is the cavitation. Even if a bullet hasn't torn apart anything vital, the *force* of it entering the body impacts all of the tissues around it, even if they don't appear affected."

"Cavitation," Graham repeated.

"A hollow is created around the bullet." Joiner moved his hands to try to convey what he was talking about. "There is a temporary 'tunnel' or cavity that is bigger than the projectile. And all of those tissues can be damaged, even though the bullet never touched them."

"Huh." Graham nodded. "I guess that's why it doesn't just feel like a little hole in my back like it is. Felt like I was beaten with a bat when I got it. Have you ever been shot?"

"No, and don't plan to be. But I've talked to people who have been shot. And to doctors and medical examiners. It's not something to be taken lightly. Not like on TV where they just get up and... jump off buildings onto racing trains and the like."

Graham chuckled and had a couple more swallows of beer. The waitress brought Joiner his drink and promised his dinner would arrive shortly.

"I don't think I'd try jumping off of any buildings or onto any racing trains even without being shot," Graham said. "But certainly not after. I'll follow my doctor's advice on that one."

They looked at the TV on the wall and made the various requisite comments on the games that were playing. Joiner got his dinner and dug in eagerly.

"I haven't eaten since breakfast," he told Graham bullishly, "and that was at the butt crack of dawn, for your information."

"I didn't say anything," Graham objected.

"I don't need a freakin' wife telling me what I can and can't eat."

Graham sipped his beer. If Joiner had gone that long without nourishment, it was no wonder he was so irritable. Joiner tucked in and didn't say anything until the first slider had disappeared.

"Sorry," he rumbled. "I know you didn't say anything. My ex-wife used to ride me about the way I eat."

"Then it's a good thing she's out of your life."

Joiner grunted and wiped a smear of BBQ sauce off his face.

"Decided to see what else I could pick up about your Uncle Boots."

"He's not *my* Uncle Boots."

"Heh. Ethan-John's Uncle Boots, then. What gave you the idea he's an old man? Does he sound old on the phone?"

"Uh..." Graham replayed Boots's voice in his head. "No... I don't think so. Just... the way he talked about things. I think he might have referred to himself as an old man once. I just had this picture of a cantankerous old guy in my mind. Too many made-for-TV movies about kids being left with the old grandpa on the horse ranch to get their lives turned around, I guess. Had that stereotype in my head."

"He's only in his forties now," Joiner said. "Which means early thirties when he had Ethan. Not that old at all."

"Oh." Graham tried to repaint the picture in his head. Not a wise old man, crotchety but kind, teaching the delinquent important life lessons. A young man. Living out on a lonely farm with an eleven-year-old troubled boy. That was probably even more difficult. A man who had never had kids of his own. "Well... that's a little disturbing. Did they really think he was the best person to take care of Ethan?"

"Did *who* think that?"

"Family Services. Whatever it is called out there. Did his case worker think Boots had the responsibility and experience to look after a kid like Ethan?"

"Family Services might have had nothing to do with it. It sounds like he was sent from one place to another without the benefit of a case worker. Just whatever the family member who had him at the time thought was the best thing to do. No government intervention. No legal guardian appointment. Just being passed from one family to another."

"How can they do that? That can't be legal."

Joiner cocked an eyebrow at him. "Brilliant deduction. In case you haven't noticed, a lot of people do things that are against the law. That's why we have cops."

Graham's cheeks warmed. He coughed. "Uh, yeah. It just surprised me. I thought they would have safeguards in place to make sure that didn't happen. I mean, with something like that... he could be trafficked all over the country. Who would know the difference?"

"Kids *are* trafficked all over the country. How do you track one kid being moved from family to family? He was home-schooled at Uncle Boots's farm, with no school oversight. Plenty of kids don't have a Social Security Number. Pay for any medical care up front, so the clinic doesn't require proof of insurance. With the number of people in this country who are undocumented, do you think anyone is going to pay any attention to some white kid whose parent forgot his birth certificate at home? If they even ask for one?"

"Boots said that he had been moved from family to family..." Graham recalled.

"I wish you could get the guy to talk to me. I'd like to get a lot more details from him about the kid's history, what families he went to, what was going on when he was at Boots's farm, and where he went after that. I can't even track him through the Family Services transfers, and we've got his correct name at that point."

"Wait..."

Joiner waited, looking at Graham.

"You still don't know his birth name?"

"No. When he went to Boots, or sometime before he got there, he was going by John Brown. But that wasn't his original name. It's on his birth certificate issued that year, so it looks like he was adopted by Uncle Boots."

Joiner took a massive bite, consuming half of the slider at once, and Graham waited for him to chew and swallow so that he could talk again.

"To find his original name and family, we have to find his hospital birth records. And like everything else in this dang case, that takes time. We have to go to each hospital in the city listed on his birth certificate to ask for or subpoena records of children born on the same day. And that's assuming that the information on this birth certificate is right. At this point, I'm not sure anything I have been told is right."

Joiner wiped BBQ sauce off of his face with a napkin.

"He might not have had a birth certificate when Family Services apprehended him from Boots. If he was born at home and never registered, they may have had a birth certificate created based on the information Ethan and Boots and other family members could provide. Bernard Brown's name is the only one on the birth certificate."

"And no mother?"

"And no mother," Joiner agreed with a sigh. "Thanks to a modern registration system that allows all kinds of combinations of single, dual, and multiple parents, you can end up with a kid with no mother or several of them."

"And you can't get anything from Boots because he won't call you back."

"And would he tell the truth if he did talk to me? I'm beginning to think he would not. If he's playing at an old man at forty, how much of the rest of it is a lie?"

"Are you going to..." Graham had been planning to ask if Joiner would go see Boots, but if he was back in Kentucky,

Graham couldn't see Joiner making that trip. "Can you find out whether Boots went back home or whether he is still around here?"

"Hmm." Joiner ate a few more bites. "Good question. If he is still in Bleeding Hearts Valley or in the city and didn't go home…"

"Then he could have Ashley and Ethan with him. He could have had something to do with them disappearing."

"But where? Not a hotel room. Not the apartment. The home of a friend of theirs? A property Boots owns?"

"Someone else in the family?" Graham suggested. "If Ethan went back and forth across the country from family to family, he could have family right here in Bleeding Hearts Valley."

"Possible. We haven't been able to nail down many details about his family or previous life. He wouldn't necessarily have told the shelter, Ashley, or anyone else if he had family in the area. If he's estranged, he may prefer to forget they even exist."

"What can I do to help?" Graham asked, draining his beer glass and setting it down with a soft thud. He leaned forward. "There must be something I can do."

"I think… we are going to have to find a way to trap Mr. Boots."

# CHAPTER
# FORTY-SIX

G raham tried to calm himself down before calling Boots. Joiner looked around the large room of the warehouse.

"Not that your warehouse isn't lovely, Mr. Hall, but don't you think we would have been more comfortable in your own living room? This is a bit... rustic."

Graham shifted. He wasn't as comfortable as he would have been in his easy chair in his living room. But he also didn't want strangers in his house. He was already dealing with anxiety whenever he got close to the spot where he had been ambushed and shot. He hoped that it would fade, but in the meantime, he did not want intruders in his living space. While Joiner was polite and friendly when he was looking for something from Graham, he was not *safe*. He could still threaten Graham with what he had found about the post-break-up war with Candice or trump up some charges if he wanted to coerce Graham into doing something.

Or worse, manage to dig up something Graham had done that could be seen in a less-than-ethical light.

Graham didn't want the man anywhere near his safe place.

The warehouse had already been violated by the burglars and

Joiner's search. Graham had decided Joiner could meet him there. Not at home.

"I didn't think you'd be here for that long," Graham told Joiner neutrally, "I didn't think it would matter to you."

Joiner nodded and didn't argue the point. Graham got the feeling Joiner enjoyed poking and prodding at him, seeing what little jabs might get a reaction. If one tease didn't get a reaction, he would try another way.

"Okay, I think we're all set," Joiner said, taking one more look around. "Let's give this a try."

Graham put his phone on the table before him and tapped Boots's number and then the speaker button. They both listened to the ringing, and Graham wondered whether Boots would pick up. Maybe he was busy feeding the horses or running errands or decided he didn't want to talk to Graham anymore.

"Yep?"

"Oh," Graham was relieved and stumbled over his words, both eager and awkward talking to the man again. "Uh, Boots, this is Graham Hall. We talked before about Ethan. Your nephew, John."

"Yeah, I remember."

"There were a few things that I wanted to ask about and clarify." Joiner had instructed him not to ask Boots whether he wanted to talk or if it was a good time. They didn't want to give Boots the opportunity to say no or put off the call to another time. "We still haven't been able to find Ethan or Ashley, and I'm really getting concerned. Even if they decided to go on a vacation or move to a different apartment, they should have popped up again by now, wouldn't you think?"

"Well, I wouldn't say so, no. They could be gone for months. A couple of weeks... that's nothing for John."

"But he has Ashley with him now. She would want to talk to her parents, go back to work, or at least tell them how much longer she was going to be. I think we need to track them down and make sure they are okay."

"That's your business. But I think you're rushing it. John's used to being under the radar for a long time. A few days is nothing."

"There is his mental health to be concerned about. I don't think he's taking his meds, and you know how he gets if he's not taking them..."

"There isn't anyone who can make him take them. He has to decide to do it himself, and before he'll do that, he's gotta hit bottom. Maybe the girl can convince him to go back on them before that, but it'll take some work."

"He doesn't have them with him, though. He left them at the apartment."

"Then he'll get a prescription somewhere else," Boots told him, irritatingly calm about it. Once Boots had seen the cycle a few times, he had probably cut himself off from getting emotional about it. If there were nothing he could do about it, then getting upset about it wouldn't help anything. It would just make him feel worse.

"Does Ethan have any family members in Bleeding Hearts Valley or nearby that he might have gone to?"

Boots didn't answer right away. Graham looked at Joiner to see what he thought about Boots's silence. He gave no sign.

"I don't think the boy would go to any family," Boots said finally. "He don't exactly get along with any of 'em."

"What about you? You still get along with him, right? He called you, you've been trying to reach him, even came all the way out here to give him something."

"Well, of course. I'm the only one who never sent him away and who he never ran away from. That was Family Services. It wasn't my choice nor his."

"But with everyone else... they always sent him away."

"Yep. Or he ran away. Either way... it's not like it was with us. Things didn't work out."

"Did Ethan tell you he was going to run away? Where he was planning to go?"

"He might have said he was going home. But then... he never came back to the farm. So I guess not."

"Home was the farm? It couldn't mean anywhere else?"

"Only place he and I would call home."

"Nowhere in Bleeding Hearts Valley?"

There was another silent pause.

"Nope," Boots said eventually. "Nowhere else."

"Or in the city?"

"The city was never home. John is not a city boy."

"He lived in the city before he married Ashley. In the shelter and then in transitional housing."

"Does either of those sound like *home* to you? You can check them out if you want. I think if he'd gone back to one of those places, you would know about it already."

"I suppose," Graham agreed. "What did you say his parents' names were?"

Boots paused before answering, not giving them the automatic response they had hoped for. He considered the question before answering. "I don't think I said anything about his parents."

"You mentioned he was orphaned, but you didn't say how. What happened to them?"

"That ain't any of your business."

"I'm just thinking it could be a factor in where he went..."

"I don't think so."

"If there was a specific place... where the accident happened, or where his parents are buried..."

"No."

"The house they lived in when they were killed?"

"Ain't there anymore, I don't think."

"It must have had an effect on Ethan. It could have affected his mental state..."

"Mr. Hall, is this all you called for? To harass me to give you private information I already told you I'm not giving you?"

"No, no. I'm sorry. I hoped to find something else that might lead me in the right direction. If he didn't go home... what if it was kidnapping? What if something has happened to him, and you're not helping us find him because you think he just ran away again? We could be wasting valuable time..."

"No one is going to kidnap John and hold him for this long," Boots said flatly. "If he was kidnapped... then it's too late. No one would still be holding him. Especially not without a ransom demand."

"Are you sure you can't think of anywhere in town he might go?" Graham pressed again, feeling like this was one question Boots hadn't answered truthfully.

"There isn't anywhere," Boots said flatly. "Goodbye, Mr. Hall."

# CHAPTER
# FORTY-SEVEN

G raham looked at Joiner, shaking his head. "I was hoping I'd be able to get more information out of him."

Joiner didn't look up from his computer. "That wasn't the purpose of that call. The only purpose of that call was to keep him talking, which you did."

"Were you able to find out his location?"

Joiner tapped a few keys on his computer. "That's what we are going to find out. If everything worked out like it is supposed to, we should have a pretty good idea of his location right now."

"It sounded like he was somewhere public. I could hear some background noise a few times. Sirens or voices."

Joiner nodded. "I heard that too."

"So he's not just sitting at home on the farm in Kentucky."

"Could have the TV turned up. But no, I don't think so. It didn't sound like a TV."

Joiner touched his computer screen. "There. No, he's not in Kentucky. He's right here in Bleeding Hearts Valley. Right here waiting for us."

"Do you think... he has Ethan and Ashley? Or knows where they are?"

"We don't know what kind of twisted situation this might be.

Maybe Uncle Boots is the one Ethan is running away from. Maybe it's who he ran to. Maybe Boots came after Ashley. Or Ethan. Maybe one of them is hiding her from the other. You never know what people are going to do."

Graham sighed. He had been hoping that the call would provide immediate answers. But it looked like he was going to have to wait for answers. And keep looking.

"He's at Bitter Bites," Joiner announced, his eyes still on the display. "We've got him."

"They've arrested him?"

"Why would we arrest him?" Joiner demanded, scowling at Graham. "We want to know where those kids are and if he's in contact with them. We're going to wait for him to lead us to them."

"You just said, 'We've got him.'"

"I mean, we have his location. We know where he is and can get eyes on him. No more chasing our tails."

"So you're going to have someone follow him."

Joiner nodded his agreement. "Exactly. Got men converging on BB right now. One will go inside for a coffee and get eyes on him. Another one outside to follow him when he leaves. We'll find out where he is holed up. And then, if we're lucky, we'll know where Ethan and Ashley are."

"You really think he has them?" Graham didn't want to get his hopes up. Maybe Boots was being completely honest and was just in Bleeding Hearts Valley to try to make contact with Ethan. Maybe he didn't have any idea where Ethan was, either.

"I think from that conversation with you... that he knows more than he has let on. What happened to Ethan's parents? Where in Bleeding Hearts Valley would he go if he wasn't at the apartment? Boots knows something, and we're going to find out."

# CHAPTER
# FORTY-EIGHT

Ethan had not calmed down when Ashley had started packing. She had hoped that he would relax when he saw that she was cooperating, but he kept switching between angrily ordering her to get her stuff packed, and pulling his hair and wringing his hands while looking fearfully toward the door.

She'd had enough anxiety herself about the safety of the apartment and someone being there while she was gone that she was amped up and expecting someone to come through the door before they were finished making arrangements.

"It's okay, Ethan," she reassured him. "We're going to be safe. You have a safe place to go to."

She didn't know what this safe place was, but if Ethan felt better there, it would help her to understand him and his past. And every bit of his past that she could learn about helped to build their relationship and helped her to find the things that would make him feel safe even when he wasn't there. She was confident she would be able to use the experience to help him.

She wasn't finished grabbing everything she needed when Ethan decided they were done.

"Close it and come on," he ordered. "We need to go now."

"I just need—"

"No!" Ethan grabbed her arm with hard, unyielding fingers, and jerked her back from the suitcase so that he could close it and do it up himself. "Now. You need to come now. We have to go."

"But—"

"Come on."

Resisting only made Ethan angry, and he jerked her harder. She was afraid he was so focused on getting her out of the apartment that they were going to leave the packed suitcases behind. She grabbed hers just before he jerked her out of reach.

"Get yours," she insisted. "Don't forget it."

He grabbed only one of the two suitcases he had packed, holding on to her tightly with the other hand, and hustled her out of the apartment. He locked the door behind him and pulled her toward the elevator.

It was all Ashley could do to keep pace with him. Clearly, he wasn't in the mood to explain himself or answer any questions. She slid into the passenger seat in the car, though she wondered if it was safe to allow him to drive in the state he was in. Ethan threw the suitcases in the trunk and started the car.

"Be careful," Ashley warned, shivering at the sudden chill of the vinyl seats.

"I'm being careful!" Ethan looked around as if expecting to be attacked or followed. He shifted into drive and, with a slight squeal of tires, pulled out.

Ashley watched out the window as they wended their way through the familiar streets of Bleeding Hearts Valley. She had expected him to make his way out to the highway, but he had not. He said he was going home, yet he didn't leave town.

They left Little Valentine and entered the Upper Commons. Ashley hadn't spent much time there. She hadn't had a lot of friends from that area. But it was not unfamiliar. It felt strange to be going there with Ethan, but not menacing.

He drove around the same block a couple of times, and she supposed he was looking for surveillance or anyone tailing them. Eventually, he pulled into a back alley and in behind a house.

"Is this it?" Ashley asked. "This is home? How are you going to get in?"

Ethan flashed her an irritated look. "Get out. Come with me."

He opened his door and stepped out of the car. When Ashley got out, he had her by the arm almost immediately. Ashley pulled back, intending to get the suitcases. But he wouldn't let her go.

"The suitcases—"

"Leave them."

He pulled her unceremoniously toward the house. Ashley's resistance made no difference; he just pulled her on.

They reached the back door of the house. Ethan turned the knob and pulled the door open. Ashley looked at it as she crossed the threshold.

"Ethan—I think someone is here—" she warned as she saw the broken frame, the wood splintered and strike plate ripped out of place.

Ethan pulled her into the house, disregarding her warning.

# CHAPTER
# FORTY-NINE

Graham's mouth was dry as they approached the house Boots had been seen entering. Joiner had already told him he would have to stay in his truck and park a few doors down the block. He was not to get out.

"I'll let you know what is going on as soon as possible," he told Graham. "This is a courtesy because you helped us get here. But you are not a cop and not allowed anywhere near the investigation."

"I know. I just want to see... when you find them. I want to know if—I want to know that they're okay."

"You have to be prepared for the fact that they might not be," Joiner warned. "Or that this might be a dead end. The fact that he came here after ending his call with you is not proof of anything."

"Okay," Graham agreed. But, of course, he hoped that it would be the end of their search and that Ashley and Ethan would be well and safe. The newlyweds could return to their life after the brief interruption. It would be a story to tell their family and friends. Maybe needing counseling for a while to get over the trauma, but able to return to happy, productive lives.

He couldn't see much from where he was. The police did not

make it obvious that they were surrounding the house. They had to keep away from the view of the windows as much as possible so that their approach would not be seen and they could strike quickly before any resistance could be mounted.

At last, Graham saw the approach. The cops knocked on the door and then pushed it in, and stormed the house when it was answered. Not flashy like on TV, but quick and efficient. Graham breathed out.

Finally.

Finally, they would have some answers.

Fifteen minutes later, Joiner approached the truck. He stood at Graham's window. As promised, Graham had not set foot outside the car, even once he knew the police were inside.

"Well?" he asked eagerly.

Joiner shook his head gravely. "No sign of them."

The letdown was almost a physical pain. "No!"

"No indication that they were ever here."

"Whose house is it? Was Boots staying here?"

"All we have been able to get so far is 'a friend,' and everyone clamming up," Joiner growled. "We have invited them to come to the police station for questioning, but I'm not sure they'll take us up on it." He gave a tight-lipped smile. "At least now I've been able to talk to Uncle Boots face-to-face. He seems like a very upstanding citizen."

It was obvious that his words were meant to be sarcastic. Graham watched out his windshield as the police left the house. He didn't see Uncle Boots or any other private citizens leaving.

"You're sure they were never here?"

"Sure? No. Can't be sure of anything. But there is no sign of them now. If they were here a week or two ago, all traces have been removed."

"What are you going to do? Can you arrest Boots for obstruction of justice? Not cooperating with your investigation?"

"No. He's not required to answer our questions. Even if he was the kidnapper, he would not be required to answer them. He doesn't have to cooperate with us. You would think that if he cared about his nephew, he would, but that is apparently not the case. He doesn't think that we are going to find him, but that Ethan will turn up on his own." Joiner shrugged. "But you already knew that."

"So finding Boots and following him here hasn't made a bit of difference. We aren't any further ahead than we were."

Joiner gazed back toward the house. "Unfortunately not."

"Who is this friend? Does he have a criminal record?"

Joiner's attention returned to Graham. He studied him. "A Mrs. Sara Lapp. No record. Do you know her?"

Graham laughed self-consciously. "I don't know anyone. Or very few. I'm still too new in town. No. I've never met her or heard her name before."

"Not an uncommon name in these parts. Might be former Amish, or her parents were. At any rate, she's determined not to talk to the police. If Ashley and Ethan ever were there... she won't be telling us about it."

Graham shook his head and sighed. He stretched and shifted in his seat, stiff and sore from sitting for too long after doing too much the previous day. His bullet wound was pulsing, and there wasn't any way to sit in the truck that didn't irritate it.

"I guess there is no point in me just sitting here. Nothing is going to happen."

Joiner nodded and sketched a salute. "It was worth a try, even if it didn't work out."

Graham nodded. He started the truck and pulled out as Joiner returned to talk to the other cops and wrap up the operation.

For a while, Graham just drove. The heated seat warmed his back, loosened up the muscles, and soothed the bullet wound. He drove in a large circle, returning to Sara Lapp's street about twenty minutes later. There was no sign of the police. Graham drove down the street slowly, looking for anyone still watching the house. One cop left there to keep an eye on things after everyone else went back to the office. But he didn't see anyone.

He circled the block, drove down the back alley, and then down the street again. He found a parking space half a block down. Still within sight of the house but not where he had been parked before.

After the excitement of the police being there, the neighbors might still be keeping an eye on the street, so Graham probably wouldn't be able to sit in the truck long without someone calling it in. And Graham didn't feel like arguing with Joiner or any of the other cops about whether he should be there or not. Of course, he shouldn't be. But it wasn't illegal for him to be there and he wasn't doing anything to interfere with the police investigation. The police had already done everything they were going to and had left.

He had been watching the house for another twenty minutes when the door opened and a man walked out. Uncle Boots, Graham had to assume. He was, as Joiner had suggested, in his forties, still young-looking. Not a baby face, but no gray hair that was visible from that distance, and he walked with an easy stride, with no hint of arthritis or old injuries apparent. He might have called himself an old man, and maybe that was how a child Ethan's age had seen him, but that was not the impression he gave.

Graham waited until Boots got in his own vehicle, an older model Ford F-150, and drove away. Graham stayed where he was, watching for a few minutes longer. No other vehicle pulled into the street. If the police were still keeping an eye on Boots, they were doing it from a distance. Maybe sitting on a nearby street, betting on which way he would drive away from the house. Or maybe they had placed a tracker on his truck while he was inside.

After another ten minutes of watching and waiting, Graham got out of his truck and went up to the door. He knocked quietly on the door.

A woman opened it a moment later, looking expectant.

Apparently, she hadn't been expecting Graham and was taken aback to see a stranger. She was a tall, spare woman with a neat bun and a dark dress.

"Oh." She looked past him and then looked Graham in the eye. "Who are you?"

"My name is Graham Hall, ma'am. I run a junk removal business in Bleeding Hearts Valley, but that isn't why I'm here. I was hoping I could talk to you for a few minutes about Ethan."

She blinked, then shook her head. "Who are you, police? I told the police I won't talk to them."

"No. I just live here. I cleaned out Ashley's and Ethan's apartment. I still have what they left there. They only took a few suitcases with them. I have all the rest."

"Oh." Frown lines appeared on her previously smooth forehead. "Well..." She looked around again to make sure there was no one behind him or with him, then stepped back, motioning him in.

The house was warm and fragrant with the smell of baking bread or buns. It was quiet. He couldn't hear anyone else in the house. Sara led him into the kitchen and motioned to the table, where he selected a ladder-back chair and sat down. He watched as she checked the oven and a bowl of rising dough. She turned to face him again.

"I don't know where Ethan is or what has happened to him and his wife. I didn't even know they were in town. I haven't seen Boots since..." she trailed off and didn't finish the sentence.

Graham leaned forward with his elbows on his knees so that his back wasn't against the uncomfortable chair and he wasn't looking directly at Sara in a way she might have found uncomfortable.

"I wish I could just walk away and not care what happened to them," he said slowly. "It was just a cleanout job. It takes a few days to get everything left behind sorted and boxed up, do a quick cleaning, and the apartment was ready to rent. But there were so many signs that they had not left voluntarily. That something might have been really wrong between them, or someone might have been menacing and harassing them. I would like to think that they are just out there enjoying themselves on a second honeymoon. But those boxes in my warehouse say they are not. And I can't bring myself to dispose of it all."

"What do you mean about signs that they had not left voluntarily? Or that someone was after them?"

Graham took it slowly and told her about the different things they had left behind, how he was convinced that they hadn't just decided to live somewhere else and left everything behind. He saw the frown deepen at the mention of the wedding album and still more at the journal stuffed under the mattress, way down so nobody could reach it, and the disturbing things she had written.

"That does sound... worrying," she admitted. "A woman doesn't just leave her wedding pictures behind. Or her journal. The only reason for her to intentionally leave her journal would be..."

"Because she wanted someone to know what had happened to her?" Graham finished. He told her about the line in her journal, begging the reader to let her parents know if something happened to her.

Sara sat down at the table, close enough to Graham for him to be able to see the fine lines around her eyes and mouth that suggested she was not as young as he had initially thought.

"And you think... someone was getting into their apartment and might have done something to harm them? Or kidnapped them?" She shook her head. "Why would anyone do that? They didn't ask for money. You don't just kidnap two adults without a reason."

"I don't know. I don't think they had anything particularly valuable to steal. I think that some of those things that upset Ashley were done by Ethan. She didn't know he was at home during the day, and he may have inadvertently moved things from where they had been. But other things she recorded in the journal... Ethan wasn't just accidentally scaring Ashley. Someone—

whether it was him or an outside party—was intentionally trying to frighten and menace her."

"Oh, this is very upsetting." Sara's hands moved as if of their own accord, grasping her skirt and twisting it around. "Boots didn't think there was anything to it. He said it was just the police making a big deal of it, and they would be fine if we just left them alone..."

"Does Boots know where Ethan is?"

"No. No, he wouldn't hide that from me." She rubbed the muscles around her eyes. "I should have known Boots was downplaying it."

"Could you tell me more about Ethan? How you know him?"

She fiddled with the back of her bun as if it might be falling out. Then, her hands were restless in her lap again. She clasped them together to keep them still.

"Ethan came here after his parents died."

# CHAPTER
# FIFTY

"I thought he went to family members. You're related, then?"

"Yes. Ethan's father was my husband's brother."

"And Boots was..."

"Boots was his mother's half-brother."

Graham nodded. Ethan was their nephew in both cases, but Boots and Sara were not related to each other. They only knew each other through the joining of Ethan's parents.

"What happened to his parents?"

She looked away. "That is something... too tragic to discuss. We put it behind us, moved on with our lives. We knew how much *Ethan* must be suffering," she said his name with special emphasis, clearly making herself use his current name instead of John, "so we offered to take him. To try to... heal what had been done."

"That was very kind of you. Was it just you and your husband? Or did you have a family of your own?"

"Yes, we had two daughters and a son. Ethan made it two girls and two boys. Easy to put a bunk bed in Roger's room. And I thought... we would just integrate him as part of our family. I knew he was hurt. That it would take a lot of love and attention to help him get over it. But we had a lot of love in our home." She gave him a wan smile. "We always had room for another child in our hearts. I thought... it was God's will that we should take him in to complete our family."

"It was very generous of you."

"It ended up being... a very difficult trial for us. It tore our hearts out to have to go back on our word and ask someone else to take him on."

"What happened? Why did you have to give him up?"

She rubbed her creased forehead, eyes big and sad. They were shiny with tears as she tried to answer him. "Ethan was only nine when he came to us. Such a tender age to have lost his parents. I knew it would be difficult to show him how much we loved him and wanted him to be safe and happy. I knew there would be difficulties, behavioral problems."

"But they were bigger than you had anticipated." It was clear from the rest of Ethan's history that he had been deeply affected by those early childhood experiences and not having a stable family.

"In the beginning, we only saw the hurt child he was. The... the terror he showed any time we corrected him, even very gently. He cried himself to sleep every night, but if I tried to talk to him about it, he would deny it. Say that he never cried; it must have been Roger. We tried to talk to him about missing his mother, but he wouldn't talk about it. Like there would be something wrong with him if he missed her. The psychologist didn't have any more luck than we did."

"What exactly happened to his mother?" Graham couldn't help noticing that there was no discussion of how he missed his father.

Sara put her hands over her eyes, sniffling and trying to keep her composure. She swallowed hard, wiped her eyes, and looked at Graham without flinching.

"Ethan's father tortured and killed her."

Graham's gut clenched. "And Ethan knew that."

"Ethan was there."

Of course he was. Graham thought back to the sketchbook. The pictures of other women being harmed. Boots acknowledged that he'd been drawing pictures like that since he was a child and that the psychologist said he was trying to work things out.

Trying to come to terms with his mother's horrific death.

Even now, he was still trying to come to terms with his mother's death.

"Oh, boy."

Sara nodded. "Looking back, I realize that we were naive. We thought that a loving family would be the best remedy for what had happened to him. A loving mother and father, loving brother and sisters. He could grow up in a home where he saw love, patience, and service modeled, and it would overcome all of what he had seen and heard growing up in that... in that home." She shrugged. "It was a nice idea. It was well-intentioned. And our pastor encouraged us. Friends told us that love would do miracles."

"But it wasn't enough."

"No. We knew he would need therapy, and he had it while he was living with us. But from what I have read and studied since then... he probably should have been put into institutional care at the start. A place with strict rules and daily individual and group therapy. Not a family that operated so differently than the one he had come from and was... soft on rules and slow on discipline."

"I'm sure that what you did was good for him."

"I'm not so sure. It was confusing for him. In the beginning, he was sad and scared, which I had expected, and we coddled and protected him and gave him special treats and privileges. Didn't expect him to be able to follow the family rules like everyone else. We didn't want to make demands on him. Then, as he became more secure... we started to see other behaviors. Instead of being protective of me and the girls, stepping in front of us to shield us if my husband or son raised their voices or got angry about something, he became volatile."

The timer on the stove dinged, and Sara stood up. She didn't say anything as she took loaves of bread out of the oven and replaced them with others. She set the timer again and paced around the kitchen, attending to other steps in her assembly line.

"He started to yell and hit. To threaten and say we needed to be punished for not following the rules. He was just a little boy, but it was frightening how strong he was when he was angry. I didn't worry so much about what he could do to me as what he could do to the girls. I could protect myself, but I couldn't always be there to protect the girls, especially if they were at school. They didn't go to the same classes, but he could still catch them unaware in the hallways, at recess, or on the way home from school."

"What did the psychologist say?"

"The girls and I had started to appear in his pictures." She licked her lips. "When he started to get violent... we had to protect them. We couldn't take the chance that he would act out what his father had done. We never knew which boy we were going to get—the scared one who tried to protect his mama or the angry one who copied what his papa did and repeated the vile things that he had said. He was just a little boy, but it would take a long time for him to get better. And during that time, our daughters would be terrorized. I would have to constantly be vigilant, standing over him, making sure he never got an instant alone with them."

She sighed and shook her head, her eyes once again sparkling with tears.

"So you arranged for him to go to another home," Graham finished. "Somewhere they would be better equipped to care for him. Where they didn't have little girls."

"Yes. We still didn't know what he needed. No one knew what he needed back then. But we could at least make sure there were not young children that he could harm."

"He went to another family member?"

"Yes. And there was a honeymoon period where everyone thought that he was doing better and we had made the right choice... and then a period where everything fell apart and they had to reconsider. And so on it went. Eventually, he ended up with Boots, which seemed to go well until Family Services intervened and took him away. Then, no one in the family heard from him again."

"Boots said that he went to various foster homes, group homes, and residential care facilities. It sounds like he was able to keep track of Ethan."

She shrugged. "Maybe. He didn't tell us any of that. Just that he was gone. Maybe he didn't want to keep reopening old wounds. It was easier not to know anything. To say that he was better off wherever they had put him."

"Did Ethan contact you when he moved back to Bleeding Hearts Valley? Or when he was at the mission in the city?"

"No. No, we never heard anything. I had no idea he was back in this part of the country. Maybe..." she stared off into space. "I have no idea what I would have done if I had known that. Would I have asked him over for a visit?" She looked at the cooling loaves of bread. "Taken him over a loaf of bread? Would I have been scared of him? I don't know. What was he like?"

Graham tried to look as reassuring as possible. "I didn't know him myself. But from what everyone I have talked to about him has said, he was very nice. He was quiet, mostly stayed in the background. He was devoted to his wife. Nobody reported him being violent."

Her use of the word *honeymoon* echoed in Graham's head. Everything had been fine for the honeymoon period, but then the negative behaviors had appeared. He tried to keep his breathing even and not think about whether everything had changed between Ashley and Ethan after their honeymoon was over and reality set in.

"What do you think happened?" Sara asked, watching him more carefully than Graham liked. He was good at keeping his thoughts to himself, but her sharp eyes made him think twice about whether he was hiding anything from her.

"I don't know," he admitted. "He had been bullied and lost his job. Boots said it sounded like he was off his meds. Ashley was being stalked and harassed by someone who could get into the apartment. It looks like they left together, but Ashley didn't take things that should have been important to her and hasn't called her parents. No one has seen either one of them. What did Boots tell you about Ethan's call?"

"Not much. Just that he had called. And Boots was worried enough about it to come out here to talk to him. He doesn't say much, but for Boots, that's pretty much admitting how worried he was about *Ethan*."

Eventually, there wasn't anything else Sara could tell him. It had been a long time since she had taken that frightened little boy into her home and then had to give him up again. She hadn't seen or heard from him in years and could not tell him where else to go.

Graham paused at the door, turning back toward her.

"What was Ethan's name originally? Before he became John Brown?"

She looked at him for a moment.

"Nicholas John Amundsen."

Ashley awoke slowly, body stiff and sore, mouth as dry as cotton. She'd had another seizure in the night, but she thought they were slowing now, that she wasn't spending as much time asleep.

She was quicker to remember where she was and how she had gotten there. He was apparently afraid to give her any more sedatives, and her brain was clearer. She had already slept through the postictal stage, and the room around her, now familiar, didn't need as much explanation anymore.

She remembered leaving the apartment with Ethan and entering the house with him. Her worry about walking into the house with the broken door and fearing that someone else might be there. But the concern, as well as her hope of discovering more about his past, was soon swallowed up by the shocking change in Ethan's behavior.

As soon as they were safely inside, he threw her down on the floor. She thought at first that it was an accident, that something had startled him or he had tripped. But he kicked her, and when she tried to rise, punched her in the face.

"No!" Ashley protested, startled. "Ethan! Ow! Stop!"

He didn't stop. He didn't respond to his name. He hurled

accusations of infidelity at her. He threatened her with punishment for her adulterous behavior. Ashley did everything she could to reach him. She called his name, wept, pleaded with him, and promised him over and over that she hadn't betrayed him.

But he seemed convinced that something had been going on at work, and her promotion was proof that she was sleeping with Mike, the director of the shelter.

And her apparent unfaithfulness when he had been fired from his promising new job, and whatever other stressors he was experiencing, had been too much.

She didn't know whether he had stopped taking his meds before that or not, but she was sure he had not taken any since they had left the apartment.

For the first few days, he had come and gone. The suitcases had been brought into the house, as well as a couple of others. She had been sure at first that someone would realize what had happened and come looking for her. Someone would see or hear something. Maybe a neighbor would call the police about lights being on in the abandoned house across the street.

But no one came, and the Ethan she had known was gone. He wouldn't even let her call him that anymore.

She was sure she had been at death's door before the beatings and brutality had de-escalated. But then she started to see more and more of the tender, frightened Nicholas and less of the monster who had no name.

Nicholas's appearance had saved her, she was sure. Without him, she would have been gone. She had been close to death and had not wanted anything but death at that point.

She looked at the man lying on the bed next to her asleep and wondered who he would be when he awoke. In repose, his face was free of any scowl or sneer, and she looked like the Ethan she had married. She could stare at him for hours.

But when he woke up, he would not be that man anymore.

A devil and an angel fought for his soul. Which one would have him in his grasp when he awoke, she did not know.

# CHAPTER
# FIFTY-TWO

G raham worked his way through the maps, census, and land records, examining each sheet critically and trying to put the Ashley Carter and Ethan Quick case out of his mind.

He had, of course, passed on everything he had learned from Sara Lapp to Joiner, who hadn't been too happy that he had gone back there on his own and interfered again with the investigation.

But how was it *interfering* if Graham stayed out of the way until the police were finished with their part?

It wasn't like he had gotten in anyone's way or planted any evidence. He had just talked to Sara. *After* they had talked to her. It wasn't his fault that Joiner hadn't gotten any information from her. When the police had talked to her while Boots had been present, she had refused to have anything to do with them and hadn't even said how she was related to Ethan.

Joiner had asked Boots to come to the police station to have a conversation with him, but of course, he had refused. And since Joiner hadn't known that Sara knew anything about Ethan, he hadn't bothered to ask her. Even if he had, Graham knew she wouldn't have gone with him. She wouldn't have left in the middle of her baking and didn't know anything pertinent to the investigation.

All Sara could tell them was what had happened years ago. It might help to put them into Ethan's head, but so far, getting inside his head had not helped to move the investigation forward. They couldn't predict what someone so unpredictable would do.

There were still too many missing years. They didn't know exactly what had happened to Ethan from the time he had been taken away from Boots until he had gone to the shelter and met Ashley. There were a lot of people he might have met and a lot of places that he might have come to consider home during that time.

It was up to Joiner to investigate further. He now had Ethan's birth name, though Graham wasn't sure that would help them. He might be able to look up what had happened to Ethan's parents, but they now had that story from Sara.

They knew now why Ethan had drawn those disturbing pictures, still trying to work through what he had seen as a child.

It was out of Graham's hands and he needed to go on with his own life. Maybe Ethan and Ashley would show up unharmed in a few weeks or months, as Boots has suggested.

Graham forced himself to study the maps, the census papers, and the deeds, trying to tie together whatever records he could. If he wanted to sell the maps and documents as sets, he should be able to match one name or address across all three, so each package was a complete picture, a slice of one person's life or a snapshot of one household.

The common names were the easiest and the most difficult. It was easy to come up with two Smith records, but if he wanted to ensure they were both the same Smith, it was ten times more difficult than matching two Shufflebottoms. And if he wanted to target buyers within Bleeding Hearts Valley, then he needed to pick the ones with distinctive family names. Who would want a Shufflebottom deed on his wall, other than a Shufflebottom?

He could put the deeds in alphabetical order. It was more challenging to sort the census and maps. Neighborhood and then alphabetical by street?

He put an Amundsen deed on top of an Andersen deed. Then he stood there staring at it.

Amundsen.

It was a name he had never encountered before coming to Bleeding Hearts Valley. He remembered seeing it when he had gone through the maps the first time. And then it had unexpectedly come up again. Ethan's birth name had been Amundsen. Nicholas John Amundsen.

Graham had assumed that Nicholas had been living out east when his parents had been killed. He had assumed that Nicholas had been born out east, not in Bleeding Hearts Valley. But had someone told him that, or had he only assumed? What if Ethan had been born in Bleeding Hearts Valley? What if when he had told Boots he was coming home, he had not referred to Kentucky, but to a house in Bleeding Hearts Valley?

He looked for the name of the street on the maps, poring over them. He picked up his phone and found Sara's number. He had been smart enough not to leave there without first finding a way to get in touch with her if he should have more questions for her.

Even though he wasn't investigating it. If anyone called her back, it would be Joiner.

But Graham didn't call Joiner with the information. He wanted to hear the answer directly from Sara.

"Hello?"

"Mrs. Lapp, It's Graham Hall. From yesterday."

Her voice was wary. "Yes, is there something else you needed?"

"I need to know whether Ethan ever lived here in town before he came to you. Did he live here before his parents died?"

"I don't know about that. Wait a minute."

He heard her muffle the phone receiver while she called out to her husband. There was a bit of back and forth, and then she removed her hand from the phone and spoke directly to Graham again.

"Apparently, they lived with Nicholas's—Ethan's—grandfather for a couple of years. I don't remember that, but my husband does. We weren't... we weren't close to his father and brother. There were a lot of family issues."

"Ethan lived here in town. At the house on Elm Street?"

"Yes, that's right."

"So he might have considered that home. Do you know who lives there now?"

"I don't have any idea. My father-in-law died a few years ago."

"Okay, thanks."

Graham terminated the call and immediately called Joiner to give him the news.

# CHAPTER
# FIFTY-THREE

The call went to voicemail. Graham hung up and tried again. And again. Where was Joiner, that he didn't notice the phone ringing? In a meeting? Driving? In the john?

"Come on, Detective Joiner," he growled, dialing again.

"Joiner," the detective barked into the phone. "What the hell is your problem, Hall? Leave a message like a normal person!"

"Ethan lived here in Bleeding Hearts Valley before his family moved out east. He and his parents lived with his grandfather right here in town."

Joiner swore. "Where?"

Graham gave him the address. "I don't know who lives there now. I asked Sara Lapp about it, but she didn't know who has the house now. The grandfather passed away a few years ago."

"All right," Joiner snapped. "I'm on it. I'll let you know what happens."

～

There was no way Graham was waiting until after everything went down and Detective Joiner got around to calling him with the details. He needed to be there to see it firsthand. He looked at the map one more time, snapped pictures of it and the deed with his phone so that he didn't have to enter the address into his contacts list, and headed to the truck.

It might take Joiner an hour or two to rally the troops. Or it might take only a minute to make the call and they would all descend on Elm Street and knock on Grandpa Amundsen's door. Graham wasn't going to miss it.

As he got closer to the address, he could hear sirens approaching. They cut off in the distance to avoid alerting anyone to their destination. As Graham pulled over down the block from the house, one car after another whipped by him and double-parked at locations close to the Amundsen address, but out of view of the house itself.

Graham saw an ambulance pull over farther up the street. His stomach clenched. He hoped that all the paramedics would be required to do was check over one healthy kidnap victim, and no treatment or hospitalization would be needed. Maybe some mild dehydration or sleep deprivation. Then Ashley could just go home to... to the hotel, he supposed, until she worked out new living arrangements.

He walked down the street, looking for a good vantage point for watching the house. Somewhere he could duck down behind a car and be out of the way of the police, but still have a good view of what was happening.

Of course, he didn't get far before being spotted by Joiner, who strode over, face an angry mask.

"Hall, what do you think you're doing here? You are not a cop. You might think you are, but trust me, you are not."

"I know. I just want to see. If they are here... I want to know about it. I have to know."

"I told you I would call and let you know what happens."

"That's not good enough. If I was shot because I was looking into this, don't you think that gives me the right to see how it all plays out?"

"What makes you think that this has anything to do with you getting shot?"

"Well, you said—I don't know. I don't usually investigate kidnappings. And I don't usually get shot. And my warehouse was broken into. Someone didn't want me looking into it."

Joiner looked toward the house. "You think he's armed? That he's out breaking into warehouses and shooting people while holding his wife hostage?"

"Just one warehouse and one shooting," Graham shot back.

"You said four guys got out of the car and chased after you."

"Yes," Graham agreed, trying to slow down his brain and think about it.

"Who are Ethan's three friends?"

Joiner had a point. From everything Graham had discovered, Ethan was a loner. He didn't have friends. He didn't have family, other than Boots and Sara. And they had not been the ones who had climbed out of that car with balaclavas on. He was sure of that.

"I Imm. Yeah. You're right."

"Yeah. You can bet that this has nothing to do with your shooting." Joiner leveled his gaze at Graham. "You're going to have to figure out which one of your enterprises that business *was* related to. You've apparently upset *someone* with what you have been doing since you moved here."

Which was not something that Graham wished to discuss with Joiner.

"I still want to see what goes down here," he said firmly. "You have to admit, I have put more effort into finding out what happened to these people than anyone else. Other than you, of course." He tried not to sound snide with the last comment. He knew Joiner had put the hours into the investigation, even if he'd had to be talked into it. Even if Graham had been the one to come up with all of the breaks in the case.

Joiner glared at him, probably guessing what he was thinking. Then he looked up and down the street. His radio was chattering as the police set up their approach. As a detective, he wasn't the one who would be knocking on the door and possibly busting it in to make entry. He would also be standing back watching as the guys in protective gear went in.

"You've got work to do here," Graham pointed out. "I'm not going to get any closer. I just want to see what happens."

"You need to go home. I'll tell you what happens later."

"I'm not leaving. You can't make me. Are you evacuating everyone else on the street?"

"No, but you're not in a house. You're out in the open where you could get hurt. Or you could run toward the house. How do I know what you're going to do? You haven't proven to be that reliable up until now."

"I haven't done anything to get in the way of your investigation. I've told you what I've found out to help you. You know I could have just come over here without telling you about it at all. Sat surveillance on the house or sneaked in to see if someone was in there. But I didn't. I want to help, so I gave you the information. I don't want this to blow up any more than you do. I want Ashley to be safe. And Ethan, for that matter."

Joiner huffed and rolled his eyes and dramatized like he was some teenager on TV, but Graham just watched him and waited. Eventually, Joiner told him, "Fine, but you stay here," and walked away to join the other cops as they made plans to approach the house.

# FIFTY-FOUR

G raham waited. He knew it would take time. Police actions took way longer in real life than on TV. On TV, there were thirty seconds of prep and ten minutes of fireworks. In real life, it was an hour of prep and 30 seconds to secure the suspect. If everything went right.

Birds chirped in the trees and a lawn mower buzzed in the distance. The police radios winked in and out with bursts of static. The afternoon sun was warm on his back.

Eventually, everyone was assembled and the cop at the front door knocked, standing off to the side so he wouldn't be in the bullseye if someone fired a bullet through the door.

Graham held his breath and watched. The cops at the front door didn't move. There was no movement from inside the house that Graham could see. The door didn't open. There was no twitch of curtains. No answer. No gunshot.

Eyes turned to the back door, located on the side of the house behind a fence. Graham couldn't see very well, but the tops of the cops' heads floated along behind the fence and in through the back door. It must have been left unlocked.

There was some activity among the police, talking on their

radios and watching the house. The front door opened to admit the cops waiting at the front.

Graham couldn't hear what was happening.

*Were they in there? If Ashley was there, was she okay?*

And then Ethan was brought to the front door. His hands were cuffed behind him, but he still struggled with the cops holding him, trying to break free, crying out in protest as if they were invaders and he was being kidnapped from his home. He looked unnaturally thin from Graham's perspective.

They brought him down the concrete steps at the front door. Graham took a step forward and stopped himself. He had promised not to move, and he shouldn't, even now that everything was over.

Then, as the cops patted Ethan down and prepared to transport him, another figure was in the doorway.

Ashley, as pale as could be, skinny and tottering, barely managing to stay on her feet. The cops tried to talk her into stopping, but gave her room to move, not putting hands on her.

She wore a blouse and dress pants, but they seemed to hang on her. What she had been able to wear a couple of weeks ago was now far too big.

"Don't," she protested, calling out to the cops who had Ethan. "Please, he needs a doctor, not the prison. Look at him. Please."

"Stay back, ma'am."

She made it down the steps without falling and floated toward them.

"Please..."

One of them was calling Ethan by name and Mirandizing him. Ethan protested and struggled.

"Not Ethan," Ashley told them. "It's Nicholas now, don't call him Ethan."

They looked at her and each other in confusion. Joiner stepped in to try to sort things out.

"Ethan is his legal name," he said firmly. "If he wants to go by his former name with friends, that's fine, but legally, it's Ethan Quick."

"But he's not anymore. Ethan is gone." She said it as passionately as if she had seen him killed, yet he was standing before them. "And this... is Nicholas. He was trying to protect me. Trying to help me. He doesn't understand why you're treating him like this."

Joiner glared at her. But there was a softness in his expression that wasn't there when he spoke to Graham. "Ma'am, we have to do things a certain way. It's the law. If he wants to plead not competent, he can do that later. Right now, he is Ethan Quick, and he kidnapped you and held you against your will."

"He needs help!"

"He'll get it. Now, please let the paramedics look at you. You can barely stay on your feet..."

The paramedics hovered, trying to get closer to Ashley, but were unable to do anything until she let them. She looked like a strong wind would blow her away like a dry leaf.

"Don't touch her," Ethan protested in a high voice, becoming aware of the activity around him rather than just the cops arresting him. "Leave her alone. Let her be. Don't hurt Mama."

Joiner flushed. He motioned for the other men to take Ethan away. He clearly saw no point in arguing with someone who didn't even know who he was, or who Ashley was.

"Ma'am, please, come have a seat by the ambulance..."

He persuaded her to sit at the back of the ambulance and let the paramedics look at her. Graham couldn't see the details from where he stood, but it was obvious that she was bruised, had lost a lot of weight, and was having difficulty staying upright on her own.

While the paramedics were examining Ashley, she suddenly stiffened and started flailing. They moved quickly to lower her safely to the ground, then got out the gurney to transfer her to when it was safe. Graham found himself beside the ambulance, trying to get close enough to talk to the paramedics.

"She has epilepsy. She's supposed to be on Dilantin. She probably hasn't had any for a couple of weeks."

"Thank you, sir, we'll take care of it," one of them acknowledged brusquely. "Just stay back, please."

Close up, Ashley looked ghostly as she gradually relaxed from the seizures. Her skin was nearly transparent. The blond hair floated around her head like an angel's halo. Her eyes blinked as she came out of the seizure and processed her surroundings.

Graham looked at Joiner. "Ethan is supposed to be on medications too. Do you know what his prescriptions were?"

"They'll sort that out at the jail."

"He should be taken to the hospital too."

"He needs to be booked."

"He's on a psychotic break, off his meds, and it's obvious that neither of them has had much to eat. He should be examined by a doctor right away. He can be booked any time."

Joiner growled wordlessly and motioned from Graham to get out of the way and stop bothering him.

"You'll be sorry if he ends up dead in a jail cell," Graham warned, raising his voice so that as many people as possible would hear him. A few heads turned toward him. The whole neighborhood was aware that something was going on now. People were standing on their porches and in their front yards watching, eyes big and bright.

"Shut up," Joiner tried to quell Graham.

"He's sick. You don't know what kind of physical trauma he's had. You don't know if someone else was holding the two of them. If you treat him like a criminal when he was a victim..."

"You have not been in that house. You don't know what went on inside."

"Yeah? Well, neither do you until you've had a chance to talk to Ashley about it. And she was pretty insistent that Ethan be treated."

Joiner shook his head angrily, but he ordered another ambulance be called and motioned to the cops dealing with Ethan not to put him in the waiting squad car.

"Keep him out. Make sure someone looks at him."

He glared at Graham. "I thought you said you were going to stay back and not interfere."

"I didn't. I just came over to tell the paramedics about Ashley's epilepsy."

"You are in the way and interfering with this matter. It's time for you to go home."

"I'll leave when this is all over."

"You'll leave now or get arrested."

Graham eyed him. Joiner was serious. Definitely capable of following through on the threat. Graham took a couple of steps backward. Joiner's chin lifted, and he nodded. But Graham didn't go any farther than that. Just far enough out of the way that Joiner would have trouble making the case for arresting him. Still close enough to see and hear most of what was going on.

Ashley moved around a little, but her gaze was unfocused, and she didn't answer the paramedics' questions. The second ambulance pulled into the street with its siren on, but shut it off quickly rather than deafening them all. Graham watched as they gave Ethan a brief examination and then spoke to the cops in voices too low for Graham to hear.

Eventually, both ambulances made their way to the hospital with the patients. Graham knew he wouldn't likely be allowed to see either of them. Not today, anyway. Ashley would need time to recover before she saw anyone other than her family, and the police would not want anyone to talk to Ethan until after he was arraigned, and then they would have to go through channels. Graham didn't imagine that they would be too happy knowing that Ethan's lawyer was likely to argue that he had been not mentally competent at the time he'd abducted Ashley.

# FIFTY-FIVE

G raham was tired as he headed home. He felt like he had been running for several days without a good night's sleep. And maybe he had. While he had gone to bed, he hadn't slept well since being shot. He didn't want to take a lot of painkillers or sleeping pills, and as a result, ended up lying awake a lot, just thinking about the missing couple and what might have happened to them.

Now, they were back. He had helped to do that. By the looks of them as they came out of the house, they would probably have both been dead if he hadn't been instrumental in finding them. The real estate agent would have had a nasty surprise when she looked at the house before listing it for sale.

Graham stopped at a traffic light and waited for the light to change. A motorcycle pulled up beside the driver's window, making a lane where there wasn't one. Irritated, Graham glanced at the motorcyclist.

Normally, he avoided meeting the eyes of other motorists, other than to nod in acknowledgment or wave someone forward. He didn't look the man in the face, but a movement of the biker's hand to his hip caught Graham's attention, and he turned his head and looked more closely.

A gun in a holster. People carried guns. But they didn't reach out and grab them in traffic unless they intended to do something with them. Graham's window was down as he had been enjoying the warm weather.

He could try to roll the window up before the motorcyclist could follow through with what he had planned, but what good would that do? The window might deflect a bullet slightly, but at point-blank range, a fraction of an inch wouldn't make any difference. Graham reached out, grabbed the closest tool at hand, and aimed a spray can at the assailant's face.

The spray can had a wider spread than a pistol, so his aim did not need to be as steady as the biker's. Bright yellow spray paint built up on the gunman's face, more concentrated in the middle and fading toward the edges.

The man shouted, swore, and immediately rubbed more paint into his eyes. He had let go of the gun and did not end up shooting himself in the head or winging Graham or some innocent bystander.

The light changed color and Graham mashed the gas pedal to the floor, launching the truck into the intersection. Luckily, it was clear of any slow walkers or vehicles that had waited too long to turn left, and he got himself out of there.

He didn't want to have to report it, and he did not want to go back to that intersection to describe what had happened. Was there any chance he could get away with not reporting it? Motorists had road rage incidents all the time. They had to be pretty common, and the police would not encourage people to report them if they didn't think they had any chance of identifying the perpetrator.

Of course, in this case, if he reported it right away, the guy should be pretty easy to spot, with a face full of yellow paint. And he had a feeling that someone would be sure to take a picture of the guy and post it on social media. "Caught yellow-faced" might replace the parlance "caught red-handed" when describing road ragers. It might become the next big trend; tagging aggressive drivers and motorcyclists with yellow paint.

Graham groaned and pulled his truck over. He called the police and tried reporting it on the non-emergency line. But apparently, the mentions of road rage and a gun got people bent out of shape, and he was told that someone would be dispatched and would talk to him right away. The dispatcher asked Graham to return to the scene of the crime, but he refused. If the biker was still there, he wasn't about to put himself in harm's way. Stepping in front of an enraged bull wasn't a good idea.

The uniformed cop who pulled over in front of his truck a few minutes later did not look happy. He removed dark sunglasses and hooked them over his collar as he looked into the interior of the car. His dark uniform shirt was limp, and sweat trickled down his temples under the gold-embellished cap. He demanded Graham tell him exactly what had happened, and Graham had to go through it three or four times before he seemed to believe that Graham was telling the truth. He looked at the can of spray paint and the other miscellany in Graham's truck.

"What is all of this stuff for?" he asked suspiciously.

Graham looked at it and didn't see anything suspicious. Was anyone possessing spray paint assumed to be a graffiti artist now?

"I was painting a sign for my business."

"With this yellow? Kind of overwhelming, isn't it?"

Graham pulled out his new business cards, designed by Perennial, and held one out to the man. "Yellow," he pointed out.

The cop looked at it and nodded.

"So this guy had a gun, and you thought it was a good idea to aggravate him by spraying him in the face with paint?"

"No... he reached for his gun, and it was the only way I could think of in that instant to protect myself. And it worked. He went for his face instead of pulling out the gun."

"What makes you think he had a gun?"

"He had it visible in a holster on his bike. I saw him grab it. I wasn't just imagining it or speculating what he might be doing. He started to pull the gun; I grabbed the spray can and sprayed it in his face. That's how close he was to me," Graham reached out his hand to demonstrate. "Right there. Right in my face. He was in my lane at the intersection, not a separate one. I could reach out and touch him. But I didn't want to do that. I wanted to be left alone."

The cop walked away from Graham to answer a call on his radio. He walked up to his own car and stood beside it while he talked to whoever was on the other end. A cop at the intersection it had happened at, Graham assumed.

The cop returned. Officer Dutton, Graham noted the name on his uniform. As it appeared he and Dutton were going to be spending a lot of time together, it made sense to at least get to know his name.

"Mr. Hall, would you step out of the car, please."

"I didn't—" Graham started to protest, then realized there was no point. It didn't matter that he had not initiated the encounter. It didn't matter to this cop whether Graham had acted in self-defense. He had to take both of their statements and investigate them with an eye to figuring out what really happened, not taking either of them at their word.

Obviously, they would each try to spin the encounter in their own favor. Each would say that they had just been defending himself. Or maybe the biker would say it was unprovoked and he had never touched the gun in his holster. *People are just crazy sometimes, officer. You never know what kind of loonies you are going to encounter out there.*

Graham opened his door and stepped out, keeping his movements slow. He held his hands at shoulder level and followed Dutton's instructions as he checked Graham's pockets. Dutton then asked Graham to sit down on the curb with his ankles crossed while Dutton looked in his car.

"What's this I hear about you being involved in another gun incident last week?" he asked.

"Uh... yeah. Four guys jumped out of a car, chased me, and shot me. You want to see the bullet hole?" Graham was aware that he sounded a little bit aggressive. But since when did being shot make him a suspect? Didn't that prove he was being targeted rather than that he had done something wrong?

"Sometimes people overreact after something like that. They get mugged on the bus, and the next week, they pull a gun on the little old lady who tries to sit down next to them. If you got shot, it makes sense that you might have overreacted to someone you thought might have been targeting you again."

"Or there was a guy with a motorcycle who tried to draw down on me while I was sitting at the red light."

"Why would he? Had you cut him off? Done something to attract his attention? It seems awfully suspicious that you would be involved in two gun incidents in such a short period of time."

Graham kept his mouth shut.

"Or, you were targeted twice by the same dudes," Dutton offered. "You double-cross someone lately? Get some mob guy upset about something?"

Graham reviewed his actions over the past couple of weeks. He had been overly involved in Ashley's and Ethan's disappearance, and he had thought it might have had something to do with his getting shot. But what kind of kidnapper sent four guys after someone for being curious or calling the police about a missing person?

Judging by the shape he was in when he was brought out of the house on Elm Street, Ethan hadn't been hiring anyone to come after Graham. And as Joiner had pointed out, Ethan didn't have one friend, let alone three, to bring with him. He had probably not left the house since he had taken Ashley there. He wouldn't have even been aware of Graham's interest in the investigation.

Was it possible Boots had been involved? He had been very quick to show up when Ethan appeared to be in trouble. He'd come a long way just to make contact with the nephew he hadn't seen in years, or to give him some memento that was supposed to anchor him to the real world. What if Boots had been the kidnapper, and Ethan had just been trying to protect Ashley? What if Boots was not an isolated farmer in Kentucky, but involved in some organized crime gang who had thought that kidnapping his nephew's wife might be profitable?

But there had never been a ransom demand. It obviously hadn't been for profit. What other reason would there be to kidnap Ethan's wife? It didn't make any sense that Boots had been involved. It had been just what it appeared to be: Ethan having a psychotic break and going off of his meds, as Boots said he had done before.

"Mr. Hall?" Dutton prompted.

"Yeah?"

"You want to tell us who you've gotten cross-threaded with? It's obvious someone is gunning for you pretty hard. If you want us to catch whoever is behind this—not just the gunmen but whoever is hiring them—you're going to need to come clean."

"I'm all about the cleanup," Graham muttered.

"What's that?"

"I'll have to think about it. I have no idea who is behind this."

It wasn't true, of course. He hadn't upset that many people in the past couple of weeks.

Joiner arrived while Graham was sitting on the curb and consulted with Dutton in a low voice, turned away from him. Joiner looked at the items in Graham's truck. He walked over to Graham, folded his arms, and looked down at him.

"So, you figured we didn't have enough excitement already today with finding Ashley and Ethan. You needed a bit more?"

"Yeah, that's right," Graham agreed with a sigh.

"You're lucky you didn't get shot again."

"I'm quick with the spray paint."

"Apparently so."

"Have you been to the hospital?" Graham asked Joiner,

figuring that was probably where he had just come from. "How are they?"

"Both will make it. Dehydrated and malnourished, but not severe enough to be life-threatening. Ashley, though, with her seizures and her physical injuries... she's in a lot worse shape. Untreated, there is always the danger that a seizure could kill her. Especially with no one to give her first aid."

"Other than Ethan."

"Other than *Nicholas*, according to her," Joiner corrected. "And Nicholas, if I am to understand it, is nine years old or younger."

"You think he has multiple personality disorder?"

"They don't even call it that anymore. And I'm not a doctor. I don't know what psychological stuff Ethan has going on, other than that he's never gotten over the murder of his mother. The name changes over the years... he keeps trying to leave his past behind, and it's always caught up with him. Maybe now, he's gone back to the beginning and trying to process what his father did to his mother..."

"Reenacting it himself?"

Joiner shrugged. "He's one sick puppy. Who's to say?"

# CHAPTER
# FIFTY-SIX

After learning from her parents who Graham was and that he had been instrumental in opening the missing person case and tracking her down, Ashley agreed to talk to him at the hospital.

Even just a day being cared for at the hospital had significantly improved her appearance. She no longer looked sunken-eyed and frail. She was thin, but her skin glowed instead of looking gray and stretched, and the hollows had filled in. The nurses or her mother had helped her to do her hair, so her silken locks were smooth and sleek around her head. Natural-looking makeup camouflaged the bruises he had seen the day before. Amazing what a layer of makeup could do.

"Hi," Graham greeted her, tentatively offering his hand. "How are you doing? You look a lot better today."

"Oh, you're the guy who told the police to have Ethan taken to the hospital! I didn't know that was you."

Graham nodded. "That was me," he agreed. "I didn't know if you would remember much of what happened yesterday. With the seizure... I know sometimes they can affect your memory."

Ashley shrugged. "I don't remember much after that. Not until later, here in the hospital."

She looked around as if to reassure herself about the surroundings and that everything was firmly aligned with her memory.

"I'm glad you're doing so well. I mean—you're looking good; I hope you're feeling better too." Graham felt a little tongue-tied. He didn't know why he should feel so awkward. This was the woman he had been looking for. He knew more about her than he did about most people in Bleeding Hearts Valley. He expected to feel like he knew her, but instead, he was surprised by the living, breathing Ashley Carter.

He sat in the visitor's chair and tried to relax and calm himself. "So... your parents told you who I am. I'm not a cop or private investigator; I just happened to get involved in this... I was hired by your landlord, Marcel, to clear out your apartment." Graham's face warmed. "He thought you had abandoned it and... run off somewhere."

Ashley shook her head, frowning. "How could he think that? He thought we would just leave it like that? We were paid up to the end of the month."

Graham told her about the "I'm sorry" note and the two sets of keys being left on the counter.

"It looked like you were apologizing for taking off and leaving everything for him to clean out. And with both sets of keys left there, it looked like you never intended to return."

"He must have gone back and done that when he picked up the other suitcases." Ashley rubbed her forehead. "I guess he never did mean to go back again."

"Why did he... take you?" Graham asked tentatively. "Was there anyone else involved?" His mind went again to Boots, so quick to travel across the country with just a phone call from Ethan.

"No... just him. But... not him. I tried to explain it to the police, but it's so hard. I did go with him willingly, but I didn't understand what was going through his head. I still don't. When we got to the house, that was the first time I realized... he wasn't himself anymore." She raised her eyes to his, dark and troubled. "I knew when I married Ethan that I didn't know much about his past, but I still thought... I knew who he *was*, and that was enough."

She readjusted herself on the bed and gazed out the window, looking away from him. Graham could see trees full of blossoms across the street from the hospital.

"But I guess... I didn't know the person he is now. Or the person I thought I knew, Ethan, was just... a mask? An illusion? Somebody he was trying to be? But with everything that happened, all of stuff he didn't tell me about, he just couldn't do it anymore..."

"Was it the job?" Graham asked. "The people at Perennial... it sounded like they were pretty nasty to him. Bullying him for being different and then forcing him out..." he shook his head. "That must have been crushing. Here he thought he'd landed this great job, and..."

"I got him that job. I thought it would be good for him. So good for him to be able to use his art for his work. He was qualified. But he said..." She swallowed hard, visibly shaken. "He said that I promised never to make him go anywhere they would hurt him, and that I put him into that place and... they were monsters." She shook her head. "He was talking to me like I was his case worker... like I had put him into another home or institution where he had been hurt, after promising I wouldn't."

"He has a long history of being moved from one place to another."

"I guess... he never talked to me about it. The past was the past, and he just wanted to live in the present."

But Ethan hadn't been able to stay in the present. He hadn't been able to leave the past behind.

"When we got to the house... he was a different person. All of this rage and violence just came pouring out. I have never seen anything like that. I never would have thought... it wasn't like he had been hiding it, like someone who has to count to ten to control his temper. I never knew him to be angry or violent at all."

She sighed and shook her head, tears in her eyes.

"You couldn't have known," Graham assured her. It was obvious Ashley was blaming herself. She was a trained social worker; she should have seen it coming. Should have known that Ethan was something other than he had seemed. "No one else I talked to thought that he could have done anything to hurt you."

No one but Sara Lapp. *She* had known. She had been the first one to send Ethan away. Everyone else in Bleeding Hearts Valley had only seen the "honeymoon" Ethan.

Ashley nodded. She rubbed the corners of her eyes, wiping away any tears before they could emerge.

"That day... I went home to tell him about my promotion. And it wasn't just that he was jealous that I had been promoted and he had lost his job. He said I must have been sleeping with the director of the shelter. And at the house, he kept saying that I had to be punished."

Graham's heart went out to her; she looked so vulnerable and confused.

"You know about his mom and dad."

Ashley shook her head. "What about them?"

"Maybe... you should find out from Detective Joiner. He knows more of the details. What I know is only third-hand."

He knew he was being a coward, but he didn't know how he could tell her about Ethan's father torturing and killing his mother.

Ashley's eyes lingered on him, waiting for him to break and just tell her what he knew.

"So... I have all of the stuff that I took from the apartment," Graham said, changing the subject. "It has been cleaned out so Marcel could show it to new renters."

She swore and thought about that, a frown line between her brows. She gathered her blond hair and pulled it all into a ponytail behind her head, then tied it into a knot in a single, graceful movement. She rubbed the frown line.

"Well... I guess I'm starting over, whether I had wanted to or not. I won't have that life I thought I would with Ethan. I would have had to go through everything anyway to decide what I wanted to keep or toss. All of those memories..."

Her life with Ethan had been short. She was young and would be able to find someone else. Her experience with Ethan, both the marriage and his breakdown, would always be a part of who she was, but it had been brief, and hopefully would not control her future.

"How do you sort things, when you do a cleanout like that?" Ashley asked practically. "Would it be easy for me to go through and decide what I want to keep?"

Graham was happy to discuss the logistics of his work rather than relationships and mental illness and how to recover from an experience like she'd had. Or like Ethan had been through.

"All of the clothing and soft furnishings are boxed together. That's stuff like pillows, blankets, throws..."

Ashley nodded. "And if I didn't want it, would you just take it to the dump, or...?"

"I had planned to take it to Scarlett's Secrets. I talked to Ms. Stone, and she agreed to look at it, buy it as a lot."

"Why don't you do that, then?" Ashley picked at the hospital gown. "Nothing is going to fit anymore and I don't really want to be reminded of our home together."

"It won't be very much money for you."

"No," she brushed this idea away with a flip of her hand. "You keep it. All you did trying to find me... you didn't get paid for that. It was just out of the goodness of your heart. You could have been doing something more profitable at the time."

"The things I thought were valuable or sentimental, that you should have taken with you if you had left voluntarily, I kept that separate. Joiner has most of it, as evidence that you hadn't left voluntarily."

"So I can ask him for that. Or at least... to see what he has."

Graham nodded.

She wouldn't want Ethan's sketchbook, of course. "And then... I have chemicals to go to hazardous materials, and a few things to go to the dump. Not a lot. And Ethan's things."

Another heavy sigh. She smoothed her sheets. "He never had very much. Maybe they could be donated... maybe back to the shelter. That's where most of it came from anyway."

Graham nodded. "Okay. I can do that. I'm... sorry for all of this. I know that doesn't make any difference. Everyone is sorry about it, but it doesn't change what happened and what you went through."

"Yeah," she acknowledged. "It was really... a terrible experience. I just lost my husband, but no one is mourning him. They are all mad at him, horrified. They can't understand how he could go from being... so quiet and tender, like he was, to... a monster. They think it was his fault. And they don't understand why I'm not mad at him; I'm sad." She rolled her eyes up to the ceiling, fighting tears. "They are all so angry."

"It wasn't... something he chose to do. The things people do when they have a break with reality... that they are not responsible for them."

Ashley nodded. "I know Ethan would never have chosen to do what he did. I *knew* him. He wasn't... that monster."

They were both silent for a minute.

"Would you go see him?" Ashley asked tentatively. "I can't, you know. Even when I get out of here, and even if they say he's better and we could start over... I know I can't. But I want someone to talk to him who understands, and I think you do, more than anyone else I've talked to."

"Oh..." Graham held his hands up to slow her down, "I don't know if I can say that."

"You're the only one other than me who isn't mad at him. If I ask one of them to talk to him, he's just going to get... dressed down. They're going to yell at him and tell him everything he did wrong, and that he should have done something to stop it. I don't even know if he'll remember anything he did. Throwing it back in his face would be cruel, especially when he had no control over it."

"I'm not a psychologist. Look, I'm just... the junk man. I don't have any training in this kind of thing; I'm just your man on the street."

"All the better," she approved. "He'll have plenty of therapists and professionals. They'll all try to use their psychological mumbo jumbo to make him feel better. But he's like you. Blunt and straightforward. He won't believe them if they tell him that I forgive him. But you can tell him. You can look him straight in the eye and tell him with no mumbo jumbo that I'll always love the man I married. And that I forgive him," she met Graham's gaze frankly. "He'll have to find a way to go on with his life alone. I don't know how he'll do that. But maybe if he knows that I don't blame him for his mental illness... maybe that will lift the burden a little."

Graham broke eye contact and looked down at his hands. He liked that he was getting callouses now. Callouses from hard, honest work.

"I don't know if I'll even be able to get in to talk to him."

"They have to let him see people. He can't just stay locked in a room by himself forever."

"But he won't even know who I am. He won't approve it."

"Please. Try. And if he doesn't say yes right away, then go back later when he's doing better and is ready for company. And tell him goodbye for me. And that I forgive him."

"You could write him a letter."

"Maybe I will. But he needs to hear it. He won't believe it if it's just written down."

Graham rubbed his face. "I'll try," he agreed finally. "But I can't promise anything. It isn't going to be easy."

# CHAPTER
# FIFTY-SEVEN

G raham was even more impressed walking back into Scarlett's Secrets the second time. After the upheaval in his life recently, dealing with all of the messiness of Ethan's life and his breakdown, walking into the clean, bright, well-organized thrift store gave him the same feeling as when he finished a big job and looked at the cleaned and organized room or home and felt a sense of pride and achievement.

He hadn't put any work into Scarlett's Secrets but still felt that same sense of peace and order. He just stood there and looked at it for a moment.

Scarlett finished with a customer and drifted over to him. She stopped a few feet away, arms folded, and looked him up and down. "Well, it's the garbage man."

"In the flesh," he agreed.

"I was expecting to see you a couple of weeks ago. Does it usually take you this long to follow through on your promises?"

"I suspect you probably heard that... there were some complications with Ashley Carter's cleanout. I got the job done on schedule, but of course, I couldn't just get rid of all the personal items I cleared out of the apartment without knowing who it now belonged to and whether I had their permission to deal with it."

She nodded slowly, green eyes bright and thoughtful.

"So, scruples too? You could have just dumped everything. The landlord hired you, and you did what you were hired to do. It probably belonged to him."

"Probably?" Graham shrugged. Rather than going for a serious discussion about legal ownership and whether it would have been right or wrong to simply deal with Ashley's possessions as if they had truly been abandoned when he had doubts about the fact. He didn't always go with the "legal" or "ethical" choice anyway, so it was disingenuous to suggest that he did. "I don't think they would have looked very good on Marcel."

Scarlett cracked a grin. She chuckled. "I'm gonna have to trust you on that one."

"Now that I have all of the issues sorted out, do you want me to bring the boxes into your back room, or come see them at the warehouse, or...?"

"Where are they right now?"

"On my truck." Graham nodded to the window so she could see it was just outside the shop.

"Why don't I just come out and look at it there? No need to move stuff back and forth."

He had half hoped that she would suggest he bring them into the store for her to look at. She would have a harder time saying she didn't want them if they were already in her store.

Maybe she knew that too. She gave him an amused eyebrow lift, then headed toward the door. "Christie, would you keep an eye on things for a few minutes?"

A younger woman near the back of the store called back that she would and moved closer to the till in case any customers should need her.

Graham put down the tailgate of his truck, and Scarlett jumped nimbly into the bed to look through the boxes. She went through one at a time, looking at and feeling the fabrics, taking a couple of pieces out to shake them out and look at the entirety.

"You're right," she agreed. "These are good pieces. But why would she want to give them to the shop now that she's back? What's she going to wear?"

"She wants to make a fresh start," Graham gave her Ashley's reasoning. "She's lost a lot of weight and says it won't fit her now, but I think it is more than that. I think... she doesn't want anything to remind her of her time with Ethan. She'll start over... maybe she'll come here to find something new."

"She'll just put the weight back on as she recovers."

Graham nodded. "Yeah. That's why I think she just wants to get rid of anything she associates with her life with Ethan."

"I suppose so." Scarlett folded the outfit she had been looking at and replaced it in the box. "How is she? Is she going to be okay?"

"She's... strong. I think she'll be able to move on without too much damage." He shrugged, not to dismiss Ashley's painful experience, but to acknowledge it wasn't any of his business. "She's focused on moving forward."

Scarlett shook her head slowly. "Stronger than I would be. If something like that happened to me... I don't know how I would move forward."

"Then again, we don't have much choice in the matter. Life demands that we keep going. Unless we make... the other choice."

He was not comfortable discussing the possibility of suicide, so he moved on with the conversation. He gestured to the boxes.

"So, are you interested?"

She nodded. "I'll take them," she agreed. "And if there are other lots you want me to look at from other jobs, I'll take a look. You're right; this is quality stuff." She jumped down from the bed of the truck. "And the fact that you cared about whether you had the right to deal with them or not makes me think you're an okay guy. Even if you are an outsider."

"Well, thanks!"

"And if you see Ashley, tell her I'll give her a special discount if she wants to come by Scarlett's Secrets to outfit her new wardrobe."

"I don't know if I'll see her, but I'll be sure to let her know. Will you know her if she comes into the store?"

She nodded. "Sure, I know who she is. And her picture has been in the Chronicle a couple of times."

"Yeah. Okay, great. Do you want me to drive around back, and I'll bring these to your door?"

Scarlett nodded and snapped his tailgate back into place.

"Haul them in, garbage man."

# CHAPTER
# FIFTY-EIGHT

Graham passed the time uncomfortably in the waiting room when he was told that someone else was already in with Ethan. Boots, probably. He wondered what the "anchoring" item Boots had brought from home was. A teddy bear? A photograph? Something that no one else would have seen the significance of, like a polished river stone?

What would Graham want from back east, if he had needed something to help him to make a positive connection with the past and move on? He had deliberately left his former life behind. Would he want something that reminded him of his ex, Candice? Certainly not. Something that reminded him of his mother or another family member? Or to the job that had done him in? Happy places he had once cared about?

Sometimes, it was best to leave the past in the past.

He looked up as someone came into the waiting room from the direction of the patient rooms.

Sara Lapp.

She saw him at the same time and stopped in her tracks. She looked at him for a moment, then came over and sat in the chair beside him, inching it away so that their elbows were not touching.

"Graham. You came to see Nicholas?"

He nodded. "I know it's kind of weird, when I don't even know him. But Ashley wanted me to see him for her. And... I don't imagine he is getting a lot of sympathetic visitors."

"No," Sara agreed grimly. "You would be surprised at all of the... hostility people feel toward someone who never did anything to harm them and who they don't know anything about."

"Maybe not," Graham countered.

"People I would have counted as friends have said the nastiest things. It is a revelation of who my real friends are. And who are... decent strangers." She inclined her head, indicating Graham with her gaze.

Graham shifted uncomfortably. "I don't know him," he repeated. "I can't judge what he did or how much control he had over it. I am only doing what Ashley asked."

"And she is probably the only one qualified to judge."

Graham nodded. "Is he... going to use *non compos mentis* as a legal defense?"

"That's private," she told him. Then, with a shake of her head. "Of course he is. It is the only option."

"I understand it's a very difficult ruling to get. Do you think he'll be able to? I mean, with Ashley backing him up... she obviously didn't think he was in control of himself when he... did what he did."

"You would have to talk to his lawyer. I don't want you to get the wrong idea, Mr. Hall. I'm not... I'm not here to act as his parent or guardian. I'm not in charge of his legal team or in their meetings. I'm just... visiting my husband's nephew, a boy I once cared for, giving him what emotional support I can." Her voice cracked.

"Sorry. I understand. And you're right; it isn't any of my business. I feel a little responsible because Ashley asked me to talk to him, but I'm not in charge of anything either. I haven't even met him."

Sara took a tissue out of her purse and blew her nose.

"He's not guilty. You know who is guilty? The people who bullied, abused, and terrorized him. His father. Everyone else who abused him." She shook her head, voice choked with anger. "I talked to Boots. You know who else? The stupid social worker who took him away from the one sanctuary he found. He had peace living with Boots, and she decided he didn't belong there."

Graham nodded awkwardly. Sara took a deep breath, composing herself.

"He's doing better right now. He's back on his meds, and he has been getting intense therapy. I don't know what is involved. But he's... acting more like himself now. The old Nicholas we used to know."

Graham nodded politely. The old Nicholas who had been quiet and sad, not the one she had sent away because she feared for her children's safety.

Sara twisted the tissue in her hands.

"I know you'll be careful with him," she said tentatively. "You'll try not to upset him, won't you? He's been through so much."

Graham wanted to point out what Ashley had been through, but Sara was fully aware of that. She knew what Ethan had put Ashley through, probably with more detail than most people in town. But she was also aware of what Nicholas had gone through when his father had killed his mother. And when he had been shuffled back and forth across the country, no one able to help him and predators just waiting for an opportunity to hurt him.

"I'll be as careful as I can," Graham agreed. "I probably won't be in there very long."

It wasn't like they would have long, soulful conversations about the tapioca pudding. Graham would do what he had come there for, and then his obligation would be over.

# CHAPTER
# FIFTY-NINE

Graham didn't know whether to expect Ethan to be in a hospital bed, a straitjacket, or a rubber room.

As it turned out, he was ushered into a room probably used for meeting with lawyers or family members. It didn't look any different from any small corporate meeting room in which he'd had dozens of meetings. Except there was no whiteboard or video equipment other than the surveillance camera. And an orderly who stood by watching them to make sure that Ethan didn't do anything disruptive. At least, Graham assumed it was for his protection and not because they expected him to do something to hurt Ethan.

Ethan was in a t-shirt and scrub pants. Not a flapping peek-a-boo gown, but nothing with a belt, shoelaces, or pockets. He walked with his hands in front of him held close together like he was handcuffed, but when he sat down at the small, round table, Graham could see that he was not. His hands were free, and when he sat down, he rested his hands on the arms of the chair and they were not chained or anchored to anything.

Graham had been expecting handcuffs or other restraints, so their absence was disconcerting.

Ethan looked him over uncertainly. Graham smiled in a way that he hoped Ethan would see as friendly and non-threatening.

"Hi, Ethan. My name is Graham Hall. I don't know if you have been told who I am? By Detective Joiner or Sara?"

Ethan shook his head slightly.

"I was hired to clean out your apartment after you abandoned it. You remember leaving a note and your keys on the counter so that Marcel would know you weren't coming back?"

Another hesitant shake of the head. "I don't remember a lot of things that happened," Ethan confessed, passing a hand over his forehead as if that might help wipe the cobwebs away.

He held something in his hand Graham hadn't noticed to begin with, and he fidgeted with it now, moving it inside his hand with his thumb.

"You knew you left the apartment and weren't going back there," Graham said encouragingly. It felt important to establish that Graham had been there for a good reason, that they hadn't just tried to steal the apartment out from under him.

"No," Ethan agreed slowly. "I was going to the house. Back home."

"Do you remember when your family lived there? With your grandpa?"

Ethan stared off into space. "It was a *long* time ago." He drew the word out.

"Yes. You would have been pretty young. It was before you went out east. But you remembered that? And you knew how to find it? You must have had the address. Maybe Uncle Boots gave it to you."

"Boots?" Ethan perked up at the name and glanced around as if expecting his uncle to be there.

"He didn't come with me today, but I'm sure he's planning to come and see you again."

If he weren't already headed back to Kentucky. Boots must have things that needed to be looked after on the farm. Now that Ethan had been found, Boots knew he would be looked after.

Maybe he had talked to Sara about her visiting Ethan in the future.

Ethan's head tilted forward, chin to chest, bottom lip protruding like a child's.

He readjusted the thing he was fidgeting with in his hand. About half the length of his finger and covered with short, white fur. Ethan stroked the soft fur with his thumb. A rabbit's foot.

Ethan caught Graham's eyes on it.

"A lucky rabbit's foot," he explained, his cheeks getting a little pink, as if he was embarrassed to be caught with it.

"Not so lucky for the rabbit," Graham quipped.

Ethan gave a short bleat of laughter. "That's what Boots said."

"Did he bring it to you?"

Ethan nodded, stroking it, his eyes far away. *Something to ground him,* Boots had said, but Ethan seemed distant as he rubbed the fur. Back in Kentucky, where he had lived with his uncle.

"Why did you go back to the house?" Graham asked. "Why did you take Ashley there?"

Ethan looked at him and didn't answer. Graham was the one to look away this time. He probably didn't want to know the answer to that question.

"Ashley asked me to talk to you. She can't come to see you, but she wanted to make sure you know... she forgives you for what happened."

Ethan's brows drew down. "He hurt her."

Graham swallowed. "You did. Yes. But Ashley knows it was because... your head wasn't working right. You didn't know what you were doing."

"He said she had to be punished for what she did."

"*He* said?"

Ethan nodded. "He said she had to pay. For what she did. She was..." His mouth formed words, but he didn't say them aloud.

Was that because the orderly would take him back away if he

used crude language? Because he didn't want to offend Graham? Or because he was embarrassed by them?

"Who said that? You? Your father?"

Ethan nodded, mouthing words. Maybe both. His father had said it all of those years ago about his mother, and then when Ethan had felt betrayed by Ashley getting her promotion, he had shielded himself by calling Ashley those same names.

"That's not important right now," Graham assured him.

Did Graham really think he was going to sort it all out? For whom? The psychologists? The police? For Ethan's court case? Besides, he didn't want to know the details. He didn't want to know exactly what Ethan's father had done to his mother, or what Ethan had done to Ashley. It was dangerous to ask. He didn't want to trigger an emotional or violent reaction from Ethan, and he didn't want to envision it.

It was bad enough that he had seen Ashley come out of that house, barely able to stand and covered with bruises.

"What's important," he said slowly, "is that Ashley forgives you. She wanted you to know. She can't come here herself, but she wanted you to know anyway."

"*He* hurt her," Ethan said. "Not me. I would never hurt her."

"No?" Graham didn't know what else to say.

"I saved her. I protected her." Ethan raised his eyes to Graham's face. "I'll always protect her. You tell her. I'll always protect her."

When Graham didn't respond to this, Ethan reached out and grasped his wrist. He held on to Graham with bony fingers like a bird's talons. "I'll always protect her."

The orderly moved in, as Graham had known he would. He touched Ethan on the shoulder. "Come on back to your room now, Ethan."

Ethan didn't move.

"Come on." The orderly's fingers tightened. Ethan still held tightly to Graham's wrist.

"Ethan."

"I'm not Ethan."

"Okay, buddy. You're not. But you still need to come back to your room."

"Not *buddy*."

The orderly rolled his eyes at Graham and let out a hissing sigh to let him know that he was not conceding Ethan's point, but merely placating him.

"Nicholas."

The patient let go of Graham's wrist and stood up. He was the same height as Graham, which surprised him. He'd thought of Ethan as being smaller and younger, a frail shadow of a man. Still half a child.

His dark, deep-set eyes met Graham's.

"I always protected her."

# CHAPTER
## SIXTY

G raham was surprised to see Detective Joiner and a couple of other cops at the bar when he stopped in for a drink. He had thought that Joiner had only stopped in on the previous occasion to talk to Graham, not that it was a regular hangout. He didn't remember seeing many cops there in the previous months.

But then, Joiner wasn't in uniform, and Graham would not previously have known he was a cop.

Joiner had a couple of drinks with his friends, then looked at Graham sideways a couple of times as if trying to decide whether to approach him.

Graham jerked his chin at Joiner, inviting him over. Joiner sat across from him and drummed his fingers on the table, glancing around.

"Not everyone wants a cop sitting with them," he commented.

"Not like I have a reputation to worry about."

"Drinking alone?"

"I usually do."

"Bleeding Hearts Valley isn't always the friendliest place toward outsiders... but you could make a few friends. If you wanted to."

"Maybe I'm not ready for that yet."

"Because of the trouble you had out east?" Joiner prodded.

Graham was still not ready to talk about that. "Because I'm not the most social guy." He sipped his drink. "Maybe inviting a cop over for a chat wasn't the smartest thing to do."

"Aw, I'm not here to give you any hassle." Joiner made a motion to wave all of that away. "In fact... I thought you might like to hear the rest of the story."

"The rest of what story?"

"Ethan's story. Nicholas's story."

"And he went to prison for the rest of his life, and everyone else lived happily ever after?"

"No, not the end of the story... the beginning."

Graham raised his brows.

Joiner sipped his drink. "Have you noticed how people talk about how his mother died, but no one mentioned what happened to his father?"

Graham nodded. "Yeah. I did wonder about that once or twice."

Joiner folded his arms and leaned forward, elbows on the table. "The police were called out to their house for a welfare check. People were concerned about not having seen them lately. They lived in an isolated area and if someone suffered an accident, it might be a long time before they got any help."

"If anyone suffered an 'accident' like his mother?"

"When they arrived at the farmhouse, they found his mother dead," Joiner acknowledged. "Starved and beaten by her husband. Throat slashed, like in the pictures. And he was also dead, a gunshot wound to the head."

"Ate his gun?" Graham asked, hating the brutal, casual way the words sounded when they came out of his mouth.

Joiner shook his head slowly. "Gun on the floor at his side. His fingerprints on it. But there was a significant amount of doubt over whether he could have been the one to pull the trigger."

Graham stared at him. "Was someone else there? He accused her of adultery, so was there a lover? Someone else who had been there and left?"

"It had been several days since they had died, which made it difficult to establish time of death, alibis, and who may or may not have been at the farm when they died."

"And where was Ethan?"

"*Nicholas* was there. Nine years old."

"He didn't know how to call for help? He'd been in the house with two dead bodies for days?"

No wonder Sara had said that it was too horrible to discuss the details.

"He was not allowed to use the phone. So he didn't. He was half-starved and beaten, too."

Graham sat there staring at Joiner for a long time. "Do you want me to think that Nicholas killed his father?"

*I always protected her.*

Joiner spread his hands apart, shrugging. "It's on the books as murder-suicide. The father killed her and then himself. Case closed. But the evidence is definitely hinky. It's 'close enough' to call it suicide. That's better than 'unknown.' Better than saddling it on the kid."

"But you think it was Nicholas."

Joiner sat back, nodding. "I do."

# CHAPTER
# SIXTY-ONE

Graham had learned a number of new skills as he had built his junk removal business. It was surprising to him how many locked cabinets, drawers, lockboxes, and small safes he encountered. He had hired a locksmith in the beginning, and as well as unlocking various padlocks and tumblers for him, Harold Beamer had shown Graham how the different locks worked and how easy it was to unlock most of them with the right tools and patient practice.

Graham didn't usually need to call Harold anymore. He still did if there were a complicated or particularly difficult lock that Graham couldn't conquer. And he sent Harold a little tip every time he picked a lock. After all, Harold had been generous with his knowledge and in doing so had worked himself out of a series of jobs. Graham felt he should be compensated for that professional advice. Harold got paid without the overhead and the time and effort of going out to the routine jobs and was incentivized to keep helping Graham in the more difficult cases. And Graham didn't have to call for a locksmith every time and paid less than he would have for an actual call. It was a satisfactory arrangement for both of them.

Despite having such a large, lavish home, Marty Ballantyne

did not have a very good security system. He seemed to think the address or the deadbolt on the front door was enough to keep out unwanted company, and that the burglar alarm was largely super-fluous. Using his birthdate for the disarming code was stupid and lazy.

The house was quiet when Graham arrived. All of the staff had left for the day, and from what Graham had observed when he had been there previously, there was no live-in staff. Marty had eaten out and it was the night for his daughter's tennis instruc-tion, so his wife and daughter were out.

When Marty walked into the house after a long day of work, he turned automatically to disarm the alarm before realizing it wasn't armed. He turned back around, his mind registering the fact that there was someone sitting in his favorite chair in the living room, the only one that was actually comfortable.

"What?" He focused in on Graham. "What the hell are you doing in my house?"

Marty fumbled awkwardly for his phone, struggling briefly before managing to pull it from his pocket. He tapped in the first couple of numbers and then stopped.

Maybe he wondered why Graham wasn't trying to stop him from calling the police. Maybe he was already thinking one step ahead, scripting what he would say to the police when they arrived. And what Graham was going to say. And the complica-tions it would cause Marty.

He stared at Graham, the phone in his hand, the call incomplete.

"I already paid you what you asked," he snarled. "I thought that was the end of our transaction."

"You made a very generous donation," Graham agreed. "I, too, thought that was the last that I would hear from you."

"Then what are you doing here?"

"Somebody keeps trying to kill me."

There was a beat of silence and just the trace of a smile flitted across Marty's face before he protested. "That doesn't have anything to do with me. A guy like you must have a lot of enemies. It must be someone else."

"My other clients know better than to send armed gunmen after me. You, apparently, need a little hand-holding."

Marty stood there defiantly at first, but his face gradually drained of color as he grappled with the gravity of the situation. If he had just let things go, no one would ever have drawn a connection between him and Graham. Graham had not hit him up for another payment, though Marty had clearly expected him to. But now at least three people, and as many as five, could connect Marty to Graham. What was he going to do to eliminate that problem?

"You know, I've gotten pretty cozy with Detective Joiner on the Bleeding Hearts Valley police force," Graham said conversationally. "He's a smart guy, and he's been curious about the two attempts that have been made on my life. I don't know how close he is to tracking down the gunmen, but there are license plates, traffic cams, potential eyewitnesses, anyone who saw a certain motorcycle rider with a bright yellow face..."

Marty cleared his throat. "What do you want?" he demanded, "Another 'donation'?"

"No, I think you have suffered enough. Unless you're stupid enough to continue on the path you have begun." This was ambiguous and could refer to Marty's old interests as evidenced by those pictures or his latest business arrangements made with armed gunmen. "I'm of the opinion that our relationship would be better served by the termination of certain activities."

Marty nodded jerkily.

"Let me be clear. If there is a third attempt made on my life, Detective Joiner or someone else on the police force will receive a letter. It doesn't matter whether I survive or not, they will receive a letter detailing our relationship and certain pieces of evidence that will confirm your guilt to their satisfaction."

"You'd better not—" Marty started defensively, then cut himself off and decided that he should not dig himself any deeper into the hole he was already standing in. His lips pressed together and he didn't protest any further.

Graham looked at his watch. "Your family will be home soon, so I should probably be on my way. I was afraid you were going to be late and wouldn't get home before them. You really should be more considerate and not spend so much time at the office."

Marty looked at the face of his phone, hit the cancel button, and put it back away.

"They could be here any time."

"Then I'll be on my way. And we shouldn't need to talk again, should we?"

"No," Marty agreed. He swallowed. "No need for that."

Graham stood up and walked out of the house.

The Sixth Street Mission had been grateful for the clothing and other items that Graham had donated. It was a small gesture, but Mike expressed his appreciation for it, telling Graham that every little bit helped.

Looking at the display on the wall that listed various large donors, sponsors, and programs that provided services to the shelter, Graham noticed one foundation that focused on mental health and recovery from childhood trauma.

"Is this a good company?" he asked, directing Mike's attention to it. "Do you work with them much?"

"Oh, yes. They provide counseling for all of our men, and they have been instrumental in getting a lot of them off the street and onto the path of wellness."

"We need more programs like that," Graham observed.

"We do. Or more funding for the ones that exist."

Graham nodded thoughtfully.

Later that day, the foundation received a twenty-thousand-dollar donation from a source that chose to remain anonymous to assist them in their counseling program.

It wouldn't change what had happened to Ashley, what had happened to Nicholas and his mother years ago, or whatever Nicholas had dealt with in foster and residential care before aging out.

But it was a start.

## Read the series

I hope *An Abrupt Departure* kept you turning the pages late into the night. If you enjoyed this story, the most powerful way to support it is with a quick review or recommendation to your friends. Your words help other readers discover the book and make a real difference.

**Please leave a review at your favorite book store**

Don't miss my next release — and claim a free book today!

Sign up for my newsletter at pdworkman.com to receive a **free bonus** and get updates on new page-turners, special offers, and more.

## SIGN UP FOR MY NEWSLETTER AND GET A FREE BONUS

NEWS • PROMOS • OFFERS • NEW RELEASES

**More books about Graham Hall will be coming soon!**

If you liked the tension and atmosphere of *An Abrupt Departure*, meet **Zachary Goldman** — a private investigator haunted by his past and driven to uncover the truth.

Start with **She Wore Mourning**,
Book 1 of the Zachary Goldman Mysteries.

**Check it out!**

# CHAPTER
## ONE

Zachary Goldman stared down the telephoto lens at the subjects before him. It was one of those days that left tourists gaping over the gorgeous scenery. Dark trees against crisp white snow, with the mountains as a backdrop. Like the picture on a Christmas card.

The thought made Zachary feel sick.

But he wasn't looking at the scenery. He was looking at the man and the woman in a passionate embrace. The pretty young woman's cheeks were flushed pink, more likely with her excitement than the cold, since she had barely stepped out of her car to greet the man. He had a swarthier complexion and a thin black beard, and was currently turned away from Zachary's camera.

Zachary wasn't much to look at himself. Average height, black hair cut too short, his own three-day growth of beard not hiding how pinched and pale his face was. He'd never considered himself a good catch.

He waited patiently for them to move, to look around at their surroundings so that he could get a good picture of their faces.

They thought they were alone; that no one could see them without being seen. They hadn't counted on the fact that Zachary had been surveilling them for a couple of weeks and had known where they would go. They gave him lots of warning so that he could park his car out of sight, camouflage himself in the trees, and settle in to wait for their appearance. He was no amateur; he'd been a private investigator since she had been choosing wedding dresses for her Barbie dolls.

He held down the shutter button to take a series of shots as they came up for air and looked around at the magnificent surroundings, smiling at each other, eyes shining.

All the while, he was trying to keep the negative thoughts at bay. Why had he fallen into private detection? It was one of the few ways he could make a living using his skill with a camera. He could have chosen another profession. He didn't need to spend his whole life following other people, taking pictures of their most private moments. What was the real point of his job? He destroyed lives, something he'd had his fill of long ago. When was the last time he'd brought a smile to a client's face? A real, genuine smile? He had wanted to make a difference in people's lives; to exonerate the innocent.

Zachary's phone started to buzz in his pocket. He lowered the camera and turned around, walking farther into the grove of trees. He had the pictures he needed. Anything else would be overkill.

He pulled out his phone and looked at it. Not recognizing the number, he swiped the screen to answer the call.

"Goldman Investigations."

"Uh... yes... Is this Mr. Goldman?" a voice inquired. Older, female, with a tentative quaver.

"Yes, this is Zachary," he confirmed, subtly nudging her away from the 'mister.'

"Mr. Goldman, my name is Molly Hildebrandt."

He hoped she wasn't calling her about her sixty-something-year-old husband and his renewed interest in sex. If it was another infidelity case, he was going to have to turn it down for his own sanity. He would even take a lost dog or wedding ring. As long as the ring wasn't on someone else's finger now.

"Mrs. Hildebrandt. How can Goldman Investigations help you?"

Of course, she had probably already guessed that Goldman Investigations consisted of only one employee. Most people seemed to sense that from the size of his advertisements. From the fact that he listed a post office box number instead of a business suite downtown or in one of the newer commercial areas. It wasn't really a secret.

"I don't know whether you have been following the news at all about Declan Bond, the little boy who drowned...?"

Zachary frowned. He trudged back toward his car.

"I'm familiar with the basics," he hedged. A four- or five-year-old boy whose round face and feathery dark hair had been pasted all over the news after a search for a missing child had ended tragically.

"They announced a few weeks ago that it was determined to be an accident."

Zachary ground his teeth. "Yes...?"

"Mr. Goldman, I was Declan's grandma." Her voice cracked. Zachary waited, listening to her sniffles and sobs as she tried to get herself under control. "I'm sorry. This has been very difficult for me. For everyone."

"Yes."

"Mr. Goldman, I don't believe that it was an accident. I'm looking for someone who would investigate the matter privately."

Zachary breathed out. A homicide investigation? Of a child? He'd told himself that he would take anything that wasn't infidelity, but if there was one thing that was more depressing than couples cheating on each other, it was the death of a child.

"I'm sure there are private investigators that would be more qualified for a homicide case than I am, Mrs. Hildebrandt. My schedule is pretty full right now."

Which, of course, was a lie. He had the usual infidelities, insurance investigations, liabilities, and odd requests. The dregs of the private investigation business. Nothing substantial like a homicide. It was a high-profile case. A lot of volunteers had shown up to help, expecting to find a child who had wandered out of his own yard, expecting to find him dirty and crying, not floating face down in a pond. A lot of people had mourned the death of a child they hadn't even known existed before his disappearance.

"I need your help, Mr. Goldman. Zachary. I can't afford a big name, but you've got good references. You've investigated deaths before. Can't you help me?"

He wondered who she had talked to. It wasn't like there were a lot of people who would give him a bad reference. He was competent and usually got the job done, but he wasn't a big name.

"I could meet with you," he finally conceded. "The first consultation is free. We'll see what kind of a case you have and whether I want to take it. I'm not making any promises at this point. Like I said, my schedule is pretty full already."

She gave a little half-sob. "Thank you. When are you able to come?"

After he had hung up, Zachary climbed into his car, putting his camera down on the floor in front of the passenger seat where it couldn't fall, and started the car. For a while, he sat there, staring out the front windshield at the magical, sparkling, Christmas-card scene. Every year, he told himself it would be better. He would get over it and be able to move on and to enjoy the holiday season like everyone else. Who cared about his crappy childhood experiences? People moved on.

And when he had married Bridget, he had thought he was going to achieve it. They would have a fairy-tale Christmas. They would have hot chocolate after skating at the public rink. They would wander down Main Street looking at the lights and the crèche in front of the church. They would open special, meaningful presents from each other.

But they'd fought over Christmas. Maybe it was Zachary's fault. Maybe he had sabotaged it with his gloom. The season brought with it so much baggage. There had been no skating rink. No hot chocolate, only hot tempers. No walks looking at the lights or the nativity. They had practically thrown their gifts at each other, flouncing off to their respective corners to lick their wounds and pout away the holiday.

He'd still cherished the thought that perhaps the next year there would be a baby. What could be more perfect than Christmas with a baby? It would unite them. Make them a real family. Just like Zachary had longed for since he'd lost his own family. He and Bridget and a baby. Maybe even twins. Their own little family in their own little happy bubble.

But despite a positive pregnancy test, things had gone horribly wrong.

Zachary stared at the bright white scenery and blinked hard, trying to shake off the shadows of the past. The past was past. Over and done. This year he was back to baching it for Christmas. Just him and a beer and *It's a Wonderful Life* on TV.

He put the car in reverse and didn't look into the rear-view mirror as he backed up, even knowing about the precipice behind him. He'd deliberately parked where he'd have to back up toward the cliff when he was done. There was a guardrail, but if he backed up too quickly, the car would go right through it, and who could say whether it had been accidental or deliberate? He had been cold-stone sober and had been out on a job. Mrs. Hildebrandt could testify that he had been calm and sober during their call. It would be ruled an accident.

But his bumper didn't even touch the guardrail before he shifted into drive and pulled forward onto the road.

He'd meet with the grandmother. Then, assuming he did not take the case, there would always be another opportunity.

Life was full of opportunities.

# CHAPTER
# TWO

M olly Hildebrandt was much as Zachary expected her to be. A woman in her sixties who looked ten or twenty years older with the stress of the high-profile death of her grandchild. Gray, curling hair. Pale, wrinkled skin. She wasn't hunched over, though. She sat up straight and tall as if she'd gone to a finishing school where she'd been forced to walk and sit with an encyclopedia on her head. Did they still do that? Had they ever done it?

"Mr. Goldman, thank you for seeing me so quickly," she greeted formally, holding her hand out for him to shake when he arrived at her door.

"Please, call me Zachary, ma'am. I'm not really comfortable with Mr. Goldman."

Telling her that he wasn't comfortable with it meant that she would be a bad hostess if she continued to address him that way, instead of her seeing it as a way of showing him respect. He hadn't done anything to deserve respect and was much happier if she would talk to him like the gardener or her next-door neighbor.

Not that there was any gardener. Molly lived in a small apartment in an old, dark brick building that was sturdy enough, but

had been around longer than Zachary had been alive. The interior, when she invited him in, was bright and cozy. She had made
coffee, and he breathed in the aroma in the air appreciatively. It
wasn't hot chocolate after skating, but he could use a cup or two
of coffee to warm him up after his surveillance. Standing around
in the snow for a couple of hours had chilled him, even though
he'd dressed for the weather.

Molly escorted him to the tiny living room.

"And you must call me Molly," she insisted.

She eyed the big camera case as he put it down. Zachary gave a
grimace.

"Sorry. I didn't come to take your picture; I just don't like to
leave expensive equipment in the car."

"Oh," she nodded politely. She didn't ask him who he had
been taking pictures of. That wouldn't be gracious. She would
have to imagine instead, and she would probably be correct in her
guess.

They fussed for a few minutes with their coffees. Zachary
wrapped his fingers around his mug, waiting for the coffee to cool
and his fingers to warm. It felt good. Comforting. He waited for
Molly to begin her story.

"You probably think that I'm just being a fussy old lady," she
said. "Imagining something sinister when it was just an accident."

"Not at all. Why don't you tell me why you don't think it was
an accident?"

"I'm not *sure* at all," she clarified. "Maybe they're right.
Maybe it was an accident. It isn't that I doubt their findings..."
she trailed off. "Not really. I know they had to do an autopsy and
all that. We waited for months for them to come back with the
manner of death. I thought that once they ruled, everyone would
feel better."

"But you still have doubts?"

"I'm worried for my daughter."

Zachary blinked at her and waited for more.

"She's not well. I had hoped that once they released the

body... and after the memorial... and after the manner of death was announced... each milestone, I thought, it would get better. It would be easier for her, but..." Molly shook her head. "She's getting worse and worse. Time isn't helping."

"Your daughter was Declan's mother."

"Yes. Of course."

"What's her name?"

"Isabella Hildebrandt," Molly said, her brows drawn down like he should have known that. "You know. *The Happy Artist.*"

Zachary had heard of *The Happy Artist*. She was on TV and was popular among the locals. Zachary didn't know whether she was syndicated nationally or just on one of the local stations. She had a painting instruction show every Sunday morning, and people awaited her next show like a popular soap. Most of the people Zachary knew who watched the show didn't paint and never intended to take it up. She was an institution.

"Oh, yes," Zachary agreed. "Of course, I know *The Happy Artist*. I didn't put the names together."

"When it was in the news, they said who she was. They said it was *The Happy Artist*'s child."

"Sure. Of course," Zachary agreed. He rubbed the dark stubble along his jaw. He should have gone home to shave and clean up before meeting with Molly. He looked like he'd been on a three-day stakeout. He *had* been on a three-day stakeout. "I'm sorry. I didn't follow the story very closely. That's good for you; it means I don't have a lot of preconceived ideas about the case."

She looked at him for a minute, frowning. Reconsidering whether she really wanted to hire him? That wouldn't hurt his feelings.

"You were going to tell me about your daughter?" Zachary prompted. "I can understand how devastated she must be by her son's death."

"No. I don't think you can," Molly said flatly.

Zachary was taken aback. He shrugged and nodded, and waited for her to go on.

"Isabella has a history of... mental health issues. She was the one supervising Declan when he disappeared, and the guilt has been overwhelming for her."

That made perfect sense. Zachary sipped at his coffee, which had cooled enough not to scald him.

Molly went on. "I think... as horrible as it may sound... that it would be a relief for her if it turned out that Declan was taken from the yard, instead of just having wandered away."

"That may be, but how likely is that? Surely the police must have considered the possibility, and I can't manufacture evidence for your daughter, even if it would ease her mind."

"No... I realize that. I'm not expecting you to do anything dishonest. Just to investigate it. Read over the police reports. Interview witnesses again. Just see... if there's any possibility that there was... foul play. A third-party interfering, even if it was nothing malicious."

"I assume you know most of the details surrounding the case."

"Yes, of course."

"How likely do you think it is that the police missed something? Did they seem sloppy or like they didn't care? Did you think there were signs of foul play that they brushed off?"

"No." Molly gave a little shrug. "They seemed perfectly competent."

Zachary was silent. It wouldn't be difficult to read over the police reports and talk to the family. Was there any point?

"The only thing is..." Molly trailed off.

As impatient as Zachary was to get out of there, he knew it was no good pushing Molly to give it up any faster. She already knew she sounded crazy for asking him to reinvestigate a case where he wasn't going to be able to turn up anything new. For no reason, other than that it might help her daughter to come to terms with the child's death. He looked around the room. There were no pictures of Molly's husband, even old ones. There was no sign she had raised Isabella or any other children there. There were several pictures of a couple with a little child. Declan and Isabella and whatever the father's name was. There was one picture of Declan himself, occupying its own space, a little memorial to her lost grandson. There were no pictures of anyone else, so Zachary could only assume Isabella was an only child and Declan the only grandchild.

"Declan was afraid of water."

Zachary turned his eyes back to her. He considered. It wasn't totally inconceivable that a child afraid of the water would drown. He wouldn't know how to swim. If he fell in, he would panic, flail, and swallow water, rather than staying calm enough to float. Molly wiped at a tear.

"How afraid of the water was he?" Zachary asked.

"He wouldn't go near the water. He was terrified. He wouldn't have gone to the pond by himself."

"How tall was he?"

Molly gave a little shrug. "He was almost five years old. Three feet?"

"How steep were the banks of the pond and what was the terrain and foliage like?" He knew he would have to look at it for himself.

"I don't know what you want to know... there wasn't any shore to speak of. Just the pond. There were bulrushes. Cattails. Some trees. The ground is... uneven, but not hilly."

Zachary tried to visualize it. A child wouldn't be able to see the pond as far away as an adult would because of his short stature. If his view were further screened by the plant life, the banks steep and crumbly, he might not be able to see it until he was right on top of it. Or in it.

"It's not a lot to go on," he said. "The fact that he was afraid of water."

"I know." Molly used both hands to wipe her eyes. "I know that." She looked around the apartment, swallowing hard to get control of her emotions. "I just want the best for my baby. A parent always wants what's best. Growing up... I wasn't able to give her that. She didn't have an easy life. I wonder if..." She didn't have to finish the sentence this time. Zachary already knew what she was going to say. She wondered if that rough upbringing had caused Isabella's mental fragility. Whether things would have turned out differently if she'd been able to provide a stable environment. Molly sniffled. "Do you have children, Mr.—Zachary?"

Zachary felt that familiar pain in his chest. Like she'd plunged a knife into it. He cleared his throat and shook his head. "No. My marriage just recently ended. We didn't have any children."

"Oh." Her eyes searched his for the truth. Zachary looked away. "I'm sorry. I guess we all have our losses."

Although hers, the death of her grandson, was clearly more permanent than any relationship issues Zachary might have.

In the end, he agreed to do the preliminaries. Get the police reports. Walk the area around the house and pond. Talk to the parents. He gave her his lowest hourly fee. She clearly couldn't afford more. He wasn't even sure she'd be able to pay on receipt of his invoice. He might have to allow her a payment plan, something he normally didn't do, but something about the frail woman had gotten to him.

He put in an appearance at the police station, requesting a copy of the information available to the public, and handing over Molly Hildebrandt's request that he be provided as much information as possible for an independent evaluation.

"You got a new case?" Bowman grunted as he tapped through a few computer screens, getting a feel for how many files there were on the Declan Bond accident investigation file and how much of it he would be able to provide to Zachary.

"Yes," Zachary agreed. Obviously. He didn't encourage small talk; he really didn't want Bowman to start asking personal questions. They weren't friends, but they were friendly.

Bowman had helped Zachary track down missing documents before. He knew the right people to ask for permission and the best way to ask.

Bowman dug into his pocket and pulled out a pack of gum. He unwrapped a piece and popped it into his mouth, then offered one to Zachary as an afterthought.

"No, I'm good."

Bowman chewed vigorously as he studied each screen. He was a middle-aged man, with a middle-age spread, his belly sagging over his belt. His hairline had started receding, and occasionally he put on a pair of glasses for a moment and then took them off again, jamming them into his breast pocket.

"How's Bridget?" he asked.

Zachary swallowed. He took a deep breath and steeled himself for the conversation. Bowman looked away from his screen and at Zachary's face, eyebrows up.

"She's good. In remission."

"Good to hear." Bowman looked back at his computer again. "Good to hear. It's been a tough time for the two of you." His eyes flicked back to Zachary, and he backtracked. "I mean it's been tough for her. And for you."

"Yeah," Zachary agreed. He waved away any further fumbling explanation from Bowman. "So, what have we got? On the Bond case?"

"Right!" Bowman looked back at his screen. "I've got press releases and public statements for you. medical examiner's report. The cop in charge of the file was Eugene. He likes red."

Zachary blinked at Bowman, more baffled than usual by his abbreviated language. "What?"

"Eugene Taft. I know, it's a preposterous name, but he's never had a nickname that stuck. Eugene Taft."

"And he likes red."

"Wine," Bowman said as if Zachary was dense. "He likes red wine. You know, if you want to help things along, have a better chance of getting a look at the rest of that file, the officers' notes and all the background and interviews. If you have to apply some leverage."

"And for Eugene Taft, it's red wine."

"Has to be red," Bowman confirmed.

"Okay." Zachary looked at his watch. "Can you start that stuff printing for me? Is there anyone downstairs?" He knew he would have to run down to the basement to order a copy of the medical examiner's report. Just one of those bureaucratic things.

"Sure. Kenzie should be down there still."

Zachary paused. "Kenzie. Not Bradley?"

"Kenzie," Bowman confirmed. "She's new."

"How new?"

"I don't know." Bowman gave a heavy shrug. "How long since you were down there last? Less than that."

Zachary snorted and went down the hall to the elevator.

As he waited for it, Joshua Campbell, an officer he'd worked with on an insurance fraud case several months previous, approached and hit the up button. He did a double-take, looking at Zachary.

"Zach Goldman! How are you, man? Haven't seen you around here lately."

"Good." Zachary shook hands with him. Joshua's hands were hard and rough like he'd grown up working on a farm instead of in the city. Zachary wondered what he did in his spare time that left them so rough and scarred. He wasn't boxing after work; Zachary would have been able to tell that by his knuckles. "Hey, how's Bridget doing? Did everything turn out okay...?" He trailed off and shifted uncomfortably.

"Yeah, great. She's in remission."

"Oh, good. That's great, Zach. Good to hear."

Zachary nodded politely. His elevator arrived with a ding and a flashing down indicator. Zachary sketched a quick goodbye to Joshua and jumped on. He was starting to regret agreeing to look into the Bond case.

~

The girl at the desk had dark, curly hair, red-lipsticked lips, and a tight, slim form. She was working through some forms, those red lips pursed in concentration, and she didn't look up at him.

"Hang on," she said. "Just let me finish this part up, before I lose my train of thought."

Zachary stood there as patiently as possible, which wasn't too hard with a pretty girl to look at. She finally filled in the last space and looked up at him. She raised an eyebrow.

"You must be Kenzie," Zachary said.

"I don't know if I must be, but I am. Kenzie Kirsch. And you are?"

"Zachary Goldman. From Goldman Investigations."

"A private investigator?"

"Yes."

He didn't usually introduce himself that way because it gave people funny ideas about the kind of life he lived and how he spent his time. Most people did not think about mounds of paperwork or painstaking accident scene reconstructions when they thought about private investigation. They thought about Dick Tracy and Phillip Marlowe and all the old hardboiled detectives. When really most of a private investigator's life was mind-numbingly boring, and he didn't need to carry a gun.

"And what can I do for you today, Mr. Private Investigator?"

"Zachary."

"Zachary," she repeated, losing the teasing tone and giving him a warm smile. "What can I do for you?"

"I need to order a copy of a medical examiner's report. Declan Bond."

"Bond. That's the boy? The drowning victim?"

"That's the one."

She looked at him, shaking her head slightly. "Why do you need that one? It's closed. A determination was made that it was an accident."

"I know. The family would like someone else to look at it. Just to set their minds at ease."

"You're not going to find anything. It's an open-and-shut case."

"That's fine. They just want someone to take a look. It's not a reflection on the medical examiner. You know how families are. They need to be able to move on. They're not quite ready to let it go yet. One last attempt to understand..."

Kenzie gave a little shrug. "Okay, then... there's a form..." She bent over and searched through a drawer full of files to find the right one. Zachary had filled them out before. Usually, he could manage to do an end-run and Bradley would just pull the file for him. Officially, he was supposed to fill one out. He didn't want to end up in hot water with the new administrator, so he leaned on the counter and filled the form out carefully.

She went on with her own forms and filing, not trying to fill the silence with small talk. Which Zachary thought was nice. When he was finished, he put the pen back in its holder and handed the form to Kenzie. To the side of the work she was doing. Not right in front of her face. She again ignored him while she finished the section she was on, then picked it up to look it over.

"You have nice printing," she observed, her voice going up slightly. She laughed at herself. "No reason why you shouldn't," she said quickly. "It's just that the majority of the forms that get submitted here are... well, to say they were chicken scratch would be insulting to chickens."

Zachary chuckled. "That's the difference between a cop and a private investigator."

"Neat handwriting?"

"Yeah. Cops have to fill out so many forms, they don't care. You can just call them if you need something clarified. Me... I know if I don't fill it out right, it's just going to go in the circular file." He nodded in the direction of the garbage can.

"I wouldn't throw it out," she protested.

"If you couldn't read it? What else would you do?"

"I would at least try to call you."

Zachary indicated the form. "That's why I printed my phone number so neatly."

Kenzie smiled and nodded. "It's very clear," she approved.

"You'll call me?"

"I'll let you know when it's ready to be picked up."

Zachary hovered there for an extra few seconds. He was enjoying the give-and-take of his conversation with her but didn't want her to accuse him of being creepy. He wasn't the type who asked a girl out the first time he saw her.

He gave her another smile and walked away from the desk. Maybe next time.

≈

*She Wore Mourning*, Book #1 of the *Zachary Goldman Mysteries* series by P.D. Workman can be purchased at pdworkman.com

≈

# ALSO BY P.D. WORKMAN

**FIND MORE BOOKS AT PDWORKMAN.COM**

*Zachary Goldman Mysteries*
*Private Investigator*
She Wore Mourning
His Hands Were Quiet
She Was Dying Anyway
He Was Walking Alone
They Thought He was Safe
He Was Not There
Her Work Was Everything
She Told a Lie
He Never Forgot
She Was At Risk
He Drowned in Memory
Their Walls Were Empty
They Came for Him
They Sought Vengeance
She Was Their Target
His Fear Was Real
She Was Out of Reach
He Was Deceived
She Once Vanished
He Broke the Silence (Coming Soon)
They Sold Her Story (Coming Soon)

He Was Not Himself (Coming Soon)

*Kenzie Kirsch Medical Thrillers*

Unlawful Harvest

Doctored Death

Dosed to Death

Gentle Angel

Rushin' Death

Posed for Death

Death of a Corpse

Endowed with Death

Shattered to Death

Captured in Death

Currying Death

Healed to Death

Death's Charm

*Bleeding Hearts Valley Thrillers*

An Abrupt Departure

*Stand Alone Suspense Novels*

Looking Over Your Shoulder

Lion Within

Pursued by the Past

In the Tick of Time

Loose the Dogs

**AND MORE AT PDWORKMAN.COM**

# ABOUT THE AUTHOR

P.D. Workman is a USA Today Bestselling author and multi-award winner, renowned for her prolific output of over 100 published works that span various genres. With a knack for crafting page-turners, Workman captivates readers with everything from cozy mysteries like the Auntie Clem's Bakery series to gripping young adult and suspense novels.

A prolific reader and writer since childhood, P.D. Workman crafts emotionally powerful stories that don't shy away from hard topics. Her books tackle mental illness, addiction, abuse, and trauma with raw honesty and compassion, giving voice to the often unheard. If you crave authentic, character-driven page-turners that hit deep and stay with you long after the final page, you're in the right place.

With each new release, fans eagerly anticipate another thrilling blend of thought-provoking storytelling and relatable characters that define P.D. Workman's brand as an author of unforgettable page-turners—gripping tales that leave a lasting impact long after the last page is turned.

Some of Workman's titles have been translated into Spanish, French, Portuguese, German, and Italian.

Workman began writing at an early age and is a prolific reader as well as writer. She is also passionate about teaching and learning, expresses her creativity through art and cooking, and loves exploring the Calgary parks and green spaces where the Parks Pat Mysteries are set. She was a legal assistant for many years and has done extensive charitable work.

Workman was born and raised in Alberta, Canada, and is married with one adult son.

> P. D. Workman, does not shy from probing the deep psychological scars of childhood trauma, mental illness, and addiction. Also characteristic of this author, these extremely sensitive issues are explored with extensive empathy, described with incredible clarity, and portrayed with profound insight.

—KIM, GOODREADS REVIEWER

Please visit P.D. Workman at pdworkman.com to see what else she is working on, to join her mailing list, and to link to her social networks.

If you enjoyed this book, please take the time to recommend it to other purchasers with a review or star rating and share it with your friends!

tiktok.com/@pdworkmanauthor

facebook.com/pdworkmanauthor

x.com/pdworkmanauthor

instagram.com/pdworkmanauthor

amazon.com/author/pdworkman

bookbub.com/authors/p-d-workman

goodreads.com/pdworkman

linkedin.com/in/pdworkman

pinterest.com/pdworkmanauthor

youtube.com/pdworkman

Find P.D. Workman's books at

**PDWORKMAN.COM**

Scan the QR code below